All
the
Finest
Girls

All the Finest Girls

A novel

ALEXANDRA STYRON

Little, Brown and Company

Boston   New York   London

First Edition

The characters and events in this book are fictitious. Any similarity to real
persons, living or dead, is coincidental and not intended by the author.

Library of Congress Cataloging-in-Publication Data

Styron, Alexandra.

All the finest girls : a novel / by Alexandra Styron — 1st ed.

p.   cm.

ISBN 0-316-89080-4

1. Family — Fiction.   2. Adult children of divorced parents — Fiction.
3. Babysitters — Fiction.   4. Funerals — Fiction.   5. Americans — Caribbean
Area — Fiction.   6. Caribbean Area — Fiction.   I. Title.

PS3569.T889 A78   2001

813'.6 — dc21   00-050051

10   9   8   7   6   5   4   3

Q-FF

Designed by Chris Welch

Printed in the United States of America

For my mother,
my father,
and
Daphne

Fiolé-e, femme, fiolé,
   Women gone away.
Fiolé-e, femme, fiolé,
   Gone, gone, gone.
Fiolé-e, femme, fiolé,
   Way off in Cayenne.
Fiolé-e, femme, fiolé,
   Tout femme ay Englan.
Fiolé-e, femme, fiolé,
All the finest girls.
   — Caribbean children's game song

The painter should not paint what he sees,
but what will be seen.
— *Paul Valéry*

All
the
Finest
Girls

I

~~~

I'VE NEVER BEEN much of a traveler, particularly not to places under the sun's fiercest gaze. So it was with a will borne of some strange and ungovernable desire that on a midwinter day I flew from New York to the Caribbean island of St. Clair.

Ssss. Lady. Whereyouwannago?

Stepping out from the terminal at the Thomas P. Rose Airport, I was instantly enclosed by a clutch of taxi drivers jostling one another for my fare. The little concrete building stood open-faced to the road, and everywhere vacationers in bright cotton and baseball caps hustled about, shouting to each other *Over here, Bill, this guy says he can take us* above the *clackety clack* of idling shuttle buses. I tried to press forward but collided with a rolling suitcase that slammed against my knee, missed only a beat, and continued smartly on. Out in the sun, the noonday heat rose and shimmered like grease in a pan.

"Someone will be picking yah up," Lou's sister had said when we spoke the day before, ringing off before I could get more detail. I looked around at the circus of people and felt a flutter of nausea. My face, caught in the reflection of a car window, was tense as a drum. After what must have been ten abject minutes bobbing around in the chaos of island reception, I retreated to a shaded bench and began searching my bag for a pair of sandals.

A sad, familiar noise, the rattle of pills against plastic, came from somewhere beneath my clothes. Oval and blue as robins' eggs, the pills were meant to soften a spur of anxiety that sometimes went for the base of my skull. I'd taken one and slept, badly, the night before, and again on the airplane, only to wake numb and blue under the blast of the air-conditioning system. In the tropical air, my medication hangover plus the two layers of wool I wore were making me feel smothered. I cursed aloud, and a woman seated next to me inched down the bench.

It was then — barefoot, my bag half unpacked — that I heard my name. A tall, chestnut-colored man with a precise flat-top haircut had planted himself before me, blocking out the sun. I stood up quickly and felt myself wobble as the blood rushed from my head.

"You Adelaide?" he said, looking not at but past me and jingling the keys in his pants pocket.

The smooth planes of the man's face were interrupted by two tight, walnutlike bunches of muscle in his jaw. I pushed my belongings back into the bag and extended my hand, but the airport PA system just then crackled to life, drowning out my response. *Ladies and gentlemen, flight forty-three to St. Thomas with continuing service to San Juan will now begin preboarding at gate two. Passengers with small children* Ignoring me, the man took my bag and walked away. I followed, shoeless, as we weaved through a chorus of gaily dressed young women holding up signs for Sandals and Club Med. Picking my way along the hot graveled road, I nearly lost sight of him. At last, on a narrow grass divider, I caught up as he stopped for traffic. His face wore the expression of a man willing himself to be alone.

"I'm sorry. I didn't catch your name," I said as we moved off again.

"Derek," he answered.

Derek; an adult face to go with the name I'd once worried like a rosary. As a little girl, I'd imagined meeting Lou's boys a hundred times, had fashioned them with thoughts and personalities as if clothing imaginary dolls. None of my fantasies had resembled this sudden, brittle truth.

The seats of Derek's car were small and close, forcing me to tuck in my elbows so he could shift as we got under way. Sweat streamed down my back. Timidly, I flapped the hem of my sweater for relief, not daring to remove anything in the tight space of the car. Perhaps meaning to be helpful, or not, Derek flipped a switch and an infernal blast of air spewed from the vents. I sat back and tried to act relaxed.

The car lurched ahead and soon we were careering along a wrecked main thoroughfare that hugged the southern coast of St. Clair. It ran like a ribbon through tattered seaside villages, opening up to sandy inlets with pink hotels, and giving way here and there to a long view of a busy Caribbean harbor town. On Derek's side of the car, the lee side, sugarcane fields ran ragged to the green hills of the north. The line between quaint and calamitous wavered with each bump and turn in the rutted road.

Feigning interest in the scenery, I managed at last to get a good look at Derek. His skin was several shades lighter than his mother's, but the features were eerily familiar. The fine, curved etches around his mouth reminded me powerfully of Lou and, for a second or two, took my breath away. I thought of her dipping her wrist in my bathwater and pausing in silent contemplation. I tried not to stare.

"When's the service?" I asked, finally, after we'd traveled a long mile in silence. The question cast a harsh glow on the ordeal ahead, a picture of which hung for a moment like a scrim between us. Derek clenched and unclenched his jaw.

"Two days' time."

"That's good," I said. "I mean, it's all a lot to handle, I'm sure." Just ahead a goat was coming down off an embankment and into the road. Derek swerved to avoid it, never taking his foot off the accelerator.

"It's just terrible what happened," I added, pitching my voice to a near shout as Derek threw the little car into low gear. He braked and, without any indication of having heard me, made a sharp turn onto an unpaved side street. On either side of the road, drab houses of cinder block and tin lined up in slack rows, one or two decorated with dirty curtains and window boxes. Halfway down the block, at a peeling yellow door, we came to an abrupt halt. Derek left me and went inside. I got out of the car to pull off my sweater and, in the sanctum of that momentary eclipse, wondered just what the hell I thought I was doing there.

~

It was just past dawn when my mother had called with the news. My bedroom was still dark, save for a wan spoke of winter light barely grazing my dirty window. She spoke quickly, wedging her words in before I could look at the clock.

"Good morning, darling, it's Mom. *Sorry* to wake you, I just thought you'd want to know Louise died."

My mother had a tennis partner named Louise, a tiny woman whose face-lifts had had the strange effect of making her look beaten up. For a moment I thought of her and could not imagine why Mom would call me with this information. We're not close, my mother and I. Not in that way. I'm not the person she would look to for comfort.

"June, you remember June, she called first thing. Isn't that dear? She's still with the Rubinsteins."

It was then that an image of Louise, as familiar as my own thumb, first appeared. Not my mother's friend, but Lou, my Lou. Dressed in her Sunday clothes, she was walking straight as a rod down my grandmother Edith's looping driveway, toward church.

"How?" I asked, lying still beneath the covers.

"You remember she couldn't swim?"

"No."

"Well, it seems she drowned."

My mother paused. The upset I heard in her silence rattled me. She wanted me to ask for details. She would have liked, I'm sure, to simply *talk* with me. And I did want to know more, but I was too far gone, too deep in my campaign of truculence to make the long march back.

After a moment, she continued.

Here we were, then, playing our parts.

"She hadn't been doing well, physically, for some time. Something about her heart, I think. The night before, her sister put her to bed but, in the morning. Well. Oh, Addy, I think it was just awful. They couldn't *find* her, if you can imagine. Someone, two boys, I think, discovered her body a mile or so down the beach. She was dressed as if she were going somewhere."

I could feel my mother straining through the telephone wires, trying to make contact with me. The phone itself seemed water-logged with her need. I worked to put all the pieces together in my sleep-bent head.

"Isn't that the oddest thing?" she said, her theatrical voice now in its upper, excited register. When I said nothing, she exhaled and re-gained herself.

"Anyway. I just thought you ought to know."

"Thanks for calling," I said. "I appreciate it. Really."

"How are you feeling? Can I do anything for you?"

"Nope." I reached over and banged on the radiator, which some-times helped to draw the heat up from downstairs. "I'm fine."

"Well, OK then. Love you," she said, her last words trolling along hopefully.

I lay in bed and felt the world zoom into excruciatingly sharp focus. A garbage can rattled. Two dogs barked. A dark, ineffable thought coiled, hissed, collapsed. I'd been sick recently, and undone more than I cared to admit. The virus had flattened me physically, but beyond that another, more persistent and scarier, germ had spread. Whatever it was had rattled my self-confidence and made me uneasy, as though someone or something were always at my back. I got better, but I wasn't the same. I felt hunted, and haunted. That morning, when my mother's news reached me, I had the dis-tinct sensation that I'd at last been caught.

I told my boss that there had been a death in my family. "Dreadfully sorry, Adelaide," she whispered, tucking her head down with perfect English reserve. Since I'd been out sick — my first leave of absence in four years with the museum — I'd detected an almost fearful courtesy from Emmeline. She gave me a wide berth, rarely checking on the progress of my work and encouraging me each day to go home early and "have a lie down." She'd even tried to pass on to someone else the painting I was restoring, evidently suspicious that the little predella itself was the cause of my undoing. But I'd refused. I needed in some insistent way to see the job through. When I decided to go to St. Clair for the funeral, Emmeline offered me as much time as I needed.

~

A screen door whined and banged shut as I got back in the car. From a cluster of bougainvillea Derek emerged, balancing a small boy in the crook of his arm. The boy, four or five years old, wore a baseball cap and red sneakers. Derek held him with casual pride, and the boy giggled and squirmed in his confident grip.

"This is my son," he said brusquely, as he lowered the boy to the ground and opened the back door of the car. "Cyril, this is Adelaide. Now get on in."

Derek walked around to the driver's side. I watched the boy as he twisted himself onto the floor to get at a plastic dump truck. When he sat up again, he looked frankly into my eyes.

"My granmumma died," he said. "She drownded."

"I know," I replied. Was I shouting?

"She was a great friend of mine," I ventured again, more quietly.

Cyril nodded and ran his dump truck along the vinyl seat beside him. Derek backed quickly down the street, then peeled out again on the main road.

"Wow. He looks just like you did," I said to Derek, taken by the resemblance.

For the first time, Derek looked directly at me. His eyes, like a Rousseau tiger's, reflected the light. They prohibited investigation.

"How do you know?" he asked.

"Pictures."

He turned his attention back to the road.

"She had them up in her room."

The road snaked north, pulling away from the coast and up a mountain pass. Every few miles, a group of weather-beaten houses appeared in a small cluster, and here and there men sat about under the high sun doing what looked to be nothing. Derek turned on the radio. A disc jockey spoke rapidly in the local dialect, and I felt the hair rise suddenly on the back of my neck.

Lawd, look me gwan on in dis kotesi kotela ya catch me happosite, an anyway me needin to mek dis girl her supper

Lou, on the phone, and me with an ear bent to the musical notes of her voice, suddenly in a language entirely other — French inflected, a word or two I'd learned in school. The sounds come out happy and loose, like dropping change.

Her voice seemed to come from somewhere inside the car — the vents, the speakers — then just as quickly disappeared, fluttering out the window into the warm air. I was tired, surely. Not myself. I fixed my eyes back on the road and we rode along, the three of us in our separateness, northward through the lush hills.

2

My mother and I stand on the stairs outside the Rubinsteins' big brick house and listen to the doorbell's tinkling chime. We have driven down from Coldbrook to New Haven in the old green station wagon, running out of gas halfway there. Before we were rescued, Mom poked gingerly with one finger under the car's hood, looking for engine trouble. Now her blouse is stained, the collar turned up on one side. She pushes at her hair and dabs at the corner of her mouth, puckering her lips hopelessly.

For a moment her hand hovers over my head. She wants to do something about my hair. I haven't allowed her to brush it since last winter, when the electricity from the brush stood my hair on end and shocked me so that I tasted metal on my tongue. The broken strands are thick and matted and won't now, I've discovered, yield to even the most gentle grooming.

My clothes, too, are long overdue for cleaning. I've taken to wearing outfits again and again, dressing myself in the half-light of morning from a pile on my desk chair. Sometimes my mother notices. Sometimes not. When she does *Snooks, I think you might want to go up and change that blouse* I explode with all my gathered strength. I howl and bare my claws.

I screech just like Cat. Cat, who shows himself only to me, circling my room at night. Howling like a dying witch when my father shouts at my mother. Plucking his way around the carpet until darkness gives into morning. I watch him all night long.

I scream until I've spent myself, till my voice is nothing but scratchy air and my head feels like a new bruise. There is no end to it, my screaming. My mother begs me to stop, in tones both gentle and harsh. She offers me things, ignores me, shouts back. *Why? Why are you like this?!* she implores, fist to her forehead, hot tears running down her cheeks to match my own. *I don't know!* I shout, each scream feeling as though I were shredding myself, piece by flaming piece.

That is it. I don't know why I am like this. I don't know why Cat torments me, why I torment my mother. I don't know at all.

"So, my lamb," she says, "you're not going to . . . are you? Remember what I said?"

I run my toe along the plastic bristles of the doormat.

"Anyway," she says, straightening up at the sound of approaching footsteps, "June is making lunch for us. Yum yum. And Max and the boys aren't home."

Finally the door opens, turning out the scent of pine and something in the oven. June, the Rubinsteins' housekeeper, stands to the side in her crisp white uniform.

June cares for the Rubinstein boys — Teddy, Ben, and Maxie — who are older than I, roughhouse boys who always smell mossy from outdoor adventures. They seem to be one unit of rapidly spinning dust and noise, like characters fighting on Saturday morning cartoons. Teasers and practical jokers, the boys give everyone a stupid name and a hard time. When June tells them what to do, they sass her, voices pitched high, imitating her accent. *All right, you buggah!* they cry, chasing her through the kitchen, breaking things as they go. *But me tellin yah, yah nutting but a tief! June, yah been smokin' dat reefah again.* They call me Sadelaide, when they call me anything at all. *Hey, Sadelaide, why are you so sadelaide? Is it because you look so badelaide?*

We haven't seen much of the Rubinsteins since last April, when Mrs. Rubinstein died. Thin and wobbly as a baby deer, the boys' mother was the only person they didn't harass. Crashing into a room, they hushed the instant they saw her. Usually, Mrs. Rubinstein was perched on the window seat or being swallowed by the living-room couch. *How are you feeling today, Mommy? Do you need anything, Mommy?* they'd say, one on top of the other. The boys fought, as they did with everything, to be the first to prop a pillow or get their mother her tea. When her heart finally gave out, Big Max, a colleague of my father's at the university, came to our house and cried in my mother's arms. Now it's just him, the boys, and June, and nobody makes jokes anymore.

"Hi, June, I'm so sorry we're late, the car just went kerflooey!"

My mother's hand darts out, nudging me along into the Rubinsteins' foyer, newly polished and still. I envy the uninterrupted quiet of this motherless house.

As my eyes adjust to the darkness, a sickening fizz rises again in my stomach. It has been sloshing inside me most of the morning.

"She's up in back. Why don't you go on and say hello?" says June to me, splitting the quiet with her brassy voice. She shouts at children, I think, out of habit.

I walk slowly through the kitchen toward the back staircase to June's room. During dinner parties, I sometimes crouch there on one of the spiral steps, hoping no one will find me until it's time to go home.

Upstairs, a woman is sitting on the edge of June's single bed. She watches a soap opera on a tiny black and white, her hands cradling a glass of water. A white cardigan sweater is buttoned around her shoulders like a cape. She turns slowly toward me. She is the darkest person I've ever seen.

Standing dumbly in the doorway, I suddenly have no idea what to do. The woman is a friend of June's from St. Clair, and Mom says we have to see whether we like each other well enough for her to come live with us. Her eyes, enormous behind their thick lenses, fall on me and hold me in their gaze. She doesn't look a bit like June, who moves about quickly, all angles and ironed edges. Instead, this woman is curved and upholstered, her lap like a love seat. She doesn't speak to me. I think to turn and run back down the stairs, but I don't. Can't. With her huge brown eyes, she's making a picture that I can see, as though her eyes are my own. I'm where she is, and across the room stands a bony girl, smudgy and colorless as cigarette smoke, done out in dusty corduroys and a crown of fermented hair. The rims of my ears go hot with shame.

We stay that way, waiting for each other, and when I think I won't stand it any longer, the woman turns back to the television. I sit down on the threshold and stare hard at the tips of my sneakers until my vision blurs.

"Louise," June calls from below. The woman walks toward the stairs, stopping for a moment in the doorway. I squint up at her, this time wearing my most terrible face. She looks back at me, soft and bottomless. Something is pulling at me, dragging me down. Afraid of crying, I turn away. The seconds tick. She moves past me to the stairs. When I hear the back door open, I stand and look out the window onto the porch below.

My mother is extending her hand to Louise, drawing her into the crazy light that seems to attract most people to her. The two of them sit down in a square of sun at the outdoor table and Mom begins making sweeping movements with her hands, talking excitedly. Louise nods. Around her I see a bright space, a reflection from her sweater, perhaps, where, in spite of myself, I want to be. June appears with a platter of sandwiches, and I drift downstairs. Taking a little triangle of peanut butter and jelly, I make a seat for myself and dangle my legs over the edge of the porch.

My mother talks and talks *A good winter coat makes all the difference. We'll take care of that lickety-split. We go away to my mother's house at the beach in the summer if I'm not working. Of course our produce is never any good up here, but we can order lots of things* as though to stop would be to die. She skitters from subject to subject, describing Coldbrook and asking about life on St. Clair. Every now and then, she offers up bits of information about me, wildly inflating my talents. *Oh, the water in the Caribbean is so lovely. Addy's a terrific swimmer, just terrific. She's like a water bug.*

I don't turn around when my mother says my name but instead count the seconds of silence before she goes off on another tangent. Louise says almost nothing, and the quiet she leaves begins, little by little, to soothe me like a language all its own. I have begun

to feel drowsy and follow the progress of a slug along the weathered porch railing.

Then I hear, ". . . June says you have children?"

"Mmhmm, yes I do," replies Louise.

"Girls or boys?"

"Two boys. The oldest is Philip. Then Derek, he's the baby.
Coming on seven next week."

I stop moving my legs. A black circle grows around me like
spilled ink. Like an inner tube. I am set adrift. There is at once the
faintest sound I must strain to hear. I pray I am mistaken. My skin
prickles. Yes, it's there. *Hoosh* goes Cat's tail, snaking through the
reeds beyond the lawn, trampling the pacific afternoon. Climbing
over the lip of the sun and into the dark, empty space around me.
Getting ever closer.

I stand and drop my plate, turn around in my dark circle, searching for him. The yard, with its budding cherry tree and neglected veg-
etable garden, vanishes. My mother calls my name, a thousand miles
away. Cat hangs above, his teeth like white needles, and now I'm
screaming, to scare him away. He draws closer and I look away. That's
when I see Louise, motionless, across the empty space, her magnified
eyes drinking me in. Her hand is over her heart. The black circle lifts
as harmless as steam from a kettle, leaving me inside the palette of
peanut butter and jelly I've splattered on the porch floor.

A chapel bell, a tree full of crows, the sounds of the neighbor-
hood clutter the air again. Mom has turned away from me, but I can
see the slightest tremble around her mouth and the whiteness of
her knuckles.

"I'm sorry, that's, um, something, that doesn't . . ."

She's looking down at the blue stones in her ring. For the first time all afternoon, Mom has nothing to say.

To my amazement, Louise smiles, revealing a little gold band between her front teeth.

"Don't trouble wit it, Mrs. Abraham," she says. "She'll be good if I be minding she."

After a moment of silence, my mother raises her head and pushes a stray lock of yellow hair from her face. "Anyway," she says, smiling again, "you were speaking of your children. I'm sure they're lovely. You must miss them a lot."

Louise nods, and the conversation moves on to vacation time and the school calendar. I run inside and settle on the bottom step of June's stairway.

By the coatrack when it's time to leave, I watch the three women. Kissing June on the cheek *Again, I'm so sorry. Remind Mr. Rubinstein about Friday* my mother turns to Louise and takes her hand in both of hers. Louise looks shyly down at the floor.

"So anyway, thank you," Mom says. "It would be great. I think. Marvelous." Turning to me, she raises her eyebrows up near her hairline.

"Addy? Can you thank June and tell Louise how nice it was to meet her?"

I do as I'm told, but I can't lift my chin from the buttons on my shirt. I don't want Louise to look at my face. I don't want her, whom I might never meet again, to see what I know only she can see.

"Nice," I whisper, and run out the door.

3

I WOKE WITH A start, drool across my cheek, when Derek pulled up on the emergency brake. Before the driveway dust settled, he and Cyril had disappeared inside the single-level, tin-roofed house in front of which we were parked. Groggy, I sat up and tried to pull myself together.

This was the second time I'd blanked out in the space of a month. It was something I used to do a lot, passing out or falling asleep at inopportune moments. People around me didn't care much for my behavior or for my lame excuses. I'd tried hard to lick the problem, and for a long time I had actually succeeded. But now I'd succumbed twice in the space of a month. It was unnerving and, I knew, totally unacceptable. As my grandmother Edith would say, this was neither the time nor the place.

The house, at the top of a steep drive, overlooked a village on St. Clair's northern coast. I could see a church steeple just below and a series of dirt roads running east and west of town. Jutting out from the cove, which was not sandy but studded with rock and coral, three docks tethered a jumble of wooden fishing boats. It was a world away from the unblemished beachfronts on the island's other

side. I unstuck myself from my seat and, stepping out, got a lung-
ful of salt air, jasmine, and the rich, fatty currents of something
cooking. Across the street a man with a cane watched me as if sizing up an unusual but not particularly glamorous plant.

Just as I felt the sun might bore a hole in my head, a woman came
out of the house, wiping her hands on an apron. Her hair, a milk
white halo, was combed back from her dark face into a tiny knot at
the back of her head. This time, I had no doubts. She was unmis-
takably Lou's sister, Marva.

"Well," she said, walking up to me and putting her hands on her
hips, "lemme see yah."

She looked me up and down, ran her tongue under her lip,
sucked a tooth. But for a large mole like a cough drop on her cheek,
and a different, sadder curve of the brow, I was looking into Lou's
face. Images, fragments of thought, clattered and snapped in my
head *I'm dreaming dem babies still, like when I left.* The sound of my own
body, rhythmic fluid and machinery, was suddenly audible. Without
ceremony, Marva broke away and turned briskly back toward the
house.

"Derek," she shouted, "come get dis frighty ting's bags now!"

I'd been to the Caribbean a couple of times, with my parents
when I was small. We would travel directly from the airport to our
hotel, where we remained for most of our stay. I remember one dinner in town, at a restaurant on a long veranda. A calypso band had
played throughout the meal, irritating my father, and I heard a par-
rot speak for the first time. It was that same trip, Barbados, I think,
that a taxi driver taking us back to the airport pulled over and used
a pocketknife to cut me a stalk of sugarcane. I sucked on the sweet,

fibrous flesh until it was confiscated by a man at customs. Never before, though, had I visited someone's home.

The cool of the entranceway was an immediate relief. I followed Marva as she moved through a little parlor at the front of the house, its dusty spareness giving the impression of a place from which life had traveled long ago. A sofa and armchair were squarely arranged on either side of a coffee table, their bowed seats just clearing the floor. At the table's center lay a Bible and a book titled *Redemption Songs.* The bindings of both were held together with tape. Nothing but a crucifix adorned the walls, the blood of Jesus' wounds pink from age. I found it difficult to imagine the room ever accommodating children, a family.

The back of the house was a different story. Continuing on, I found myself at the kitchen's threshold, where sunlight and a breeze came through the open windows. An old radio played softly from its perch above the rusty refrigerator. Long and narrow, the room seemed barely wide enough for anyone to navigate between the counters and the linoleum-topped table, but Marva, her back still to me, moved about it effortlessly. She opened cabinets, reached without looking, found work space on the jammed counters. This was her kitchen.

"Gwan and sit down," she said finally over her shoulder, and as I did so, I realized what was in store for me.

Platters and casserole dishes lined every flat surface. Boiled vegetables, fish and curried chicken, stews and compotes, all bumped up against one another. Cakes with icing running down their sides and glass bowls of carefully cut fruit. Serving plates in neat towers. It was, of course, a house to which death had come. And so neighbors had come as well, hoping to ease the burden. The smells that hung in the air were unfamiliar, intense. Marva ladled food onto a plate, and I began to feel distinctly nauseous. To my left, down a darkened passageway, I could hear Cyril talking loudly and a woman responding in a hushed voice.

"Please don't. I had lunch on the plane," I lied, hoping that would be enough to save me from the dish, brown and glutinous, over which Marva was now pouring a piping-hot red sauce. "It wasn't very good. I'm sorry if I'm not hungry."

Marva forced a disapproving burst of air through her nostrils. From the refrigerator she drew a green glass bottle and placed it, with the steaming plate, before me. Then she sat down across the table, quiet descending about her suddenly, and folded her arms. There was little question I'd have to eat, unappealing though the idea was. I wasn't used to being a guest and remembered quickly why I didn't accept, or receive, many invitations.

I looked down at a little dune of speckly rice. Marva jutted her chin out and poured me a glass of tea from the bottle. I drank and felt the tea travel down in a cool stream, slaking my suddenly astounding thirst. While she refilled my glass, I tried the simplest meat dish on my plate. It looked like chicken, firm and unadorned, topped with a yellow sauce that I suspected was curry. I chewed but didn't breathe. Finally, little by little, my tastebuds connected to my brain. The food was better than anything I could remember having eaten. A long time seemed to pass before I thought to look up and say something. Marva was studying a fray in the trim of her apron.

"My condolences. For your loss," I offered, remembering the phrase from some long-ago exchange I'd witnessed, or a movie I'd seen. The words spooled out as weightless as thread and lay there for an instant before blowing away. I wished immediately I could take them back in favor of something better, more my own. But nothing appropriate came to mind. If Marva found my sentiment wanting, she showed no sign in her reply. Neither did she look at me.

"When I told Papa, him sit up in bed all night calling Mumma's name. *She* been gone nearly twenty years."

"You still have your father with you?"

"Whatever yah want to call it," Marva answered with a sigh, pushing herself up from the table. I could see the years of work in the backs of her sculptured, masculine hands.

Marva turned her back, and it suddenly occurred to me that maybe Lou's sister didn't like me any better than Derek did. Perhaps she was just being polite. I began to imagine the worst was yet to come and felt the sudden deadweight of the situation into which I'd maneuvered myself.

After I ate, we walked out back where the roof extended over bare earth and a few rattan chairs were placed in the shade. Marva bent to pick up a piece of trash from the dirt floor. I felt compelled to say something.

"It's really pretty, this place."

"Dis was Lulu's spot," she said matter-of-factly. "Got to where I'm setting her here in de morning, retrieving her when de sun go down."

"What was wrong with her?"

Taking a dish towel off her shoulder, Marva smacked roughly at the chairs, scaring up a small cloud of reddish dust. She sucked her cheeks as though only a fool would ask such a question.

"Well, she lost her head enough to fall in de ocean, didn't she?" Turning her gaze out to the horizon, Marva lowered herself into a seat. I followed suit. "I don't know," she continued. "Cancer took at her a few years back. Dem saying dey ridded her of it. But me never trusted dem."

I didn't know how my mother had gotten the idea Lou had heart trouble.

"You think it had spread?"

Just at the cliff's edge a donkey strained on a short rope, twitching his lips to nip at the leaves on a flowering bush. Marva picked up a clump of dirt and tossed it at him, and the animal lazily backed off the red petals.

"Me not saying dat," she answered, annoyed. I nodded quickly. Marva looked at me. "Anyway, she wasn't right past dat time."

Below us, the town had gone silent in the midday sun. I felt the closeness of Marva's grief, and the peculiar distance of my own. Taking a seat, I slowly rolled the cuffs of my pants.

"I should have tried to stay in touch," I said. "When my parents divorced, I went away to school. Everything changed a lot."

Getting no response from Marva, I continued.

"After college I moved to New York. I'm an art conservator. I fix up old paintings."

"Dat's nice," she said, nodding slowly, uninterested. "Paintings."

"Not as nice as this," I prattled on, gesturing out at the view. "Time hasn't changed anything here, I bet."

Marva gave an unfocused look at the crooked hillside.

"Well. I guess not," she said hazily. And then she pointed east. "Except de plantation. Used to have de Buxton Plantation, dere past Billy Point. Bananas used to make money for people here."

Grainy black-and-white photos from a high school history book came suddenly to mind. Women in long skirts spread out in a field, bent over their work. A mule and a wooden cart standing by. Plantations, I thought, were a ghost of some other era entirely.

"Shut down?" I asked.

Marva laughed and sat back in her chair. "*Blew* down. De day Lulu arrive. September the fifth. Nineteen forty-tree. Lawd, dat girl would have to arrive in a storm."

Marva's brow lifted, revealing a more youthful face, as an intricate yarn unwound. Any trace of reticence disappeared in the focused light of her memory. Her West Indian accent bloomed as she spoke.

"Me six but gwan grow big already. Hurricane coming like *noting* we seen before." She leaned in and made a broad sweeping motion with her hands. "We was watching it for two days already. Nineteen forty-tree. You cyan even see it now inna history books. Lawd! Went right tru here, tore up St. Vincent, St. Lucia, clear tru Martinique. It dead a lotta people, you know. Right here in Pville two men dem friends of Papa's went under wit deir nets just off dat beach dere. Papa was away working onna freighter and nevah home but maybe once a month. Seems de baby weren't due fi two weeks. But just when de storm gwan heading for us? Mumma started getting pains." Marva shook her head and I got another spectacular flash of Lou. "Jes' me and Mumma, Auntie May, and me brother, Michael.

What a piece a rain! Me trew every pot and bowl onna floor but still cyaant catch all de water coming tru de ceiling."

"May sent Michael to fetch de doctor, but it weren't no use. De doors dey banging like a drum and de trees pulling down till everyting was darkness. May was lighting lanterns and putting water on fi boiling. Me cyan still hear Mumma screaming same like de wind outside. Den May made me go inna back room. Back dere where Cyril is now. I lay onna floor watching May's feet and de light coming from de fire and de sheets dropping fresh wit blood. Me cyan still cry tinking about dat night!"

Marva smacked her cheek and let out a deep, rolling laugh.

"Well, she lived, yah know. We all lived. Inna morning we look out and weren't but a few houses still standing in Pville. Water come up and *boom* — everyting washed away. De houses, de old church, mules. And de Buxton Plantation where me grandpappy and uncles worked. Big boats, for transport, yah know, lying down inna street like lazy horses. Up here was different. Here we arright. And Lulu, her quiet like a mud crab. Always was."

"What about Michael?"

Marva sucked her teeth.

"Michael what. Him fine."

Looking exhausted again, she stood up. When something over my head caught her eye, I turned and saw Derek standing in the shadow of the doorway. The features of his face shrank from me, sewn up tight with scorn.

"Cyril's in back wit Floria," he said to Marva. "I'm going down to see about de headstone."

Derek walked around the house, and I listened to the little car whine backward down the driveway. Regaining her composure, Marva looked down at me.

"I have some work to do, if you'll excuse me."

"Can I help?" I asked, not, I hoped, too visibly relieved when she turned my offer down. I was feeling overwhelmed and found myself desperate for some distance from that house. "Maybe I'll take a walk, then. I could use some exercise after the plane ride."

Marva pointed me toward a footpath that led to town along a sloping green bank. I walked away from the house, ignoring the heat and letting the steep grade propel me forward.

4

~~~~~

U NDERNEATH THE GRAND piano, in the corner of the living room of our house on Marbury Road, I lie with my face pressed between the brass bars of the piano's pedals. I can see, from here, my mother, her long legs curled beneath her on the couch. She's gesturing with her cigarette and laughing. The smooth gold bangles that she wears jingle as she waves her arm, and at her feet sit two men, their eyes fixed upon her like magnets. A sad, tipsy melody comes from the record player. Two more people, a lady and a man dressed all in black, stand against the French doors that lead out to the back porch. The man kisses the lady's neck while she closes her eyes and tilts back her head.

There's a curly thread come loose in the rug just next to where I lie. It once made the border of a pale yellow rose. I like to pull at the yarn when I'm underneath the piano, though I know it's naughty. The bald spot has grown over time, the flower spiraled down to a small dark bud.

"Not that anyone's actually read it. I *did* overhear Jacques Cassal say he was using it for a doorstop."

My father's voice, coming from just above, sounds like a color to me. Silver, like the train we took when I was still practically a baby. Three years ago, when I was only five. I closed my eyes as the train arrived and stood so close I smelled the metal and heat. The silver roared in my ears till I was pulled back by the collar and the train clacked to a halt. *All A-board! YAN-kee Clipper to WASHington. UN-ion Station!*

At the Capitol, I crushed up against the legs all around me until my father lifted me onto his shoulders. *This way, Mr. Abraham,* said the man with hair down his back who picked us up at the station. From the top of the white stairs that I thought might climb to heaven, beneath the huge white dome, I could see forever. Below us stood men and ladies, their bodies against one another as far as I could see. As far as the curve of the earth. A people lawn. American flags rippled in the breeze, and people waved cardboard signs with vivid letters I couldn't read. I saw, below, every person in the world. Almost. They looked up toward where we were. Looked toward me on my father's shoulders *Let me now bring up here a personal hero of mine, one of America's leading young minds. A philosopher, a peacemaker, and one seriously hep cat, Professor Henry Abraham* until he put me down. Next to us, two men sat in wheelchairs, one leg where there ought to have been four. No knees, but instead rounded knobs, puckered and sore. One man, the color of chocolate in a jacket made all of patches, caught my eye and smiled. Mom squeezed my hand. *Don't stare,* she mouthed as my father began to speak into a microphone.

From where I stand, I'd say the world was upside down. Upside down because Daniel Berrigan, Father Daniel Berrigan, is in jail and J. Edgar Hoover is free

All the people in the world cheered, and my father's silver voice sounded like thunder I smelled in the air.

Upside down because Dr. King is gone and the leaders of the free world are still here behind these marble facades, mocking the doctrine they are charged to uphold, that all men are created equal. I say, I say just who do they think they're fooling?

When the rain began, a lady in a tangerine-colored dress made a poncho for me from a garbage bag. Later, a butterfly landed on my arm, the very same color orange.

~

"Anyway," says Daddy, laughing now, "fuck 'em. Fascists. Fascists and imbeciles."

With my hands on the piano's brass bars, I'm nose to toe with my father's scuffed brown shoes. His fingers are around a thick-bottomed glass. Fresh fat blocks of ice crowd in with the amber liquid, bleeding slowly. A woman's legs, in shiny ankle boots, are next to his. Very close.

"*I've* read it," she says. Peeking, I can see her hand on his shoulder. "Well, started it, anyway. And I think it's brilliant."

"Nice. You're nice. Not to worry, though. At least I won't go hungry." Daddy raises his voice and the silver runs upward like the inside of a thermometer. "Will I?"

His shoes turn out toward the rest of the room.

"My wife, you know, is an heiress. Isn't that what you're called? Baby? Isn't that right?"

Mom looks up, her brows coming together in confusion. *Heiress,* whatever it is, sounds just right for my mother. Something light, spun like a spider's web, blowing about on a breeze.

"Isn't Baby wonderful?" asks my father. The men at my mother's feet nod enthusiastically, sip from their drinks. "Gorgeous, isn't she?" Daddy's brown shoes turn back to ankle boots. "Very high bangability quotient," he whispers. Shoes point back out again. "Rich as Croesus. Pays for all that swell swill you're imbibing."

Dad walks over to my mother's side, his legs, body, head, coming into view, and sits on the arm of the couch. His hair, soft and brown, drops down over his glasses as he takes the cigarette from her hand and raises it to his lips. He scratches his back, showing the white underbelly of his arm and a lock of hair where it meets the sleeve of his T-shirt. Smoke curls around his face and through the haze he catches my eye. Only the music can be heard.

"Look who's there." He unfolds his big arm and gestures toward me. "The wild child. That's our daughter, Addy. Adelaide. Named after my mother, God rest her benighted soul. Hello, Adelaide."

I press my face further against the cool metal and hold my breath.

"Adelaide Kane Abraham. Should have done it the other way around. Abraham Kane. Give her all the help she can get."

Mom rolls her eyes, laughs.

"Oh please," she says, and rubs my father's knee.

"Please what, Baby?" he asks, bending down to kiss the top of her head.

"I'm sorry," he says, "I know you hate it when I do that. No, listen now, here's the thing. I *don't* think it's so terrific. Actually, actually, I'd like to talk about this." Dad springs up and walks in a tight circle, rubbing his hands together. "*This* is interesting. OK. Fanny, let me ask you something. Do you think it's possible to be a great artist as the progeny of one? I've been thinking about this. Because you know Baby, Baby's a good actress. Well, you've seen her. You know. Very good. Committed. I've always thought that. But Christ, I don't know." The woman called Fanny watches Dad walk back and forth. When he is up close to the piano I can feel his nearness on my eyelashes. When he moves away I see my mother, looking down, picking at the polish on her nails.

"You sort of feel like, well, *I* don't, but you might say Kane was this very important painter, you know. Talented as hell. And made bucketloads, which is amazing. And he made it possible for Baby, his daughter, to live life free from those concerns. Baby *never* has to work. You know? She can do as she pleases. And she does! Of course that's wonderful. We should all be so lucky. But I think the big question is this: Can Baby be an artist? Can she succeed? I'm not an artist myself, but I've given this some thought and I just wonder. Can you *portray* suffering if you haven't really suffered? You know? All that privilege! All that moola!"

Ankle boots has left the piano and is squeezing the shoulder of one of the men at my mother's feet. She bends down and whispers something in his ear. Dad takes another drag off my mother's cigarette and hands it back to her. She leans forward, her face bright and urgent.

"No, don't go. Please!" She reaches for a bottle of wine at her feet and points the neck in the couple's direction. "Here. Stay. It's all right. Hank's just, he's like that. We'll talk about something else. Please stay."

"Yes. Stay! Baby's right," Daddy says, flinging his arms open wide. "I'm like that. I am. Forgive me."

He stops, rubs his jaw. "Anyway, Baby needs you to stay. She's schooling Addy. In the fine arts of the leisure class." Laughing, he bends over and squints at me. "Addy's here as an observer. Isn't that right, babe? That's why she isn't in bed. She's on reconnaissance, as is her birthright."

Dad rocks back on his heels, and when he looks at Mom again, he sees something in her face that makes his silver voice wind down to a gray trickle.

"Oh," he says, and scratches his cheek. "Oh dear."

One by one, each man and woman walks by the piano. The record ends, the arm returning, and begins again. Mom is still, looking out the glass of the French doors. She sighs. In the lighted reflection, her blond hair is on fire.

I hear Cat. He's dancing across the roof beams. I close my eyes.

～

Hmm. Do you think it was something I said? Here. Where's your glass? Oh come now, don't pout. Baby? Please. I'm sorry

Cat is turning into the hallway. I see him in my head. His back an exaggerated curve, he stops and flicks his tail. Licks something from his paw.

Oh Baby, don't cry here here I'm sorry. I'm a fucking asshole, right? Isn't that what I am? I'm sorry

Thirteen more steps down the worn floorboards, sidestepping the one that creaks. He sets his nasty yellow eyes on the door to my room and flip-flop goes his tail, to and fro. Back on his haunches, he makes a slow, deliberate decision. The bed? The desk? The closet?

Why, Hank

The closet. I know all this. I know where he is each second, upstairs making his move. He crawls to the back of the overhead shelf, pulls his claws through a sweater, plants himself, and settles in.

Don't, Baby

His eyes are on my pillow, waiting for me to go to bed. The pillow where I will have to fight to keep myself awake, knowing he will strike, watching as the sky turns from black to blue, then pink for just an instant before day. Cat is cleverer than I. He'll land on my chest, claws out, if I let myself drift off. Yawning, he stretches his wet tongue, waiting patiently for me to come to bed.

∼

I open my eyes again and look through the piano's pedals. My father is on the couch. My mother is at his feet, her head in his lap. She is crying. He leans down and whispers something I cannot hear, lifts her head and kisses her mouth. The room is cold and big, and I can feel the winter air slipping around all the glass panes of the French doors. There is a circle of inky darkness between me and them. Only Cat can get through. Cat is waiting for me upstairs. I want to be nowhere. I close my eyes.

∼

I have dozed and the rug's made a bumpy pattern on my cheek. My father, walking toward me, lets go of my mother's hand. Bending slowly, he holds the piano for balance. His breath is warm and a funny kind of sweet.

"Come on, peanut." His mouth is a loose-lipped smile. "Your beautiful mother and I are going to bed."

He reaches out and puts a hand around my ankle. Upstairs I hear

Cat knock over a bottle on my dresser. I scream and try to pull away.

"What?" says Dad.

I continue to scream.

"What the hell is it?!"

My father is pulling me by the foot out from under the piano. He picks me up and I stiffen flat as a board so he has to struggle to keep hold. I see his eyes darken, go from gray to jet where no light gets in, but I can't stop my hollering. I want him to hold me, but I know what waits in my room. I want a moment to think, but there isn't time. Cat is slipping under the bed skirt, I'm certain of it. He howls and I howl too, kicking at my father's side.

"Ow. Damnit!" shouts my father, dropping me to the rug. "Fine. Stay there. Sleep on the fucking ground for all I care."

I stay where I am, with my face beneath my elbow.

"Sweetheart," says Mom, bending down to me.

"Let her stay there."

"What is it, Snooks? What's the matter?"

"She's OK. Just leave her."

My father pulls my mother to her feet and puts a hand beneath the hem of her dress. She steps away from him.

"Fine," he says.

"Hank, I just need —"

"No. That's fine. Go to hell. Both of you."

"Don't be like that. Please."

"Fuck. You."

A glass breaks against the wall and it's like a kaleidoscope coming down, all icy shattering onto the floor. Mom's shoulders stay pitched forward toward the door where Dad has exited.

"Why must you ruin everything?" she says quietly. I don't know which one of us she means.

When the door upstairs has slammed, Mom sits down beside me. All her features turn down toward the ground. The shiny white fabric of her dress is flecked with wet brown droplets. She strokes my back, burnishing me with the heat from her hand till I feel a kind of glow along the length of me.

"OK. It's OK." She speaks with renewed energy, wiping her face. "He doesn't mean it. He doesn't. Daddy just . . . oh crum! He gets cranky. He's been working hard. He loves us, Snooks. Daddy loves us so much." Her voice is strange, quavery. "Hey. You know what, Snooks? Louise will be here soon. Two more weeks. Two weeks." Again and again her hand runs along my back, her eyes still fixed on the doorway. "That will be fun, won't it? Funsy. Won't it?"

Inhaling deeply, I take in her smell. Smoke and wine and lavender. The muscles in my chest quiver. In time, my breathing becomes the long, slow rhythm of my mother's caress, and I pretend I'm asleep.

~

There's no sun the next morning, just a low, flat March sky and the dull reflection of early light on the pond at the foot of our hill. I've been watching for hours. Dilly, who does yard work for my parents and drives me to school, stands in the doorway of my bedroom. Dilly at my bedroom door. It's late.

"Addy?" he whispers.

His shoulders are pulled down, hands sunk into his denim and fleece vest. From my bed I can smell coffee and gasoline.

"You up? I'll meet you in the car in five minutes."

Using the top of my bedsheet, I wipe the sweat from my face, then dress quickly in yesterday's clothes. I grab the satchel that holds my books and last night's homework assignments, untouched, undone. At the end of the hallway, I pass my parents' bedroom, their door wide open. Except for a tangled sheet, the bedclothes have fallen to the floor, so I can see the whole of them asleep. My father's face nestles against the curve of my mother's neck, his arm across her bare torso like a fallen tree limb. My mother's pale, fine hand rests on my father's naked hip. Her face is turned away from him toward the wall. I take the stairs on silent feet.

5

～

PETIONVILLE WAS SHAPED like a mutant nautilus shell, all the roads bending at broken angles but eventually leading east to the town's hub, near the wharf. I walked down the hill from Marva's house and crossed the main road onto a narrow street. On either side, shacks leaned helter-skelter against one another, and where a thin strip of front yard might be, scabby dogs lay asleep in the dirt. Out there at midafternoon, life was almost imperceptible. The air hung rotten and briny.

Perched on one foot in the entryway of a house on the corner, a woman watched me with an expression as blank and shutterless as the door in which she leaned. Balanced on her hip was a reedy little girl with plaited hair, her smooth body naked from the waist down. The baby reached for her mother's hair, but the woman took hold of the girl's hand and shook it. She broke into a smile, dandling the baby on her hip, cooing in her ear. I could tell by the softness of the woman's mouth that she was younger than I. I smiled, tight lipped, and looked at my feet as I kept walking.

My thoughts were fitful and unmoored, drifting here and there in the quiet gulf of early afternoon. I was feeling bad for myself. I guess I'd wanted the Alfred family to like me, though I've no idea why I thought they should. Lou's face flickered before me, its tender expression hewn to some terrible murky sensation that caught me under the ribs and made me wince. When the vision dissolved, I had another. In three-quarter profile, swinging a twisted magazine like a bat, I saw in my mind's eye Daniel Moss. Daniel, to whom, by sadness, I was also bound. My waist felt the warmth of that little girl's legs encircling me. And then, with a little self-preserving shove, I landed back in the concrete center of my new surroundings.

Coming to an intersection and a broader avenue, I saw before me a grassy lot bordered by a rusty fence. Back from the fence down a mottled path stood a church. Two stories tall, it soared above the other buildings, looking bravely dignified despite the white paint that peeled away from it in big flocked patches. Its roof, a red tin cap, shone bright with a fresh coat of paint, and the yard grew green and thick. Rows of lilies turned their wimpled heads toward the sidewalk. In the upstairs window of the adjoining parsonage, a young man in a black suit polished a silver chalice. He looked down at me, then slipped back into a dark room. In here I figured, inside the walls of this strange place, Lou and I would soon be together again. I turned away and felt a quickening cold down my spine.

~

I was just at the edge of the town's center, within sight of the wharf, when I turned to a hissing sound behind me. Two boys in school uniforms stood watching me with wide eyes. Another boy, taller than the pair and holding his shirt and tie, appeared from a doorway. He pushed between the two boys and walked toward me. I

looked at my watch in a vain attempt to appear late for something.
The taller boy let out a laugh. Within moments the street was alive
with children fresh from school and brimming with stifled energy.
They all seemed to be pressing toward me, though I had turned my
back and kept walking. A chubby girl ran up next to me. She was so
close I could feel her breath on my neck.

"Whereyoufrom?" she asked, pulling lightly at the hem of my
shirt.

There were shops and businesses here, but the shutters and
doors were all closed.

"Excuse me?" I backed up against a wall to look at her.

"Excuse me," she mimicked, tittering with a hand over her
mouth. The other girls on the street laughed in chorus.

"Ex-cuse me," said another girl, following me as I began walking
again. The children, about a dozen, were on either side of me now,
unified in a hungry pack. Fixing my sight ahead, I stepped off the
sidewalk and began crossing to the other side of the street. Over my
shoulder came the sudden, eardrum-piercing screech of a vehicle's
brakes. I backed up, stumbling on the curb and falling onto my backside. The car, an old Cadillac pulling behind it a trailer and a battered
skiff, swerved to avoid me and landed with a crunch. Its nose rum-
pled up against the concrete storm drain that ran along the opposite
side of the street. Teetering briefly on its trailer, the boat toppled and
fell to the ground. The children screamed with enthusiasm and
rushed to inspect the damage, leaving me alone in the shade.

A white man in rolled shirtsleeves and a loosened tie came out of
the Cadillac, hand on his head.

"Shit, mon," he said, looking from the front end of his car to the overturned boat. Two boys, one with a surprising red Afro, stood by his side and nodded vigorously.

"Yah. Shit, mon," the redhead offered in agreement while the other boy hopped into the driver's seat and pulled on the wheel.

The man turned and his eyes fell on me. Coming quickly over to me, he squatted by my side.

"Are you all right? Can you move your neck?"

He held his palm to my forehead, then made an examination of my shoulders as though he half expected to find a couple of jagged bones sticking through my shirt.

"I'm fine," I said, rubbing the gravel off my hands and trying to get up. The man was clearly not a doctor, and I felt foolish and vulnerable there on the curb. He held me in place.

"No. Don't move! Are you sure nothing's broken?"

"Yes," I said, freeing myself. "I'm sure."

Across the street, a small girl was wrapping herself in the boat's luffing sail as though it were an ermine cape. The man was sizing me up from head to foot.

"Jesus Jumpin' Judas," he bellowed, "what the hell were you doing in the middle of the street?"

I felt a rush of anger.

"Why were *you* driving so fast?"

The man stood back, mouth agape. His clothes were well worn but of good material, and they hung on him with a what-do-I-care messiness. I figured him for the sort of expat I knew gathered like barnacles down here. Beach bums who came for the sun and rum, too bleached and stupefied to go home again.

"You could have killed one of these kids," I said, high now on making my point, despite the fact that the children I was defending didn't seem to me particularly defenseless. "How dumb can you be?"

I crossed the street to inspect the damage. Except for the curling flakes of paint that had come free and scattered on the sidewalk, the boat — already well weathered — seemed OK. She lay on her side, blocking the road, her keel sticking up like a fin. At the stern, the name of the boat was painted in a faded, curving script. *Cinema Girl.* The skiff's owner was now leaning over the dented front door shooing a flock of children from inside the car.

"Gwan out of there, all of you," he shouted, "before I tan your hides!"

His aggravation didn't have much impact on the children, who had dissolved not into fear but fits of giggles.

"Is there someone I should call?" I shouted to his broad shoulders, head gone inside the Cadillac's interior. I was anxious to be gone from there, to find a quiet place where I wouldn't be the object of attention.

The man stood up and thought, filling his mouth with air like a blowfish. Finally, he exhaled.

"I don't know. Shit. I'm supposed to be picking out my mumma's headstone a half hour already gone. My brother's gonna dead me." He looked at his watch and shook his head. "Damnit!"

I tried to see beyond his rough facial hair and shaggy ringlets, which fell in a mess over his glasses, but it was difficult to imagine. This had to be Philip, Derek's older brother, but he looked nothing like Lou. Though not as fair as I, the guy before me was white. Or nearly so. Something flickered in my memory but hadn't time to catch fire. My mind raced.

"Oh wow," I heard myself murmur. "I'm so, I'm so sorry."

Jesus Christ, I thought, what were the odds? The children had by now piled out of the car and were watching the two of us, their mouths slung open in fascination. Other people emerged from shops and houses onto the sidewalk, standing in groups taking in the spectacle.

Touching his lips in a gesture of private thought, Philip leaned against the Cadillac's wrinkled hood. The car wobbled and he laughed ruefully. Behind his back, I could see the busted fender, crumpled like tinfoil into the driver's-side headlight.

"Can I get you a cab?" I asked, immediately aware of my stupidity. It didn't take a native to see that taxis weren't in abundance in Petionville.

Studying his feet, Philip waved off my question. At last, composing himself, he looked over to a half dozen men standing in the shade of a shop awning, already mobilized to come to his aid. Within a few minutes, they had made a circle around the little boat and were lifting it with a collective heave back onto its trailer. When the trailer rig had been disconnected from the car, it was rolled out of the street, and the men let it rest while one of them went to fetch a mechanic. Philip, in a rush now, reached into his car and grabbed a briefcase. Then he was off, halfway down the block in a loping run before I could introduce myself. Feeling a bruise begin to swell on my behind, I stepped gingerly inside a narrow storefront that was now open to get something to drink.

It was a dank affair. The store's rickety shelves held a row of dusty household goods, boxes of Hollywood chewing gum, and plastic crates filled with scratched Fanta bottles. An old top-loading cooler hummed behind the counter. As I reached into my pocket, the chubby girl who had badgered me before appeared at my elbow.

"You gwana have a Coca-Cola?"

Behind the register stood a boy no older than seven, a little half-moon of snot dried beneath his nose. He waited patiently, picking at a scab above his elbow. I looked at the girl and raised an eyebrow.

"Maybe," I answered, feeling punchy from the sudden ebb of adrenaline. "Why do you want to know?"

"No reason. Me usually *love* Coca-Cola."

She turned her head to one side and shot me a sly close-mouthed grin.

I bought two Cokes, and soon the girl and I were sitting in a patch of shade on the sidewalk next to Philip's car. She smelled unwashed, sweetish and a little gamey.

"Whereyoufrom?" she asked again.

"New York."

"Dat's where Donald Trump lives."

When I laughed, she set her mouth in a hard line.

"Why do you know that?"

"Him rich. Me have an uncle dat went dere once. In Queens."

I asked the girl, who had moved close to me now and was touching and inspecting my hand, what her name was.

"Lyris. Me mumma name Lyris same. She work a Sunny Bay. You know it? Big hotel a Oriente. Me live wit Granny-Jean. Where you chilren live?"

"I don't have any."

Lyris whistled and shook her head.

"Why? You cyaant? From sickness?"

"No," I answered with a brightness trying to veil my indignation. I had an urge to defend myself, to explain to this kid that in America, thirty-two was not so very old to be childless. "I just haven't," I replied instead. "Do you want another Coke?"

Two of Lyris's coterie came down the street, barefoot, breaking into a run when they saw us on the curb. Lyris held up her soda bottle as a shield.

"Gwan," she said, warning them away and grabbing tightly at my arm. "She me new auntie. Me white auntie."

Lyris turned to me and grinned. Her smile revealed a mouth full of snaggleteeth in a kind of pitched battle with one another, and with uncharacteristic shyness, she tried to press her lips closed around them. She was a beautifully, spectacularly ugly girl and, despite her peskiness, I liked her quite a lot. When I stood up to get three more sodas, the girls began to chatter like gulls.

I hadn't yet managed to move from the curb before Derek's blue car rounded the corner. I watched as it neared, sunlight glinting off the windshield. Philip was gesturing from the passenger seat, and before long the car idled beside me, Philip and I looking at each other through the open driver's window. I thought I saw Derek ever so slightly shake his head, though he kept his attention on the empty road.

"For true?" Philip said to Derek, laughing now at a conversation the subject of which I had no trouble guessing. I felt the heat of my embarrassment flooding up from my shirt collar. Derek didn't bother to reply to his brother but addressed me through gritted teeth.

"Yah wanna ride back to the house?" he asked.

Philip was laughing harder now, holding one side as he unfolded himself from the tiny seat.

"Jee-sus Jumping Judas," he crowed, glancing over at me again and splitting up with guffaws. "It *is* her."

Between the two, I couldn't decide with whom I would fare worse. Pulling himself together, Philip sighed and hitched up his sagging trousers.

"No, no, I'll bring her back up," he said, relieving me of having to make a choice. Coming around to the curb, he banged on the hood of his brother's car. "Hey, mon," he said to Derek, "check out the *Cinema Girl*."

Derek eyed the Cadillac instead.

"Fender looks pretty bad. Better find Clifton. Out by Billy Point."

And with a rev of the engine and a plume of exhaust, Derek pulled away and headed out of town.

Standing close to me now, Philip studied me carefully and then, again, began to laugh. A fraying wire switched in me and sparked.

"Sorry, sorry," said Philip placatingly. "Who needs a drink?"

Moving off down the street toward the waterfront, Philip looked like a giraffe, his long legs independent of him, knobby knees akimbo. I was still rooted to the sidewalk when he turned back.

"Come on, Connecticut!" he shouted, smiling.

I handed Lyris the dollars I was clutching and told her to buy her friends each a soda.

"See you later, Auntie!" Lyris cackled over the heads of her school-mates as I walked away. Her hand, holding my sweaty bills, slipped deftly into the pocket of her skirt.

6

G ONE TO THE city," Dilly says when I ask if my mother is
home. We're coming in the front door from school. Tight
black buckle shoes. Third grade. Last night, my father's words came
up hard through the loose planks of the floor, followed by the
crunch of gravel and burn of motor from his little red car zipping
up the road. After he left, I listened as Mom stacked records in the
living room, the click and hiss of each disc moving into orbit. She
played her sad music, lonesome melodies with no voices. I never
heard her come upstairs. Cat kept at me all night, fussing and taunting. In the morning, a fog lay on the Schroeders' pasture and everything was hushed.

At the doorway I drop my schoolbooks. I fell asleep at school
again, during reading hour, and I've a note in my pocket for my
mother. But it's a crumpled, smeary ball now, and I don't think she
could read it even if I gave it to her. So I won't. Taking it to the
trash, I pass the dishes from last night's dinner, still on the table. A
carton of cream is spilled on the counter, and coffee grounds lie
like potting soil on the floor.

"I'm going to the bus station," says Dilly, looking around and pushing back his cap to scratch at his head. "Be good now."

In the TV room, I turn on the television and wait for the pop of the tube and the voices to kill the big silence around me. I hear Mom's voice in my head. *When she comes we'll be at our absolutely best to make her feel at home.* Now I'm looking at the TV screen but I can't see anything except the wrecked kitchen and a space where my mother should be. Outside, the sun begins to slip behind the top of the hill and Mr. Schroeder's cows are funneling into their big white barn. I go back to the kitchen and pull a chair up to the sink.

The first spray of the faucet drenches my blouse. I turn the knobs this way and that till the water runs steady and warm. Squeezing the detergent bottle tight between my hands, I watch dreamily as the white liquid makes creamy streams around the saucers and pools inside each cup. I push a sponge around the dishes and let them sit beneath running water.

At the bottom of the sink is a large skillet filled with something stiff and white like mashed potatoes, but not potatoes. I reach into the pan to scoop it clean. The buttery clush cakes on my hands. I run water over them, pull at one with the other, but still my hands don't come clean. Steadying myself on the edge of the sink, I slip and my hand drops into the basin, breaking a glass. Blood rises in pink swirls from the dirty water. I leave the water running and stand, arms raised, in the center of the room.

Well, it's an opportunity, really, a film, and the pay is
Oh for God's sake, Baby, don't pretend it's the pay
But it matters to me, it does

A red stream like Peter Coolley's bloody nose in math class wends its way along the cakey white banks of scum, around my fleshy knuckles.

Anyway, it's just a meeting. Jerry

Jerry is a parasite

Turns thin when it mixes with the water on my wet wrist and runs in a sheet down my arm.

Jerry said the director asked for me, and I don't always want to be saying no. Besides, now we'll have Louise

My heart is racing, racing. My finger throbs, feels hot.

You don't care what I think. Why are you asking me

I do, I'm

You're a cunt

Sparks and spangly pictures crowd outside my vision, and the kitchen begins to disappear behind the black spilling around me.

⌁

"What's happened to you, lickle one?"

It's her. She's bent over me, wearing a long brown overcoat and a delicate hat. The chain on her glasses swings above my face. Dilly is in the doorway and he's dropped her bags. In an instant Louise has lifted me by an arm and is shoving my hand beneath the faucet.

"It's OK. It's arright," she says, her voice soft as a bunny's fur. She's wiping the waxy clots from my fingers onto her own. "Lemme see. You're OK. Jes' a lickle glass. Jes' a peeny-weeny piece. But yah hand's so greasy."

She looks back at Dilly, and then she looks me in the eye and smiles. Gold.

"What yah doing the dishes for? Dat's not yah job."

～

Dr. Goodman has hair like cauliflower. He holds a needle up to the light, so big he could use it to make clothes for a giant. The room is chilly and smells like my father's favorite drink. I'm sitting on a table covered in paper that crinkles under my legs, and I'm frightened and my finger throbs. Louise holds my good hand in hers. Together they look like chocolate and butter. We left Dilly in the waiting room, twisting his cap.

"Don't watch," says Dr. Goodman.

I try to concentrate instead on the zigzags in Louise's coat.

"Still now."

I hold my breath. Louise has said it's all right to cry, but I've decided I want to be brave, for her. The first stitch feels like burning water. Louise holds me tight. Zigzag, goes the cloth of her coat. Zigzag. Zigzag. Louise smiles at me. Zigzag. On and on, the burning water on my hand and zigzag. Zigzag.

"That should do it."

Dr. Goodman is finished. I look at the fatty part of my pointing finger. It's rusty brown from the medicine the nurse swabbed on, and across it run four black X's, just like the stitching on the back of my blue jeans. It's swollen and pulses with heat. The nurse has begun to gently roll gauze around my hand when the door springs open. All in a sweet-smelling rush, Mom appears, waved in I think by an unseen magic wand. Her butterscotch hair is falling from its twist.

"Oh, Snooks!" she cries. When I look at her, her eyes are drowning. They're swimming with tears and a dark kind of trouble that wakes Cat and frightens me. I turn away from her, toward Louise.

～

Back at home, Mom rushes about, turning on all the lights till the house glows like a birthday cake. She shows Louise her room and then spreads a picnic on the living-room floor. Everywhere around us are paper parcels from Schwarz and Bonwits and the food shop in the basement of Bloomingdale's. The kitchen is still a mess.

"It's grand, just us girls. Right?" Mom says, pouring grape juice into a wineglass for me.

She pushes the plates of salmon and cheese toward Louise and, from time to time, glances toward the front door. The brimmy, drowning look in her eyes hasn't quite gone away. *I wonder where my Hank is. Addy's father is wonderful, Louise, an absolute genius. You'll like him, I'm sure.* Louise drinks water and sits carefully, her legs tucked beneath her. *When I'm away you may have to fill in for me a bit, but he cooks, mostly looks out for himself. Right, Addy?* I lie on the floor and train my new binoculars on Louise's face. She has a mole like a pencil eraser just above her lip.

When Louise goes to unpack, my mother takes me to bed. She tries to help me undress, but I pull away from her, not wanting to look into her eyes.

"I'm sorry, Snooks. I really am." She sits on the edge of my bed. "You're cross with me," she says softly. "So is your father."

My pajamas are in a heap on the floor and, feeling cold now, I get into them quickly. On the other side of the wall, I can hear bureau drawers opening and closing. Louise hums a pretty tune. I imagine her moving gently about, floating like a dancer. Mom is crying now, and the sound of it makes me feel sick. Keeping my back to her, I get into bed and snap out the light. I'm achy and tired and want to go away from the day.

"Everything is going to be fine, Addy. I promise," she says in the darkness. "It'll all be just fine."

I listen to the sounds on the other side of the wall and find I cannot keep my eyes open. It is much later, I think, when my father returns home.

Jesus, this place is a fucking pigsty
Please keep your voice down, Hank. I got back late and
Look at this. Look at this!
It's my fault. I said I'm sorry. The meeting went on
Thank Jerry for me, will you? Tell him I couldn't be more pleased. Really.

Up rises furry spine. I wait for the scratch of his sandy tongue, for nails on the bedpost, for the long night ahead. But when my father's voice recedes, I hear only the sound of Louise's steady breathing, close by. Cat turns and takes his leave.

7

SEE THAT MOUNTAIN over there?" Philip said, pointing to a tiny island just off shore. Together, its two uneven hillocks resembled a sleeping woman, her back to us. "It's called Morne des Serpents. It used to be a volcano. A long time ago a giant boa constrictor, four hundred feet, crawled from the sea and settled at the bottom of the hole."

We were sitting at a table that had been plunked down in the sand outside a waterfront bar, waiting for word on the Cadillac. My head now cooled, I was just about to apologize for the trouble I'd caused and insist on paying for the damage when Philip began to describe our surroundings. He leaned in close to me, his expression grave.

"She stayed in there and, over the years, had thousands of babies. Twisting and turning on top of each other. Serpent stew."

My flesh crawled. Philip brought his voice down to a whisper.

"If you're foolish enough to go up there? Well, my aunt Marva knew a lady who did. If you go up there and look down on them, you die RIGHT ON THE SPOT!"

With the last words he slammed his palm down, making me jump, the uneven legs of the chair pitching me sideways. I hung on to the table to stop myself from falling over. Breaking up with laughter, Philip reached out and helped me right myself, then smacked me on the shoulder. I watched him as he kept laughing, his gangly legs poking up around the sides of the table, and thought he looked about twelve years old, which was around the same age he was acting. Philip, it seemed, had a unique way of making me feel stupid. He was beginning to get on my nerves.

"Don't worry," he said, grinning now. "He never bothers with white people."

"That why you're still alive?" I asked, unable to check my sarcasm.

Philip tucked his chin back in an attitude of mock indignity.

"Shit, no. I ain't white. I'z a nee-gro!"

Between our table and the water, a man in dreadlocks and a threadbare UC Berkeley T-shirt squatted on the beach, scaling a pile of fish. He dropped his head, trying to hide his laughter. Until then, I hadn't known he was listening to us.

I was flummoxed by Philip's looks. The photos of the boys that Lou had had in her room were small and, as I remembered them, bent and faded. I couldn't even say for sure, after twenty years, if they were color or black-and-white. Maybe I'd seen only what I'd expected to find.

So what of Lou's husband, the father of these men? I recalled his name suddenly. Errol.

Errol.

Lou's voice again, clear as the sound of seawater washing the shore just ahead of us. I closed my eyes for an instant and a figure, entirely in shadow, came to me. That's all there was. In my mind,

Errol had always been a dark man in darkness and nothing more. I knew the boys had a father but — now I wondered why — I had pretended he didn't exist. For me, there were only women on St. Clair. Women and boys. *Errol.*

I turned my attention back to Philip, who was bugging his eyes out at me and grinning like Stepin Fetchit. I had dozens of questions, but I didn't want to ask any of them. I resolved to keep quiet and ignore Philip's patronizing. He didn't seem to notice or care what I was thinking. Finished with his routine, he cuffed me lightly on the arm.

"You sure you don't want a beer?"

I swirled the ice around in the pulpy bottom of my pineapple juice and shook my head.

"I got the good skin. Like my pappy," he said, stretching himself and revealing his tanned, hairy stomach.

Philip, it was plain to see, had a beautiful body. I looked away and out at the little whitecaps in the harbor. Three pelicans swooped down, dropped their prehistoric beaks into the water, and took off again. Deeply uncomfortable, I felt compelled to talk.

"Is that why Derek's so angry?"

"Oh, *Derek* woulda been pissed if he'd been born the Duke of Windsor."

"So I shouldn't take it personally."

"Well, yeah, you probably should. But so what."

I turned back to Philip, who was smiling warmly at me now. My curiosity was beginning to get the better of me.

"Has he always been like this?" I asked.

He gave my question some thought and shrugged.

"Yeah. No. Probably. I didn't really grow up with him, so I can't say for sure. But he wasn't so mingy, tight like that, when we were real small. He's suffered a lot of disappointment, my brother."

"What do you mean you didn't grow up with him?"

"I grew up with Errol in Eldertown, mostly. With my step-mother, Patrice, till she sent me to school in the States. I never spent much time with my real mumma till the last few years, after Patrice died and a lot of shit started to come down."

"When did they divorce?" I asked, trying hard now to recall what I knew.

Philip began to laugh again. But this time he wasn't mocking me. I'd struck a nerve.

"Oh, they weren't *married*, Errol and Louise! Don't you know what they say down here? 'If you're white, it's all right; if you're brown, stick around; but if you're black, GET BACK!'"

"Wait, is your father white?" I asked, incredulous.

Sobering up, Philip leaned on the table and looked down at his arm and mine.

"Nah. Not white. He's like me." He ran his finger across my hand. The contrast was great. "He's not real white, like you."

Reflexively, I pulled away, and we both turned to look for the waiter. Just then, a man who had helped with the boat came into the bar and told us that the tow truck had arrived. Philip thanked him and proffered a crumpled dollar bill.

"Let's go see what this Clifton has to say."

I followed Philip back to the car, where we found a man in bare feet squatting down, inspecting the fender. Half of his ass was exposed above the top of his ripped denim shorts, and his chest was bare. Philip caught my eye and, trying to make me laugh, stuck out his tongue and waggled it obscenely. The tow truck, a rusty jalopy, was fitted with a winch made of recycled metal and old rope.

"Hey, boss," Philip said, eyeing the hook suspiciously.

"Yah, boss," replied the mechanic, standing up and stroking the scraggly hairs on his chin.

"What yah say?"

"Mmm. Yah needing a new headlight, leastways," he said, showing as he spoke a broad hole where his four front teeth should have been. "And a fender. Gonna need some front end work too. Big job, boss."

"Well, can you get it running again or can't you?" asked Philip, anxiety creeping into his tone.

"Me try."

"You call up by the Alfred house and let me know."

Clifton gave a toothless smile.

"Got no phone, Bakra Man."

Philip sighed, took a wad of cash from his back pocket, and peeled off a few bills. I pulled out my own wallet, but Philip waved me away.

"Do what you can, then," he said to Clifton. "I'll check you later."

When we got down the street a ways, I asked Philip the meaning of what the mechanic had called him.

"Nothing," he said, stiffening.

"Come on."

"It's what slaves used to call plantation owners. It means well-endowed white guy. A jerk, basically."

It was my turn to laugh, discovering too late that Philip's sense of humor failed when he himself was the subject. We returned to the scene of the accident and I helped him wrap the sail, securing it across the boat's little open hull. Philip walked around to her stern. Running his hand over a row of dislodged, chewed-up nails, he looked bereft for the first time since we'd met.

"They met in a movie house," Philip said quietly.

"In the summer, we used to go nearly every night," I told him, remembering the evenings at my grandmother's beach house.

"Guess he wasn't seeing her too clearly, in the dark," he said, his mouth turned up in a smirk. His mind was a long way from the sidewalk where we stood.

Philip and I walked a circular route back through town and he gave me a bit of St. Clair history, a thumbnail sketch of its passage through Dutch, French, and English hands. He impressed me with the breadth of his knowledge. When I told him so, he shrugged.

"I was prelaw in college. Thought I'd come home and shake my fist, become president of St. Clair!"

"So what happened?"

Philip laughed.

"President of St. Clair? Please. I mean, who gives a shit? Anyway, I had other things to do. Family business to run. I'll leave the showboating to my papa."

~

Errol, his son told me, was once an entertainer. He'd also been a politician, a taxi driver, a doorman at the Hotel Caribe, and a restaurateur whose famous charm had made him a minor Windward celebrity. All that was gone now, replaced by age and grief. Errol had probably earned his unhappiness, Philip conceded, though he really wasn't a bad man. He had just, over a lifetime, let a lot of people down. Not the least being, of course, the woman he loved the most.

In 1964, when Errol Hodge met Louise Alfred, he was already a couple of years into a gig that seemed to suit him perfectly. Three nights a week, he headlined at Foxy's Palace, thrilling to the attention and making enough money to spend the remainder of his time in other, more idle pursuits. "Back then, Foxy's was the number one," said Philip, with a touch of pride. A swank watering hole, it was the kind of place where tourists and locals mamboed and cha-chaed under the stars, and big-name performers regularly stopped in on their way back from Havana. With a limited vocal range and a couple of enormous feet suited to only the simplest of steps, Errol wasn't exactly Harry Belafonte. But no matter. His light skin and devastating smile had a mesmerizing effect on the ladies. And Foxy, who discovered the young man wasting his looks as a shoe shine, paid him an enviable wage to headline when the big bands weren't in town.

On his nights off, Errol invariably went to the movies. Down at the Eldertown Cinema, the only movie house on St. Clair, first-run American pictures played on a wide screen just weeks after their stateside debut. "Everybody got together there," said Philip. "Catch the picture and then just hang around outside, liming, chatting each other up, till it was time to go home." Errol loved the movies, but he loved people more. As popular offstage as on, he was at the center of any group and the very last one to depart when Bobsled began turning out the lights. "Like I said," Philip reported with an ironic chuckle, "he was an entertainer." Errol was thirty years old, with no inclination to change, till the evening when an argument with Bobsled Terry turned his life upside down.

Friday night was always a double bill. Not, as Bobsled would grouse, to be confused with a two-for-one. "If yah staying, yah pay-ing," he'd warn each and every customer as he ripped their stubs. Unfortunately, the man had a couple of enforcement problems. "Bobsled was cheap *and* he was nearly blind," recounted Philip. "They say he had a old piece of cane, for getting around. And he would throw up the lights between shows, then go down each aisle, knocking it back and forth, sweeping the place for cheaters. Then everybody'd go hiding in the bathroom or crawling up this ladder he had and hanging all in the beams of the place. Everyone cheated Bobsled."

Except Errol. Errol liked Bobsled. Their fathers had been friends, and the men had known one another since grade school. For years, Errol maintained that on the night in question a jealous boyfriend must have given Bobsled some bad information. When Bobsled shined his flashlight on Errol halfway through *Viva Las Vegas,* he stared into the spotlight in disbelief. Bobsled tapped his knee with the cane and told him to pay up. Errol swore he already had. Their argument became a shouting match and, with the rest of the house hissing its complaint, Errol flew up the aisle after Bobsled. He was well inside the tiny office behind the projector, still cursing Bobsled a wicked mile, before he saw the young woman bent over the accounting books. She wore a simple gray blouse buttoned high, and at her left elbow was a Bible. When she looked up at him with her enormous eyes, he felt as strange and new as if he'd just been born.

" 'That girl *saw* me, for true.' That's what Papa always said. Like he thought no one had ever actually seen him before. Like *everyone* was blind but her."

Despite his way with women, Errol's powers failed him when he met Louise. Miraculously, she wasn't interested in him. Not in the least. This, however, didn't deter Errol; it emboldened him. "They both of them stubborn as mules." Errol had never really been in love before, and the effort required to catch Louise's eye served only to convince him this was It.

"So Papa got religion," Philip said, laughing, as we drew up to the footpath I'd taken down the hill.

In the twenty minutes since we'd begun our walk, a canopy of clouds had draped the sky, portly and gray.

"Mumma, I'm told, did her best to ignore him. She was living down with my uncle Michael and studying to be a teacher. Going to be the first in the family to go to college. In Jamaica. My grandmother had it all planned. But Papa followed her home. Every night for two weeks, professing his love. Mumma just smiled at him, barely said a word, ducking inside quicklike when they made it to the door. He wasn't getting *anywhere*. Until he started studying the Bible. He got the spirit, you could say, quoting scripture to her, preaching the virtues of humility, the works. I suspect he was hard to resist, even for someone serious as my mumma. She finally invited him in for tea and introduced him to Michael. After that, Papa asked her and Michael to come to Foxy's and hear him sing. That's when Michael decided *for* Mumma. I think my uncle Michael had plans for Papa from the very beginning."

With rain threatening, Philip picked up the pace, moving ahead of me as we wound uphill. Listening carefully to his story, I took my eyes off the steep path and several times stumbled on rocks and old roots. At one point, Philip reached back to help me over a particularly steep embankment. I thrilled at the warmth of his hand, surprised by my reluctance to let go. I was entranced, by him, by the story, so much so that we were a good way up the hill before I realized how difficult a hike it was for me. I stopped, sweating and out of breath.

"You ain't much of an athlete, are you?" asked Philip jovially.

"What makes you say that?" I responded, bent over, hands braced on my knees. We probably hadn't climbed more than fifty yards.

"A hunch is all."

"I'm not a billy goat. But I get by. What did Michael think?"

"Michael thought he'd caught himself a big fish. My uncle was agitating for independence. Needed a front man, someone to sponsor for Parliament. Soon as he saw the way everyone fell all over Errol, he figured he'd found his man."

I was still working for breath.

"You need stamina," Philip said, touching his chest. "You got kids?"

The question jarred, and returned me to a self I'd momentarily left behind.

"Why does everyone ask that around here?" I snapped.

"Don't know," he replied. "Everybody's got someone."

"It's rude, I think."

"Sorry. I just figured."

"Figured what?"

"I don't know. That you did. Sorry."

"No. I don't. OK?"

Philip stopped and let me catch up, then touched my arm.

"Christ," he said, his voice soft. "Lighten up, will you? Your pretty face gettin' all pruney."

I felt myself blush violently.

"Hmm. Lighten up?" I replied. "OK. Yeah."

Feeling dumb, out of line and awkward too, I tried to be funny. Flapping my arms, putting on a face. We rose to the top of the hill and, though I was still short of breath, I took his hand and did a goofy kind of jig. I'm not sure what had gotten into me. Philip appraised my moves.

"Now you're in business. Look out, don't give yourself a heart attack!"

I was aware suddenly of my body and how shapeless it appeared in the oversized clothes and hat I was wearing. Philip caught me looking down at myself.

"Did you meet Floria?" he asked, gesturing toward the Alfreds'. "She's big as a house and she's still foxy as hell."

"Floria?"

"My wife. Due in two weeks." He held out his arms from his stomach. "Now that girl's got stamina!"

The rain, which had been out over the water, edged closer to us. I watched the fast-moving clouds while Philip kept talking, about what I'm not sure. The sound of my own voice inside my head was too loud. Just before we got to the Alfreds' backyard, Philip asked me a question, bringing me around.

"Hey, Connecticut. Let me ask you something. Is it true you were . . . sort of crazy? When you were little?"

His words stabbed the woolly fuzz of my thoughts, but I couldn't focus on them. I wanted to be alone.

"Yeah," I answered vaguely. "Sort of, I guess."

" 'Cause I was expecting, well, sorry, but a real cuckoo kind of girl."

I pretended to laugh as, just then, the skies broke open with fat, slow drops of rain. Philip pulled on my sleeve, but I stopped by the back door and told him I'd be right in. The downpour began in earnest, and I took shelter under the house's metal eaves, sitting down to rest on Lou's rattan chair. Way out on the horizon, it was again a fair day, the setting sun fanning out in a citrusy pool.

It hadn't been much. No more than a minute of, what? The most casual flirtation? But I began to burn, sitting there, set upon by a rash of anger and embarrassment. My feelings crept up my neck like an allergic reaction, making me want to remove my own skin. Fuck you, I thought, blood throbbing in my head. I don't need your charity. And I don't want your friendship, either.

Eventually my childish temper gave way to something else, more closely resembling fear. A lack of control seemed to be dogging me, overtaking my usual equilibrium with way too much frequency. I'd just barely pulled myself back together — it had been less than a month since my sickness — and here I was threatening to fall apart all over again. Was I still feverish? Or was this some bigger calamity?

The story of Lou and Errol, of their courtship, arose again and played over my dismal concerns. I rubbed my thumb along a smooth spot on Lou's armrest, where the same repetitive motion from her must have worn thin the veneer. I wished she were there, to calm me. Closing my eyes, I could just about feel the whisper of Lou's skin against mine. *Lickle Miss Shirley Temple, you so baaad.* I sat and breathed, listening to the rain taper as the clouds moved through.

8

I T'S SUNDAY MORNING and Louise is taking me to church. She tells me which kind, but I can't get the word off my tongue.

"Apixilan," I say while she stands above me and holds open the waist of my tights so that I can step into them. I lean back and she braces me between her arms.

"It's jes' a certain kind of Christian. And yah got it here like we do at home."

Spring has begun to surface in the weeks since Louise arrived. Daffodils are showing their buttery bonnets out on the lawn, and the tree outside my window blossomed overnight into cotton candy. The soft petals brush against the window screen, disappearing behind a blue veil as Louise pulls a jumper over my head. My clothes are fresh and smell of morning.

I've never been to church before. June told Louise that my family doesn't practice religion. And when I asked my father what we are, he raised an eyebrow and laughed.

"Cynics," he said, turning back to his newspaper, in a voice that made me decide not to tell Louise the answer. The word sounded wicked and echoes grimly in my head.

Louise keeps a Bible by her bed. Some nights after dinner she leaves me alone in front of the television while she goes upstairs to read. If I follow her she lets me stay, rubbing my back while she keeps her head bent, slowly turning the delicate pages. The book's leather binding is soft and dark, like Louise's hand. Its gold-edged paper catches the light. When Louise reads, I'm inside a warm hollow, like a giant's palm, and the ceiling is raked with stars. I have had a wish, one I made and then buried, that my mother would go away.

Two days have passed since Louise spoke with Dilly about church.

"Dilly," she said, drying a plate and looking out the window over the sink. Dilly had come in for a cup of coffee and was on his way back out the kitchen door. "I'm wanting yah to carry me down to de Anglican." Louise stopped and sucked a tooth. "Hear me now, Anglican, I mean Episcopal, church on Sunday. Down by de market."

Whenever Louise speaks, Dilly's face turns very serious. His eyebrows shoot downward and he pulls at the corner of his mustache. I watched him concentrating hard on Louise as she spoke.

"You want me to take you to church on Sunday? Is that it?"

"De service is at nine, for an hour. Den I'll be ready to come home."

Dilly nodded slowly and walked out the door, where I could see him scratch the top of his head and adjust his cap before getting back on his mower.

Sundays are Louise's day off. Mom says we're not to bother her on those days. We're all to make do, she says. But so far, Louise has been just the same on Sundays, spending the day with me as always. Maybe it's because there's nothing to do in Coldbrook. Today, though, she wants to go to church, and she's invited me to come along.

Louise walks me into the bathroom and sits down on the lid of the toilet.

"Commere witcha razzy head," she says reaching for the hairbrush resting on the sink. I back up toward the door. She holds the brush high.

"Yah not entering de house of de Lord wit yah head like dat. So if yah wanting to come wit me, let me do my work."

Until now, Louise hasn't said a word about my hair. I'd thought she didn't see the fuzzy knots, the patches that had become sticky to the touch. Or maybe I looked like a black girl now. I wanted her to notice, but now that she has, I run to the bed with a screech.

I stuff my head beneath a pillow. The truth is I hate my hair this way but can't admit it. I keep it wrecked for my mother, because it makes her sad. Too many ideas and feelings jab at me. I'm anxious, unhappy, and I'm ashamed for disobeying Louise. But what is strangest is what I cannot find. There's no red anger rising, no prickly skin, no sandpaper tongue of the enemy. I wait for Cat, but he doesn't come. Louise doesn't sit on the edge of the bed the way Mom does, doesn't plead, doesn't offer a leg for me to kick at, an arm to twist away from. With Louise, there is no inky darkness, no place to go. I'm at loose ends, and the air beneath the pillow quickly becomes hot and thick.

I turn the pillow aside in search of fresh air. Beyond the open bathroom door I can see Louise at the mirror, adjusting the pins in her small round hat. In the reflection, she catches my eye.

"Yah don't wanna be raging against me," she says, her voice quiet and simple. "A child's always got the power to break her mumma's heart. But yah cyaant break mine; not yet, Addy."

I lie on the bed and listen to a bird calling outside the window. Bob White, says the bird. Bob White.

"All right den, Addy, I'll see yah after service."

Before she can walk away, before I can think anymore, I walk, head bent, back into the bathroom.

The first stroke of the brush brings tears to my eyes, and Louise must take a scissors to three impossible nests. When she's done she fastens the top of my hair with a blue ribbon. I can't stop a smile when Louise looks at me head-on.

We walk down the long hall that separates our rooms from the big center of the house. I get up on my tiptoes as I pass my parents' door and am rounding the corner to the top of the stairs when I catch the smell of frying bacon coming up the stairwell. Louise's eyebrows are raised in surprise. Grabbing the bannister, I clatter down the stairs.

The kitchen is a cloud of blue-brown smoke. Louise pushes past me and turns off the burner that flames beneath a cast-iron pan. Five or six tar black strips of bacon spit their last, drowning in a pool of hot grease. I look to the far end of the room, where the table is set for four, crowned at the center by a clutch of forlorn daisies in a crystal vase. Mom sits at her place with her back to us, turned to face the sliding glass doors that open to the back lawn. A half dozen sooty cigarette filters fill an ashtray at her elbow. In her lap is a script open to the last pages.

At the sound of my hard-soled shoes on the tiled floor, Mom turns around. Her skin and lips and hair seem to disappear, papery and pale against the blushy collar of her robe. The delicate skin beneath her eyes is ashy gray.

"Good morning!" she calls out, her voice faltering on sleep and smoke. Her face looks confused when she notices the haze between her and us.

"Oh," she says, frowning. "Whoopsy daisy."

She walks to the stove, and Louise steps out of the way. When she finds the knob already in the off position, she tugs on it anyway and then peers into the bottom of the pan.

"Oh, well," she says turning to us with a quick, tired smile. "My gosh, Addy." My mother looks me up and down. "You let Louise brush your hair!"

I feel I've lost something. I turn my ankles and say nothing.

"Thank you," Mom says to Louise, extravagantly. "Well. Hmm." She turns back to the stove, as if she is looking for something but not sure what, then returns to us, her greenish eyes watery and bright. "Don't you look lovely. Where are you off to?"

"Church. Dilly's coming to carry us dere. Addy says she's never been."

My mother laughs gently.

"Oh Louise, that's totally unnecessary. It's your day off. I'm going to do lots of fun things with Addy. You go on."

I make a squawking sound. Louise squeezes my shoulder.

"Now baby, remember what I told you about Sundays," my mother says, pushing a lock of hair from her eyes.

"It's no bother," Louise says. "I asked she to come."

My mother looks from me to Louise and back again.

"Addy. Don't you want a yummy Sunday breakfast?" she says.

I turn my face into the folds of Louise's dress and begin to holler. Louise pulls me away from her and squats down.

"Stop it, Addy. Now listen, don't yah want stay wit yah mumma?"

I look up at Mom, shake my head.

My mother frowns, sticks her lower lip out. Like children do.

"Okeydokey," she says, sighing and turning away. She scouts about for a place to put the ruined frying pan. "You go with Louise. We'll do something together later. That's fine."

~

When we get in the car, Louise sits with me in the backseat. Dilly pulls the car out of the driveway and we head down the road toward town.

"Yah a hardheaded lickle ting, aren't yah?" she says, watching the Schroeders' farm passing outside her window. I think she must be angry with me, but I don't care. I am with her and we are driving fast away from home.

Ten minutes later, we're in Coldbrook center. Dilly drives around the green and onto Ford's Hill, where the grocery store, the elementary school, and the town's three churches are. Ford's Hill is all of Coldbrook center. Don't blink or you'll miss it, Dilly says.

We pull up to the front of an old white church next to the market. Louise looks out the window and eyes it from steeple to steps.

"That's it," she says, clutching her purse in her lap. Behind her glasses, the corner of her eye twitches almost imperceptibly. "An hour's time, Dilly."

Dilly drives off, leaving us on the sidewalk. Little bunches of snowy clouds sail along over the roof of the church. Lilacs bloom in purple profusion on either side of the building's big red doors, and I hear simple chords of music float out from the darkness inside. Louise takes my hand and we walk up the rutted cement path. Off to the side in the parking lot, people are nodding, waving to one another, saying hello.

The two Wyant boys, Kurt and Eddie, stand on the church's stone steps. Kurt is a fat boy with a blond brush cut. His face, always flushed, looks today like a cherry red balloon squeezed by the knot of his brown tie. The buttons of his shirt strain across his soft belly. Kurt's younger brother, Eddie, has the same yellow broom of hair and enormous eyes that roll in his face like a doll's. When Kurt sees us, he sticks an elbow in his brother's side and puffs out his cheeks. Eddie's eyes jump out another inch from their sockets.

Louise and I follow a line of people up the stairs. When we reach the top, I'm a foot from Kurt and Eddie. I look at the legs of the man ahead of me. A noise I've known since the beginning of second grade, like something gnawing through paper, comes from the boys' direction.

"Fff-fff-fff-ff," comes the sound. "Rat Girl. Rat Girl. Fff-ff-ff." Eddie meows like a cat.

"Rats don't go to church," Kurt whispers. "Who brushed your hair, Rat Girl? Is that your new mommy?"

The boys begin to snort and laugh. On the other side of the doors, a skinny man in a tie and cowboy boots is handing out programs. He looks over the heads of the people filing in and cuts his eyes at Kurt and Eddie. The boys quiet down, but when I glance over, they're still looking at me. Kurt's lips are pursed together to keep from laughing. The man in the cowboy boots hands Louise a program and nods his head in silent greeting.

Inside the church, Louise guides me to an empty row near the back and follows behind me, directing me to sit down. The big open space hums and rustles with the settling of people in their seats. Up in the balcony Mrs. Labenski, a teacher at my school, plays the organ. Louise has gotten on her knees and is praying silently. As she does so, a man in the row in front of us turns his thick neck and peers over his glasses at her. When his eyes catch mine, he twitches his mouth and turns quickly away.

Across the aisle ahead of us, I see Mrs. Chisolm, who owns the market, in a yellow suit and a giant green hat wreathed in fake flowers. Her daughter Amy baby-sat for me a few times before Louise arrived, but I've never seen Mrs. Chisolm herself outside of the store. When I go shopping with Dilly, she presses the buttons of the cash register and asks me questions about my family — how my mother is feeling, what big travel plans we have coming up — but when I'm with my mother, she sneaks glances at her over her half lenses and says nothing. Since Louise has come, Mrs. Chisolm lets her glasses dangle on their chain and leans her elbows on the worn linoleum counter.

"She treat you good? She sure got the money to, right?" I heard her ask Louise one day, her voice low like they were sisters.

Louise nodded just barely and began to scoop up the grocery bags.

"God bless you," Mrs. Chisolm said, leaning back and patting her breastbone. "Suits me fine my Amy not working up by there anymore. She says that house is a godalmighty wreck."

Now Mrs. Chisolm is sitting next to her husband near the front of the church and she is waving at me with a hand up tight by her shoulder, like the wing of a wounded bird. Mr. Chisolm, out of his bloody apron, is bending his bald head awkwardly over his shirt collar as he peruses the program. While Louise prays, Mrs. Chisolm continues to watch her, craning her neck to get a view between the shoulders of the people behind her.

A man in a white robe, his waist cinched with a length of rope, emerges from a side door and walks up to the platform. His face is round and flat and white. Like a dinner plate. Everyone rises at once, including Louise, who touches my arm. *The minister,* she whispers. Mrs. Chisolm turns around again, breaking into a broad, lip-sticky grin when Louise finally returns her gaze. Arm still close to her chest, Mrs. Chisolm is flapping her hand now. *Hi, Louise,* she silently mouths, then nudges her husband. Mr. Chisolm turns his shiny head and nods once, then looks away.

While the music from upstairs continues to play, the minister stands with his hands clasped, looking out at all the people. Two girls older than I, also in robes, stand behind him holding candles on brass poles. A boy carries a gold cup to a table. The minister's eyes land on me and Louise, and stay there. When the music ends, the people shuffle their feet against the wood floor and sit down.

"Good morning," says the minister.

"Good morning," respond the people, all together.

"And what a good morning it is," the minister continues, his voice simple and clear. "We are truly blessed by this beautiful day, a gift of God's creation."

He smiles, his teeth like cubes of yellow cheese.

"I want to welcome you all here today, those from our parish, as always, and most especially warm greetings to visitors from other parishes, as well as new members of our flock." He spreads his arms wide and casts his eyes about the room. "Welcome to you all."

As if they were responding to a loud sound or flash of light, the churchgoers turn toward Louise and me. More eyes than I can count, some friendly and others wide with wonder, look out from faces I don't recognize. Louise stares straight ahead and holds a handkerchief tight in her hand. The minister raises his voice and the people turn back around and face him.

"As I took my morning walk an hour or so ago, I noticed, as most of you likely did, that the fields of Coldbrook are particularly ripe with promise this spring." The minister's voice fills the church and fastens the people's attention. I lean forward and watch their quiet, upward-turning faces.

"I know for those parishioners who work the land how important this verdancy, this blossoming, is each year. Reaping the harvest puts the kids through school, replaces the worn muffler on the family car, adds to the kitty for that long-awaited Florida vacation. But what of the rest of us? How often do we take time from our busy day to marvel at this great bounty? The wondrousness of God? I'd like to begin today with a reading from Ezekiel. 'And the word of the Lord came unto me, saying . . .'"

There isn't anyone else, not another pair of eyes or back of a head, that looks like Louise. No one has skin that is dark like hers, no one has a nose so broad. There isn't a shiny and curly head of hair in the church that resembles hers. I look down at Louise's hand resting on my knee.

"And they were scattered, because there is no shepherd, and they became meat to all the beasts of the field . . ."

Louise is different, I think. Louise is different and I am different.

But Louise is stranger than I.

The idea rushes my senses, making me sick with the sudden excitement.

For once I am not last.

"Therefore will I save my flock, and they shall no more be a prey . . ."

In the back of the church, a baby begins to cry.

"And I will set up one shepherd over them, and he shall feed them . . ."

Sunlight filters through the red and gold stained glass on one side of the church, spilling colored light across the floorboards, playing across Mrs. Chisolm's green hat, casting a picture on the far wall like a slide show. A woman holding her baby, the baby Jesus, I think, both of their heads surrounded by crowns of gold. Their skin, made of dusky triangles of glass, is neither dark nor light.

Heat from the sun waves the picture against the wall, like water, and I imagine swimming in the currents of color.

"And the tree of the field shall yield her fruit, and the earth shall yield her increase . . ."

I am lost in the gold, the amber, and green. Organ music begins again and Louise is tugging at my arm. The people are on their feet.

"Joyful, joyful, we adore thee . . . ," they all begin to sing. Louise sings too. I don't understand how she knows the same words to the same song when she's never been here before. It seems a kind of magic, a mysterious circle I'm being drawn into. Louise's voice is high and clear, and impossibly sweet. Leaning against her, I close my eyes and feel the vibration from her voice in my own chest.

When I sit up again, Kurt Wyant is craning his head around in the pew in front of us, baring his teeth at me, *ff-ff-ff.* The people are making a line up the center aisle, walking to the raised platform up front. Once there, they kneel and sip from the cup made of gold. The Chisolms make their way to the altar. The Wyant boys waddle out with their mother. But when I try to follow Louise, she stays me with her hand.

"Yah cyaant take communion," she whispers. "Stay right here."

My face goes hot, my mind is racing with confusion. I can't drink from the cup of gold. I can't drink from the cup, but the Wyant boys can. The Chisolms can. Louise can. When she returns I latch onto her arm.

Louise is guiding me out of the church. At the door, the minister stands in his white robe, shaking hands and nodding. He holds a Bible just like Louise's. When the service ended, I saw Mrs. Chisolm scurry out the far end of her pew. Now she is standing just inside the red doors. I can see her smiling and laughing with people as they leave, but she breaks off several times to look toward Louise and me. When we arrive at the doorway, Mrs. Chisolm cuts through the line to the minister's side.

"Here, here," Mrs. Chisolm says, breathy as if she's been jogging. Her face is orangey, wrinkled, like a rotting peach. She touches the minister's elbow.

"Reverend Malone, I want you to meet Louise, who I told you all about. She's the new maid, um, help, living up at the Abrahams'. Louise, this is the Reverend Harold Malone."

Several people already outside in the sunshine turn around to watch us. Mrs. Chisolm's lipstick has worked its way into red veins running outward from her lips. While Reverend Malone shakes hands with Louise, Mrs. Chisolm takes a cigarette out of her shiny purse and lights it, blowing the smoke out the door.

"Welcome to our parish," says the minister, his cool blue eyes dancing in his platter face. "Delightful to have you. Delightful."

Louise offers him a tiny close-lipped smile, saying nothing.

"I hope our service didn't disappoint you," the minister continues, still holding Louise's hand, "that it compares acceptably with your church back home?"

Louise is looking down shyly, away from the minister's gaze and speaks just above a whisper.

"Yes, thank you."

"And this is the Abrahams' girl, Addy," Mrs. Chisolm says, grabbing at Reverend Malone's elbow and pointing at me. "Amy cared for her some. I don't know as they've ever been in here. *Such* busy people. Isn't that right? *She's* from New York."

The minister bends down.

"Well, nice to meet you, Addy. Welcome to Coldbrook Episcopal. Hope to see more of you."

His breath smells like sour milk, and I step back into the legs of a man behind me. Louise has moved down into the churchyard. I lurch forward and begin to run out after her when I feel a burning, like the twist of a rope, on my upper arm. Mrs. Chisolm has her hand around me and is pulling me in to her side. Her nails dig hard into my flesh.

"You ought to tell your mother to give that poor colored lady a break," Mrs. Chisolm whispers in my ear, her breath hot and cigaretty. A slash of red stains Mrs. Chisolm's front teeth. I try to get away.

"Having to bring you along on a Sunday. *Shame* on them."

When my mouth meets Mrs. Chisolm's skin, she lets loose a shriek that bounces against the high ceiling of the church foyer and out the front doors. Louise is back up the stairs in an instant, but not before I've left a perfect imprint of my teeth on the fat of Mrs. Chisolm's upper arm.

Louise will not speak to me on the way home. Alone in the back of the car, I want to say I'm sorry. I roll the word, heavy as a stone, around on my tongue, where the tastes of blood and talcum powder linger. Instead I keep my lips closed, and *sorry* lands with a silent splash where it always does, in a dark place beneath my heart.

9

I REENTERED THE ALFREDS' house that evening just in time to hear my name being spoken somewhere within.

"Addy, not Annie. Adelaide, Papa. But dey call she Addy."

Marva was in the living room, tucking a blanket around an old man's legs and shouting to be heard by him. The soles of my wet sandals squeaked against the wood floor.

"Here, Papa."

She guided me in front of her father's cloudy eyes.

"Do I know her?" he asked, his head and neck bobbing about in the collar of his shirt like a turtle's. Marva propped and adjusted him with swift efficiency.

"She's de girl Lulu cared for in de States. 'Member when Lulu went in de States?"

Mr. Alfred shook his head dismissively and looked toward the side of his chair, as if searching for something else to engage him. With no teeth to support his mouth, his lower jaw folded up like a brown paper bag.

"Don't know no Lulu."

Marva looked at me and rolled her eyes.

"Well, yes yah do, Papa. Lulu was yah youngest. Louise. Derek's mother. And she jes' pass away, jes' now. Addy's come fi go to de funeral."

His head continued to shake — up, down, sideways. Parkinson's, I guessed. I began to get a fairer idea of Marva's life, day-to-day.

"Don't know no Lulu," Mr. Alfred repeated.

"He gets some better dan dis," Marva said, moving off toward the kitchen. "Him at his worst when he first wakes up from his nap."

Mr. Alfred turned his head back in my direction.

"Thank you for stopping by," he said in a deliberate, practiced way. He sounded like a Berlitz student. "It's very nice to be seeing you again."

I took a seat on the edge of the sofa and thanked him for having me, finding that soon I was bobbing my own body, emphasizing my appreciation with a sympathetic sort of mimicry. I made myself stop, but soon, hopelessly, began again. Mr. Alfred's eyes were set on a place over my head. When I was quiet, he moved to fill the gap, pulling lines from some amnesiac's phrase book.

"Where are you living now?"

"I live in New York City," I shouted. "It was eighteen degrees when I left this morning."

Mr. Alfred nodded vacantly. "New York City. Yes."

"It's lovely here. You have a great spot on this hill."

"Yes." He nodded. "Lovely. Lovely. Now tell me, where are you living now?"

As I answered him again, he brought a withered hand up to his mouth and froze suddenly with a look of quiet alarm.

"Can I get you something?" I asked.

His hand stayed in front of his face. Marva halted at the threshold of the room, holding a cold drink.

"What is it, Papa? Yah teeth? Yah want yah teeth?"

Mr. Alfred studied his lap while Marva put down the drink and went toward his bedroom. I studied the bald nails in the floorboards and found, emerging out of my anxiety, a freshly buried memory of my own father. Our most recent meeting. The images shuttled by, rickety like old movie frames, then faded out. My head felt light, spinny.

"Sorry, Papa," said Marva, returning with a glass full of plastic teeth, magnified in water. She was laughing. "I know yah hate to entertain witout yah teeth."

Marva slipped the dentures between her father's lips and wiped at the corners of his mouth with a dishcloth. While he shuffled the teeth around in his face, she turned on a lamp above the old man's head, suffusing the room with a yellow glow. Mr. Alfred looked in my direction and, seeing me fully for the first time, knit together his eyebrows. The light had done nothing to dispel the darkness in my eyes, which I'm sure Mr. Alfred could not help but see.

"Why is she here?" he asked, looking up at Marva.

"I told yah, Papa." She threw her dishcloth over her shoulder. "She come fi de funeral."

"I didn' do anyting," he said.

Marva handed him the glass of tea, and he held it between his shaky hands but didn't drink. He looked at me again and his eyes welled with tears.

"I didn' take 'em," the old man moaned.

"Arright, Papa. Let's not get inna foolishness. Addy's been telling me she fixes up old paintings. Makes dem new again. How about dat?"

Mr. Alfred's Adam's apple bobbed up and down beneath the papery skin of his throat.

"It weren' me. I cyaant even reach de tree," he said, his drink tipping precariously in his hands. "It's Roly Bennett steals de limes, Mumma. It's Roly. It ain't me."

Marva rescued the drink just as it began to spill on Mr. Alfred's lap. He continued on, his weeping eyes now fixed on his daughter's, imploring.

"Don't mek me go wit her; don' wanna go to de big house. Please, Mumma. It weren' me!"

As the old man's voice grew louder and began to trill like that of a captured bird, Derek entered swiftly from the direction of the kitchen and walked straight to his grandfather's chair.

"What's all dis about now, Pappy," he whispered, squatting and stroking his grandfather's head. Mr. Alfred's hand came up, fluttering.

"Tell Miz Buxton I didn' do it! I didn'! I DIDN'!"

I motioned to Marva that I was going to step out. Derek kept his eyes locked on his grandfather, continuing to caress him.

"It's yah grandson Derek, Pappy. It's Derek. Don't yah worry about Mrs. Buxton. She won't harm yah."

Slipping away, I moved into the dark of the hallway and stood motionless while Mr. Alfred continued to shout. I could see through the front door the day's last light playing on the trunk of a poinciana tree and for a few minutes indulged in a fantasy of walking out and leaving the Alfreds' house for good.

Follow the road back south until you get to a phone, then call a taxi, I thought. Or maybe find a bus stop and chance the kindness of local people to guide you back over the mountains to the other side of the island. I saw myself dropping my bags in a clean little hotel room out near the airport. I could take a night walk along the beach, circumnavigating the sunburned couples and their tropical drinks lighting up the poolside bar. When the Alfreds discovered me gone, their surprise and disgust would be quickly overshadowed by their own more profound concerns. In a day's time I'd be back at work and my visit to St. Clair no more than a big, but brief, mistake. Just do it, I was thinking. Cut your losses.

And then, as if from a dream, laughing, came Lou. *Gwan now, Addy, and don't yah be a Frighten' Friday.* It's not that I thought she called to me from the dead, a ghostly apparition. Nothing so daft as that. It was something closer to me. *Upon* me, in fact, like her fingerprint might have been, long unseen but alive again under the ultraviolet light of the crazy day. There was no mistaking the fact that I could hear Lou again, when for so many years she'd been utterly lost to me. I could not but obey her.

Mr. Alfred was quieter now, his monologue mingling with the alarm of a confused rooster, somewhere sounding a continuous reveille.

"What is what is —" he said as Marva and Derek hushed and clucked. "How old I am I is old I what —"

Not wanting to hear any more of him, I moved off down the little hall and turned into an open doorway. There I discovered Cyril sitting on a dingy red carpet in the middle of a cramped room, his head tipped back beneath a bag of potato chips. Watching him from her seat on one of two single beds was a thin woman with a huge belly. She stood up gracefully despite her size and stepped lightly around the boy. Even under the unflattering glare of the overhead bulb she was ridiculously beautiful, her caramel skin set off by eyes of almost cornflower blue. I touched at my bedraggled hair, half expecting it to have fled with the rest of my dignity.

"Hello, I'm Floria," she said, her tone polite and perfect in a way I'd never heard anywhere but the Caribbean. Miss St. Clair, I thought. Or pretty close to it.

"Pardon me," I said, though I'm certain she did not catch the gravity of my meaning. Something about Floria, her eyes or that she was a woman close in age to me, moved me dangerously close to some sort of surrender.

She pressed her palm into mine.

"Not at all. I was just going."

For the first time since I could remember, I thought I might cry. And though I'm sure Floria would have comforted me, I didn't particularly want to break down, especially in front of the boy. Before anything too humiliating could happen, Floria turned back to Cyril.

"You're not going to have any room for dinner," she said, removing the bag from her nephew's face. "Go on and wash up."

Cyril wiped his hands on his T-shirt and picked up his truck. Looking back from the doorway, he stuck his tongue out at me and disappeared. Floria gestured toward the bed upon which my suit-case had been placed.

"There are towels for you in the bathroom," she said, heading after the boy. "Dinner will be in half an hour, I expect." Quietly shutting the door, she left me alone.

It was obvious, with one quick look around, that I was in the bedroom Lou and Marva had shared. The signs were everywhere apparent, spanning the decades without account for the years in which either woman had been away. Mismatched bureaus, beds, tables, and shelves were all squashed against one another, leaving no corner uncovered. A squat bookcase listed against one wall, shoved tight with dusty lesson books. On top, a vase of plastic flowers weighted down a yellowed and crumbling mimeograph of some-one's high school graduation program. Hung on another wall, across from the window, a poster boasted of "The Fair Isles of En-gland," with rolling hills bleached gray by the direct sunlight. And above the bed on which I was to sleep, a series of newspaper clip-pings were pinned to the wall with rusty thumbtacks. I picked my way across the room and leaned over the bed. As I did, the scent of something artificially sweet knocked me back a step, revealing an obscure memory that took me a minute to trace.

~

Lou's hair.

The dark of my room. Late at night.

A chest cold.

My breathing slow and thick. Lou bends over me to rub something icy, minty, on my chest. Her hair glistens in the light from the moon and gives off a candy-sweet smell.

Put yah head back, lickle one

The smell of her hair is frozen, vanquished by the menthol she dabs gently beneath my nose.

In the morning, my mouth waters when I look at the glass jar in her bathroom, filled with the pink jelly that sweetens her hair, so inviting I can already taste it on the back of my throat. Dippity-do.

I fumble with the top, dippity-doing my finger in the cool, soft gel. Slip my finger between my lips.

Candle wax, fire, and alcohol.

BUCKS BEAT ROYALS IN LITTLE CRICKETEERS SEASON OPENER

So read the headline on one of the crumbling brown clippings. The short account praised the teamwork and batting skills of several boys, including Philip Hodge. Under Philip's name was a line where a now-faded ink had once drawn attention to the spot. Along the edge, in the same nearly invisible pen, was a handwritten comment that I didn't read. I stepped back a bit to take in the entire wall.

CHALWELL ACADEMIC PRIZES GO TO LISTON, HODGE
YOUNG BATTER NAMED ALL-ISLAND
THREE SET FOR FALL STUDIES AT AMERICAN UNIVERSITY

Here and there were pictures of Philip, circled in faint lines. His little-boy face staring out from a team picture. A strip of photo-booth shots, mugging, adolescent. The clippings dated mostly from the late sixties and seventies. One, less damaged and with a date only three years past, was posted below the others.

MISS LETTSOME TO MARRY YOUNG HODGE IN MAY

Mr. and Mrs. Gerald "Sugar" Lettsome, proprietors of Sugar's Construction Ltd., in Carrot Bay, have most happily announced the impending wedding of their daughter Floria Hyacinth to Philip Arthur Hodge, son of Mr. Errol Hodge of Eldertown.

The groom, a graduate of Emory University in Atlanta, Georgia, is the chief financial officer of the family concern, Foxy's Ltd., owners of the legendary Foxy's Palace. Foxy's doors were first opened in 1943 by Clemont "Foxy" Rose, father of Errol Hodge's deceased wife, Patrice. Mrs. Hodge was a descendant of Thomas P. Rose, and a valued member of the Eldertown Garden Club.

Miss Lettsome is an afterschool teacher at the St. Clair Boys and Girls Club, where she met the groom-to-be, as he is a member of that organization's board.

The groom is also the son of Miss Louise Alfred of Petionville.

Near the foot of the bed, the cardboard sleeve of a record album was propped against the slatted glass of the window. In the cover photograph, six dreadlocked men posed along the length of a limousine. The car and clothing styles were at least a decade old. *RUDE BOYS*, read the lettering in red, gold, and green above the picture. I looked closely at each face until I found a familiar one. Derek's tiger eyes looked warmly at the camera. He was leaning on the man next to him and laughing. He was in motion, handsome and joyful. If it weren't for his eyes, I might not have recognized him.

There among all the news of her children, I scanned Lou's wall for some evidence of me. Lord knows I should probably have been concerned with something more profound, mindful of the sorrows of others. But I wasn't. Lou had always been a keeper. In her room on Marbury Road, on a shelf with pictures of the boys, she kept a little trove of clippings, trinkets, and ticket stubs arranged just so. If you signified in Lou's life, she had evidence. She had bought me my first diary (white leatherette with a little gold lock and key) and taught me how to press sticky corners on blank pages to make my own photo album.

There was no reminder on that wall of Connecticut, of my family, of me. A dry, crackling vent of air, pollenated with unsavory feelings, blew through me and pitched me back on my heels. I sat down on the bed and rested my head against the wall. I couldn't help but think of my father again. In the stupor of my recent illness, I'd managed to block out our chance reunion. It made me laugh to think I could have forgotten. Maybe the two things, my sickness and Hank's cameo, were directly related. Perhaps the threads of events fit into some natural, mysterious pattern. Hank, the pragmatist, would scoff at such a notion. But how could it be otherwise?

10

~

I RAN INTO MY father on Valentine's Day, less than a month before Lou's death. I remember the afternoon as snowless but
bright and clear cold, the kind of day that makes New York side-
walks glitter like tinsel. That morning I'd woken up and known
something wasn't exactly right. My ears were clogged and there was
a stiffness about my chest, as if some incubus had made a midnight
visit and sealed me in a plaster body cast. I thought about calling in
sick, but with a new collection to be hung, there was just too much
to do. I thought that I was doing just fine, but Emmeline must have
felt otherwise. At noon she made a definitive shooing motion and
sent me out for a break.

I followed the museum's tunnel system as far as it would go, then
pushed my way out onto Fifth Avenue. The bitter wind immediately sprang teardrops to my eyes and froze them on my cheeks. Actually, I remember thinking, I really *don't* feel so hot. Taking a stool
at the closest coffee shop, I hunched over a cup of thin tea and ordered from Rene, the counterman, some toast I knew I wouldn't
eat. The restaurant was freezing, arctic, like a goddamn icebox. Was
the heat on the blink? I wondered, looking at the back of Rene's

sweat-soaked shirt. I swiveled around and was puzzling over the condensation fogging all the plate glass windows when Hank walked through the restaurant's double doors. His face was lost behind an enormous paper cone bearing the name of a Madison Avenue florist, but I recognized instantly his chapped fingers and the wristband of his old Timex.

He took off his winter hat and I watched him, undetected, while he shifted his parcel around, waiting to order. I was amazed at how vulnerable he looked, standing there alone. His white hair, which he'd always worn long, was cut close, exposing his ears in a boyish way. The glasses were the same time-worn tortoiseshell, dull and speckled along the arms from years of being dangled from his mouth and chewed on when he wanted a cigarette. And though the cold had flushed his cheeks, I thought I could see a faded tan from perhaps a tropical vacation not long past. He looked attractive, approachable.

When he spoke to Rene, I leaned in to hear him over the lunchtime din. His voice was soft, almost apologetic, not the deep bass I'd remembered it was but scratchy and thin, as though he were straining against some terrific heartbreak and had to marshal all of his courage just to get to the sentence's end. *Where's my Quiet Boy?* my mother used to say ruefully, dumbfounding me. The father I knew was distant, and at times silent, but even then he was, to my ears at least, thunderous. He was *never* quiet. I was shocked to hear this gentle voice. He sounded like someone thoughtful, decent, a man to whom a young woman might easily be drawn.

It struck me suddenly, seeing him there, how much I resembled my father. We looked like each other but like no one else I knew. I

used to think every older man looked like Hank, and he like them.
They were Fathers, and shared the same Fatherness. I mistook the
back of every graying head for his. But I'd never seen a family resemblance between the two of us. And I knew no other Abrahams
who might have given additional clues, Hank being an only child
whose parents had died long before I was born.

On my mother's side of the family, nobody looked alike. Where
other families are known for how their members resemble one another — generations of golden hair or button noses, square jaws or
widows' peaks — the Kanes resisted replication. When I was a little girl, my grandmother Edith was squat and muscular, wearing her
red hair no-nonsense short like a man's. My mother was all long
legs and blond tresses, her siblings a variety pack of brunets. And
then me, hair black as pitch and skin so blue white that for a time I
misread the label on the milk my mother drank, thinking it was
named for the pallor it resembled. Skin milk. Even my grandfather,
whom I knew only from pictures, was wholly dissimiliar to anyone
else. Like a loose confederation of changelings, we were none of us
alike and startled even ourselves that we shared a family tree. It is
why, I've often thought, my grandmother seemed always disap-
pointed in us but never surprised.

That day at the counter, something particular in my father's
countenance got me up from my stool. His eyes, gray like mine,
held a queer startled expression. The quality made me think of a
face trapped inside a scientist's jar, a mad scientist whose victims
were preserved at the moment of capture. The hint of panic was
entirely familiar. I saw it all the time when I looked in the mirror.

I began to make my way over to him, a little slick of sweat erupting on my forehead. Nerves, I suspected, since my teeth were chattering like a teletype machine. The meeting suddenly seemed lucky; I'd actually had Hank on my mind just a few days before. He'd recently published a new book, the first in ten years or so. *Morality and the Millennium* was a collection of his more recent essays, most of which were political in nature. A disciple of James and Dewey, Hank had taken his former pragmatic position — that the intellectual left could no longer afford to wait for the Ignorant to see the Truth, that time was past due to concentrate on the suffering of our poorest citizens — and turned up the heat to a full scorch. I hadn't read the book myself, but from the damning reviews, I gathered that Hank had attacked not only his enemies on the right but his friends and compatriots as well. I remembered one critique in particular by the conservative commentator Arthur Block in a newsweekly. Block dubbed the book peevish and a flaccid effort from an old warrior. He also scolded Dad for wandering far afield from the courage of his lifelong convictions, even though those convictions had always been disagreeable to Block. He charged Dad with regressing into an "infantile rant" and feebly bolstering his argument with attacks on the Republican congress that were "beneath reproach."

I had also read a quote somewhere from my father's old friend Max Rubinstein, whom Hank had apparently excoriated as a coward. Hank labeled him a cop-out who'd gotten fat in the groves of academe.

"Hell was his heaven and earth," Max rejoined. "Thus spake Zarathustra."

I felt sorry for my father, knowing how sensitive he was to criticism. And I figured as well that at his age, a radical intellectual with unpopular views had a pretty dark future himself. I'd considered calling him but decided that that would only make him feel worse.

When I got around the crowd at the counter, I touched his elbow. He immediately recoiled. It was too late to turn back.

"Oh. Addy," he said, peering over his misted lenses. "Jesus. I . . . I thought you were trying to mug me."

"No, Dad. Just saw you and thought I'd say hi."

The frame of his glasses had broken and was being held together by a fat swatch of duct tape. They bent as he took them off.

"Right, right." He blinked at me like a soft, caged animal.

"What brings you over here?" I asked. My father and his wife lived on Upper Central Park West in an area I took great pains to avoid so as not to run into them.

"Nothing special. Nothing much. Just, you know, errands." He glanced at his package. "Anemones for Linda. She loves them."

Hank had a green thumb. In and around the garden on Marbury Road he could make anything grow. Trembling wisteria, flaming red hibiscus, polyanthus, larkspur. He would lift his worn nylon gimme cap and garden shears from the hooks in the muck room and wander the property every afternoon when the weather was fine. I followed behind at a discreet distance, rapt. It was part of our game to pretend that he couldn't see me. But when he walked through the wooden gate and inside his seedling patch, he always shut the door behind him and held up a hand to stop me following. The first summer after Dad left us, the garden was set upon by rabbits, destroying inside of a month what it had taken him a dozen years to create.

He shifted his parcel, fiddled with the paper.

"Have you a beau these days?" my father asked, careful not to look at me.

I laughed, a phlegmy hiccup, really, shook my head. In the two years since my final breakup with Daniel Moss, I could not claim I'd had so much as a date. Nor had I wanted for any kind of attachment. But it was difficult not to take my father's question as a loaded one and be conscious, as usual, of my failings.

Hank chewed the inside of his lip. I searched for something to say.

"Well, you look really good," I finally ventured, trying not to inflame the situation.

"Thanks, thanks. We went over to Korea, Pusan. You know Linda's family is still there."

I did not know. Linda had been Dad's teaching assistant, and he'd moved from our house directly into her apartment. When he left the university four years later, they moved to New York. I hadn't met Linda more than a handful of times.

"Just got back," he continued. "The food was extraordinary. Extraordinary."

"Great, that sounds great."

My father stole a glance over the cash register and in through the short-order window.

"How's your work? Still at the museum?"

"Yeah. It's good, busy. I'm assistant director of paintings conservation now. So. That's good."

"You sound like you have a cold."

I nodded, waved it off.

"It's really going around," he said. "Linda's got it, Dr. Orkin . . ." My father stopped himself and looked toward the kitchen again. He cleared his throat, adjusted the paper around the flowers. I felt an unexpected wave of dread.

"Who's Dr. Orkin? Dad? Are you sick?"

"No, no. Dr. Orkin's a . . . whatever. He's a psychotherapist." He smiled sheepishly, blushed. "Linda thought I might find it interesting. I've really just started. I don't know if I'll continue. But it's been . . . amusing."

I looked out the window and up the avenue. Shrink Row.

"Wow."

"Is it so surprising?"

"Kind of." I imagined my father in a dimly lit room, wringing his hands in a confessional mode, lightening his load. The idea was grotesque, obscene. And I was stung suddenly with a hot flame of envy.

"But I don't really know you," I continued, trying to be helpful to both of us by closing the subject, "so what do I know."

My father grimaced and shook his head.

"What does that mean — you don't know me?" The woman behind the counter brought out a brown paper bag. He lowered his already low voice. "I'm your father. Jesus, Addy," he hissed, "that is so like you. Always apart. Always judging."

A businessman in an overcoat who'd been waiting behind my father pushed between us with an exasperated shove of the shoulder. Hank picked up his bag and clutched the flowers. I felt the blood leave my face.

"You ought to talk to someone," he said buttoning up his coat. "It can be very instructive."

Hank backed toward the door. With his hat back on, he looked just as he had when I was small. Cloaked and impermeable.

"I wish . . ." he began, and then stopped, fumbled with his packages. "In any case. Good to see you. I'll be in touch." Before the door shut behind him, he turned around.

"I'm sorry," he said.

I waited till I was sure he was gone, paid for my tea and toast, and headed toward the museum.

~

The predella was a Flemish work, in tempera and oil, and I'd been restoring it for a couple of weeks. The panel, along with the triptych it fronted for, had survived a major fire that ravaged a sixteenth-century Italian villa. It was a small miracle that the paintings had made it out at all, and at the pleading of the English auction house that had rescued them, our atelier had agreed to make a restoration effort. The work was tough, not only because of the smoke and fatty deposits that obscured much of the painting's detail, but also because I had no conclusive evidence as to the artist's identity.

I spent the first few days viewing the panel and doing research. The scene was of a figure at sea, with his sail blowing out in tatters. Taken with the other panels — one of a man on bended knee receiving keys from Jesus, another of a white-haired figure enthroned — I figured that the artist had rendered several images of Peter. In each small painting the sky glowed luminously, even with the smoke damage, and featured a corona of light, a dove issuing forth from the circle's center. The influence of Van Eyck was obvious, but I began to think that maybe the artist was a closer disciple of Juan de Flandes. The exceptional detail and the strangely unreal quality of the water and sky seemed more in keeping with de Flandes. But there was little to go on.

I removed the frame to study the best-preserved portions. It was immediately apparent that there had been no previous restoration done on the panel. Usually with a work that old, restoration involves as much effort undoing other people's mistakes as bringing it back to its original state. Inch by inch, I worked on the painting, making use of a new resin developed in Pietrasanta.

For the first week, I felt confident that I was cleaning back to the artist's final glaze, preserving the patina while returning most of the contrast and color to its former refulgence. I had removed the top coating of smoke and was beginning to get a fuller sense of the work's original color and shading. Though slow going, the project was similar to many other restorations I'd made. But one day, coming in as the early morning light was banking off the west wall of the studio, I saw that I'd made a terrible error. A portion of sky, about the size of a dime, was reading much brighter than the rest of the painting. Initially I hoped the difference was caused by the slow drying time of the resin I was applying. But soon I became certain I'd gone too far and removed a layer of varnish. In fact, it seemed that I'd gone straight down to the gesso when I thought I was merely clarifying a section of cloud. If I was right, the area would never age again at the same rate as the rest of the work and would be irrevocably changed.

It's impossible in my line of work not to make the occasional mistake. One always hopes that it will happen, like this, with a small and unimportant work. Anyone else in our department would have shrugged off the discrepancy, but I couldn't let it go. The spot had begun to flash at me like some kind of sinister searchlight, focusing on me and my imperfections. I tormented myself with the problem, sat at my desk at night making notes, questioning whether I could do a repaint or whether I'd only make matters worse. My experience had taught me that with rare exception, once you had cleaned a section it was extremely difficult to resurface without treating the whole work as well.

As I walked back to the museum after seeing my father, my mind again fastened on this foul-up. I thought about making a quiet call to an old professor of mine at the National Gallery. My stomach felt unsettled; something in my mouth tasted rank.

When I got to the studio, Emmeline was in her office consulting with Mark, our antiquities man. Through the open door, I could see a bouquet of red roses surely sent by Emmeline's husband, Felix. On the windowsill next to my easel, I discovered two of the same roses placed in a glass bud vase. It was a gesture typical of Emmeline, simple and thoughtful, of which she would not want me to make much. I moved the flowers aside and looked at the altarpiece. Inches above the sapphirine sea, the medallion of sky glared an unlikely chalky white. Picking up a cotton swab, I leaned in to work a lower corner of the painting but began to feel very strange. All in what must have been a second or two, I was overwhelmed by exhaustion. My hearing went funny, my eyeballs felt covered by itchy wool, and the painted sea I was focused on turned suddenly from green, to gray, to a spangly, dusty sort of nothing at all. Before I fainted, I remember stretching out a steadying hand and the sound of my palette clattering to the floor.

Mark knelt before me, and Emmeline had my head in her lap. I must have been out for at least a couple of minutes.

"Too much naphtha," I said, trying to pretend that I was not lying on the floor of the studio but actually standing professionally before my incredible fuckup.

"You're not supposed to drink the stuff, Addy," said Mark, fiddling with his earring and giving me a gentle wink.

"I've ruined it," I said.

Emmeline laughed softly.

"We all make mistakes, darling. No point in killing yourself over it."

"Nah. So messy," seconded Mark.

I sat up and shook them both off, though I felt sweat dampening me from scalp to toe. When Emmeline insisted that I go home and get some rest, I simply didn't have the strength to argue.

～

I boarded the crosstown bus, but as the doors began to shut, I felt sure I would vomit. I remember yelling to the driver to let me off. A handful of private school teenagers, trussed up with huge backpacks, lumbered away from me in attitudes of contempt and disgust as I made for the door. Afraid of being trapped again in a closed space, I walked home and tried to calm myself by repeating the words "It's OK, you'll be fine." One more mad person in the park.

What occurred after the first day of my illness was evident to me only in the aftermath, when I began cleaning up my wrecked apartment. But the first stages, though uncomfortable, remain clear enough to recall.

I sat on the floor near the radiator for what seemed like an eternity. My fainting spell had left me feeling numb, evacuated, and as I sat there I had a strange kind of out-of-body experience. Like a pathologist inspecting a cadaver, I could see and feel my body expanding, firing, warming under the blaze of the coming fever. Blood ran slow, molten, through slackening valves. My heart, totally out of sync with my breathing, felt as if it were thudding against the bars of a cage. Each bone in my body hung from its net of tendons aimed toward the floor in a bid for eternal rest. My very scalp felt inflamed.

I thought of what my father had said to me in the coffee shop, replayed the whole encounter over and over. Backward and forward, slow and fast, I dissected the scene like a film editor making the final cut. I spoke the lines out loud, substituted my wan, stuttering pleasantries with zingers and wicked one-liners. And all the while, I felt a fireball of heat gathering inside of me, a hailstorm of anger and vitriol. I could not have deciphered anymore whether my sickness was physical or mental, but it had soon consumed me utterly. The rage I felt was nearly erotic in its intensity, the flames of it licking at me as I lay there on the worn rug in my clammy little apartment. It had been years since I'd felt anything so acutely.

Some undefinable time later, before night came and threw my apartment into total darkness, I pulled down from the bookshelves a stack of philosophy books I'd acquired in college. Flipping through Durant, I came upon the lines that were flickering around the back of my overheated mind but had continued to elude me. In an angry letter to her son, Arthur Schopenhauer's mother once wrote:

You are unbearable and burdensome, and very hard to live with; all your good qualities are overshadowed by your conceit, and made useless to the world simply because you cannot restrain your propensity to pick holes in other people.

This struck me as hilarious, and I had to lie down on the floor again from the strain of laughing. I remembered vividly the night I'd first discovered that line.

When I was a sophomore in college, emboldened by the delicious freedom those years give a person to investigate — and cultivate contempt for — one's parents, I took a kind of antiseptic interest in the subject to which my father had devoted himself. I read Kant, Hegel, Schopenhauer's *The World As Will and Idea.* I enrolled in a couple of courses in the university's philosophy department, gathering a slow appreciation for the discipline. I thought I might gain some insight into, if nothing else, what I believed was Hank's impossible nature. I felt very grown-up, investing myself in this analysis. Clearly, however, I was leading up to some far more dramatic effort.

One night, facing finals and stirred by what the psychiatrist at Health Services called my "routine anxiety disorder," I charged into the university library. During these attacks, I found that light of any kind made my already throbbing head feel as if it were going to implode and so I'd taken to wearing sunglasses until the episodes passed. I can only imagine what kind of lunatic I looked like darting through the dimly lit stacks, squinting behind dark shades as I ran my finger down the titles. I searched out two volumes of my father's work (noting with satisfaction that neither had been circulated in a half dozen years) and hustled them to a study carrel. I had of course seen the books — his Ph.D. thesis on Schopenhauer and another whose subject I forget — on my parents' bookshelves for years. But it had never occurred to me before that I might read and understand them. Throwing my coat over my head to block the fluorescent light, I dug into Hank's works, making angry notes in the margins as I went along.

Dad made a name for himself by anticipating the chaos and violence of the sixties. During the midfifties' sock hop of optimism, Henry Abraham was crooning gloom and doom, his message amplified by McCarthyism and the country's combustible racial divisions. His Ph.D. thesis warned against an ahistorical approach to morality, suggesting that mankind would repeatedly commit atrocities against one another because we continued to divide our species into the "subhuman" and the "morally right." Hank sought to transcend the argument that such a thing as human rights even existed and concentrate instead on our protean ability to become what as a society we deem acceptable or necessary. He made quite a splash; his scholarship and keen intelligence were difficult to ignore. But, in a post-Holocaust world, Hank's philosophy was ultimately totally unpopular.

It wasn't until the end of the decade, when black men and women took seats at lunch counters demanding to be served, that Hank was "discovered." A tiny swell of support moved in his direction, consisting mostly of fellow academics and black intellectuals who foresaw terrible trouble ahead. At Columbia, where he had studied

Dewey and stayed on as an associate professor, his colleagues began to talk him up and by 1962 he was hailed as a minor oracle. It was during that time that he and my mother fell in love. An actress with a promising theatrical career, as well as the beautiful daughter of a famous artist, Barbara could by all accounts have had her pick of New York's bachelors. But at a smoky party on Riverside Drive, she chose Hank and sealed her fate. He was, she once told me, "simply the most beautiful, fascinating man I'd ever met."

When I was very young, Hank had taken a prestigious chair in New Haven and become an impassioned political activist, teaching to packed classes. The students embraced him as a happening counterculturalist. Selma, Vietnam, Cambodia — Hank saw it all coming; he knew the score. Of course, he hadn't prophesied the mellowing of the nation's consciousness a few years later. In the self-improvement seventies, Hank's point of view became at best irrelevant and at worst a real drag. By the time the tall ships sailed up the Hudson in all their vain Bicentennial grandeur, Henry Abraham had flamed out.

I read my father's work until the library shut down. Then I went back to my dorm room, pulled out a couple sheets of notebook paper, and wrote him a long letter, posting it to Vermont, where he was on sabbatical with his bride, Linda, whom he had finally married. He'd sent me a postcard with news of his wedding and a return address, "if you need anything." Mercifully, I've forgotten much of what I wrote. I did devote some space to an exigesis of my father's hypocrisy, enumerating the ways in which he had betrayed his own philosophy. I questioned why he had married my mother, a rich woman, why he had married at all, given what we knew of the horrors of Materialism, the deceptive nature of Love, man's propensity for cruelty. "You seem, ultimately, to have missed the point, Professor," I wrote with such fury that I can still remember how the ballpoint pen dug into the page. As I recall, I signed off the letter with one last toxic dart. "I hope your honeymoon offers you the kind of rest you so richly deserve. Perhaps you'll be glad to know just how big a break you're getting. I've enrolled in a snappy little course on contemporary American philosophy. You are not on the syllabus. Your loving daughter, Adelaide."

Not surprisingly, I didn't hear much from Dad after that. He tried some — a phone call every birthday, notes attached to a magazine piece or newspaper article he thought might interest me — but I wasn't very encouraging, and after a few years he gave up. What I knew of his life came from my mother, who, for her own complex reasons, kept in occasional touch with him. Eventually, he moved back to the city, where Linda had been offered a high-paying job as a translator for a large corporation. My father took a position teaching undergraduates at a college up the Hudson, where he no doubt waited for the cycles of history to spin around and lift him up again to his brief, former glory. For my part, I took comfort in a philosophy constructed in direct opposition to his beliefs: I embraced my own very human right to ignore his existence.

~

I'm sorry.

So now I was sick, really disgustingly sick, and my encounter with my father ran a viral course through me.

I'm sorry.

103

These last words of Dad's played like a scratched record in my head, in the end drowning out the rest of our exchange. His thin lips moved, disembodied, before my eyes, exhorting me, taunting me, until I was cramped with nausea and crawled to the bathroom, where I began to expel everything my body could offer up.

For the next few days, I was in and out of consciousness. I guess I had surges of physical strength, because I managed to move around the apartment with some indeterminate purpose. I pulled a few things out of the refrigerator — milk, jam, a jar of honey — and left them, untouched, on the counter. I ran a bath, probably hot at one time, but I doubt I ever stepped into it. At one point, I remember waking and striking my head on something flat. It took a few moments before I could figure out that I was wedged for some reason partway under the couch. A clot of dust had lodged between my lips.

Boxes were removed from the cramped storage spaces in my closets, cleaning products unearthed from beneath the sink, sofa cushions reassigned to the floor. Were a stranger to have wandered into my apartment after these four days (and a stranger was exactly what I felt like when I returned to reality), he might imagine that whoever created that mess was either crazy or had been searching long and hard for something. That, anyway, was my conclusion when I stood on the fourth morning, my legs weak as two blades of grass, and surveyed the scene. If I had found something, though, I have no idea what it was. My place looked like a hastily planned yard sale.

I had a little patch, a half day or so, of wellness toward the end of my odyssey. I remember taking some soup and aspirin, changing into a fresh nightgown, and answering the phone once when it rang. My friend Reid (we'd met in a cooking class at the New School —

my last attempt at clubby socialization — and he was the only person with whom I spoke on a regular basis) offered to come take care of me, but I was too embarrassed by the bizarre state of my apartment to accept.

My fever spiked again on that last bad day, and then I had a night of dreaming that I can still recall with almost perfect clarity. In fact the very obviousness, the almost hyperreal quality of the images is what made them hard to forget. They didn't show much creativity. If anything the dream seemed pedantic, designed to insure I didn't miss a thing. It was as though, in all that retching, I'd popped the top on some moldy, musty trunk full of my uninvited past. When I awoke, I felt buried by the dust of it all.

In the dream I was well again, and returning to work after all those days off. I showered and had coffee, caught the crosstown bus, did everything suggestive of an absolute reality. It was that kind of a dream. The sort where you tell yourself, *Well, I know I'm not dreaming, that's for sure.* At the south entrance of the museum, Segundo the guard was minding his post, his dolorous face fixed on the surveillance television. Life as usual. When he saw me on the screen, he swiveled on his stool and raised his bushy thatch of eyebrow. *Good to have you back, Addy. Your show is very fine,* he said. *What show?* I asked. *Your show,* he said. His opacity confused me, but thinking little of it, I crossed the Great Hall and took the elevator to the second floor. Making a left, I walked down through the Japanese Gallery and was just outside the American Wing when the landscape suddenly got strange.

Where usually there hung Binghams and Bierstadts and Eakinses, I saw instead the distant outline of figures that appeared intensely, personally familiar. I stood back and looked above the doorway. In gilt gallery lettering were these words:

Adelaide Abraham: A Life

How clever, I said to no one. Just like the title of my grandfather's biography. *Noah Kane: A Life.* Did they know? Never mind. The rooms were empty and quiet.

On the first wall I discovered a white tapestry featuring an intricate pattern of multicolored balloons. I leaned in close to inspect the cotton fibers and their patches of age and discoloration. Without any surprise I acknowledged what I was actually viewing: the top half of a set of bedsheets from when I was very small. On more than one occasion I'd woken up in the middle of the night and screamed, mistaking the balloons for an army of bugs. Eventually the sheets had been thrown out. Or so I thought.

On the succeeding wall hung a Lucite box and inside it, an unframed painting of my mother on a beach towel, rubbing oil into my father's tanned back. At the bottom of the picture were a toddler's toes, as though I'd grabbed the family camera and sloppily snapped a photo. Beyond the box, a small pen-and-ink in an oversized gilt frame depicted a scene from a similarly childlike perspective. A gas pump and the white clapboard of the station were background for the red sleeve of a child's coat pressed up against a car window. Rain streaked the glass. Yet another, gouache, was an angle of my grandmother's wide front porch and the blur of a dark, skirted leg crossing the threshold into the day's waning light.

On and on went the show, some of the pieces mundane and others rich with drama and danger. Although the media were various, all of the work was masterful and precise, and difficult to turn away from. Some felt like tableaux vivants, and more than once I expected the people in the paintings to talk to me. *They're paintings, Addy,* I had to remind myself. Each one was carefully hung, and I was horrified and a little excited to think that they would be admired and rejected, analyzed and dissected by the museum-going public. I forged ahead for what seemed like an eternity, until an ear-piercing caterwaul froze me in my place. Looking up to the cross-hatch of gallery skylights, I saw the dirty pads of an alley cat striding across the glass. I woke with a jolt, my heart pounding. The feline wail of an ambulance passed by my building and continued down Broadway. On my pillow was a stain, a small, angry fist of blood, the source of which I couldn't find. It was early morning, and my fever had broken.

~

I returned to work for real that morning. But I don't suppose I was ever the same. I didn't feel like me at all, but as though I'd been kidnapped from myself and dropped at an unmarked crossroads with no identification and no map. The museum struck me as completely alien terrain, some unfamiliar, nearly lunar plane. It frightened me. That place of infinite beauty and perfect light suddenly became my betrayer. I had always relied on the museum as a place where I could disappear. I felt cradled and cosseted there, as though the vast scope of the place could minimize, annihilate my anxieties and fears. Now I saw the museum as something else, wholly indifferent to me. A place of cold marble and ghosts. Tombs. Dead things.

Emmeline admonished me for not allowing her to visit, a decision I didn't remember having made or uttered. I knew I'd lost some weight and probably didn't look terrific. But it was her tense solicitude, and the repeated suggestion I see a doctor, that convinced me how truly bad off I must have been. Something weird and mighty had gone to work on me, and it showed all over my hollowed face.

~

When my mother called me with news of Louise's death, I'd been back at work, in a desultory daze, for two weeks. The information lit a fuse in me, one I was seemingly powerless to extinguish. I called Marva and shamelessly pressed myself on her. I spoke of my grief and expressed my condolences until she was nearly forced to make me an invitation. When she did, I accepted immediately. Of course I changed my mind the minute I hung up, but I knew that by then it was too late.

I told Emmeline that an aunt to whom I was very close had passed away in the deep South, bought a ticket, and got on a plane. It's likely Emmeline didn't believe me, by which I mean she didn't believe any relative of mine had died. I'm not a very persuasive liar. But she probably figured I was heading toward some place for deep psychiatric evaluation or intensive cure. If that's what she thought, then she wasn't entirely wrong. I guess I was making a bid for self-preservation, backing out like a mole from my tunnel of darkness. Whatever. I had to go, and so I did.

II

~

"Nevah mind her."
Lou squeezes my hand as we step off my grandmother's porch, her fingers wrapped around mine in a brown-and-pink fist. The field that separates Further Moor, Edith's summer house, from the Bay Shoals Road is parted by a long driveway of sand and broken clamshells. We walk quickly, Lou's whole body pitched forward in a dark slant. It's our second night in Bay Shoals, and Lou and I have plans to see a movie. But now we're running late.

August.

Here's the familiar long slatted shadow, like a picture negative of the widow's walk, laid across the heather in the late afternoon. Here's scrub oak, and goldenrod, and fat, goosey gulls cruising inward from beyond the cliff. Blackberries, thorns, halyards pinkeling against their masts, the briny intake of sea air. Here is *Van Riper, your lunch is ready* that comes like a yodel through the privet from the beach club just next door. Sand in my bed, sea monkeys growing like germs in a mason jar on the windowsill, Orange Popsicles, stacks of library books dragged back to Edith's in a red wagon, the forever unfinished *Self-Portrait* under a curtain of dust in my grandfather's studio.

Further Moor is far enough away from Coldbrook to stop twice off the highway for bathrooms and lobster rolls. *WELCOME TO MASSACHUSETTS!* Miles and miles along Basket Alley, a two-lane highway strung together by shops selling saltwater taffy and wicker. A long road away from *You imagine I don't know what you think of me, but I do, I do know exactly* and *Darling, what are you saying* and *Your contempt is positively viscous; I do believe it's choking me* and *You're crazy; what are you saying* and *Fuck you or fuck whoever it is you're planning on fucking, I'm sure*

My father almost never comes here *I'd rather put a bullet in my head* and now he's too many miles away to think about. I imagine unweaving every basket until the brown threads are laid end to end. Unimaginably far, that's how far away we are. We have arrived for August at Further Moor and I am with Lou.

I have her.

She is mine.

The smell of summer berries in the warm after-dinner air hangs juicy, blue. Mom is in California, acting in a movie. She's playing a mother. *Don't even have to try,* she says. Neither do I. I've wished her away, and she is gone.

~

Edith was in the kitchen and that's why we're late.

"Good God, what is that?" she said, looking at my Mocko hat.

"Keeps the Jumbies away," I told her, running a tongue over and over through the hole where my two front teeth used to be. Lou and I had made the hat that afternoon. It was the Jumbies, Lou said, that had been at me. Evil spirits giving me badways. The hat would make me scary, like the Mocko dancers back home in St. Clair. The dancers dress to chase the Jumbies away.

This will set yah right again

The detergent box that makes the base of the hat sprouts two horns, branches from an apple tree on the back lawn. Seaweed hangs down in soggy strips from the crown, and a veil of moth-eaten lace we found in the attic droops down the back. I painted the sides yellow and brown and pasted macaroni on the front. In the hat I see myself toothless, smelly. It makes me feel strong.

"Ugh," said Edith, backing away from me, her lips stitched up at the corners. She was wearing her red dress, the one that makes her look like a fire hydrant. Edith was going to a party.

"You're not wearing that out, missy. Take it off."

I didn't take it off. Edith's dog, Constable, nudged at me, sniffed up my legs. I scratched a Jumbie in my armpit.

"Take. It. Off."

A fat fistful of the creatures wriggled in my ear and laughed. I trembled, smacked my head.

"Stop that Addy. She can't wear it out, for Christ sake."

Edith looked at Lou, standing behind me. I felt the hat lift from my head. Edith sighed and popped a handful of peanuts in her mouth.

"It's for your own good," she said, looking down to rub salt off the front of her dress. "You're no Shirley Temple as it is. Really. Why add insult to injury?"

Lou tugged at me and we slipped out the kitchen door.

"Nevah mind her."

She looked back over her shoulder.

"Ol' pissy ting."

At the foot of the driveway, we turn onto the rutted sidewalk of Bay Shoals Road. Lou's chin juts out of her sweater, the chain on her glasses swinging as we navigate the street signs and stout lamp-posts. In the morning when we went downtown to do errands, Lou stopped short in front of the town hall. Up the outdoor stairs and beyond a small landing, movies are shown on summer weekends. Lou gazed at the poster on the sandwich board and lifted her hands to her cheeks.

"Yesss, I've *got* to see dis flim."

"Film. Not flim," I said, tugging at her skirt. I had my eye on Ben Franklin's at the end of the street, had been waiting all year to cruise the bins of licorice and jawbreakers, Matchbox cars, plastic pranks, needlepoint kits, and rubber animals. I'd been telling Lou about the five-and-dime for months. How could she stop to read a movie poster?

"I'm wanting to see dat flim tonight, Addy," she said when she finally caught up to me, down the block. "Yah gonna love it."

I didn't look at the poster. The evening didn't matter to me as long as we got to Ben Franklin's.

~

I'm glad not to be wearing my Mocko hat when Lou and I are in sight of the movie theater. The sidewalk is jammed with people out for the evening. Tourists with sweaters tied like necklaces tilt their heads, smoothing ice cream paths around the rims of soggy cones.

Ladies push strollers. Old couples lean forward, shuffling slowly, while big boys in bell-bottoms lean back and amble just as slow. I keep close to Lou's side as she gently threads the traffic.

The ticket seller is getting ready to close the theater doors. In a circle of light at the top of the stairs, a group of kids is in conversation with two grown-ups. Beach club kids. Elizabeth Dalley, Sarah Conway, Danny Leahy, who hasn't grown an inch over the winter. There's another boy too, older, with hair black as coal. He's hanging off to the side, apart, and I can't place him. But it is Sarah, in braces and barrettes, whom I have my eye on.

Sarah Conway is hard and shiny, like the center of the tires on a brand-new bike. Everyone else moves around her like a spoke on her wheel. She keeps Elizabeth Dalley beside her, tells her what to do, how to walk and what to say. On the beach, Sarah instructs Elizabeth to keep her back to me. She commands the other kids too. Except for me, whom she doesn't talk to at all. I have not minded. Until now.

I think of Coldbrook, of the Wyant boys, and I fall a step behind Lou, who is bounding up to the box office. I don't want her to see, don't want her to know it's the same in Bay Shoals as it is in Coldbrook. While she buys the tickets, I lean over the railing and look at the brick sidewalk below.

"You just buy them and we all walk in together, like we're with you," Sarah is explaining to the man and woman.

"No biggie," interrupts Danny. "Our parents know it's rated R and everything. They're just busy tonight."

"Really," Sarah says, her voice with a touch of boredom now. "We do it all the time, just about every night. So . . . OK?"

"Addy!" Lou calls. I cringe when I hear my name.

Pulling my sweater slowly over my head, I turn around. Through the fabric's loose weave I can see the kids following the couple inside. Lou pushes a ticket into my hand and leaves me. Within an instant, she has disappeared, nothing more than the corner of her skirt left to follow into the darkness.

~

Lou sits forward in her seat, looking as though she's been shot through with electricity.

A red eye fills the screen.

The face of a woman, as dark as Lou, is lit beneath by fire. She stands and dances, flames covering her nakedness. Her head melts and becomes a skull.

A man in a suit aims a gun at us.

The numbers 007 zoom into view.

"BAYAAAH!" shouts Lou, her face lit up like a sparkler. I hear a chorus of laughter in the back row and slide down low in my seat.

~

The movie is strange, sinister, the first grown-up movie I've ever seen. The story has lost me, so I watch Lou instead. She grins and rubs her hands together, rocks back and forth in her seat, warns people on-screen of danger they can't see. *Yah! Watch out for Mr. Big. Catch him, Bond!* She laughs, slaps her head, thrusts her fist in the air. When I crawl into her lap, she wraps a tight arm around me but keeps her eyes riveted ahead.

We are the last to leave the theater, Lou and I. Slung back in her seat, she watches the screen until the projector stops. The lights of the house make my eyes hurt. Outside we walk slowly up the street, wet from passing rain. Lou has my hand and is swinging my arm.

"Yes, Addy, I'm telling yah dat was a different James from de other one me seen. Me cyaant *wait* to tell Errol, for he won't be getting dat flim for a while now."

At the end of the block, Sarah and the others are clustered around a bike rack. Elizabeth wrestles with Danny, who is sitting on her bike and pulling the spangles on her handlebars. When we cross near to them, Sarah begins to giggle. I catch Elizabeth's eye.

"Hi, Addy," Elizabeth says.

Two summers ago, Elizabeth and I took swimming lessons together. Afterward, we collected periwinkle shells beneath the dock or raced in our wet suits for milkshakes and BLTs. But that was before she fell in with Sarah. When she greets me now, I am stunned. Before I can respond, Sarah thumps Elizabeth on the back.

"What?" says Elizabeth, turning to Sarah and rubbing her back. "What?" she says again, and begins to laugh. Sarah whispers something in her ear, but Lou is dragging me away now. She stops abruptly and turns around.

"What yah laughing at? Yah bunch of jackasses. Y'all pass stupid."

There is no sound at all, it seems, though the street is still alive with people. No sound except the crickets scratching in the elms above our heads.

We are well up Bay Shoals Road before Lou speaks again.

"Bayaah! Damn nasty chilren! Should have smacked dem up deir backsides."

It is Lou who is upset, I think, a crease furrowing her brow. I'm not upset. I don't care because I have Lou.

"Bayaah!" I say, trying to make her laugh. "Watch out for Mr. Big!"

Lou pats me on the behind and dances away, her gold tooth glittering in the lamplight.

"Yah naughty ting!" she says, wagging a finger in the air, as the crickets sing another chorus.

"Jes' remembah, yah no Shirley Temple."

That night, I take my Mocko hat to bed with me and sleep a long and dreamless sleep under a blanket of stars.

12

~

SOMETHING LIKE ROUTINE appeared to be in full swing when I entered the Alfreds' kitchen for dinner that evening. Cyril and his great-grandfather were both seated at the table, napkins tucked into their collars. Derek moved between the two of them, cutting up stewy pieces of meat and potatoes, while Marva, rooted at the stove, spooled out her thoughts in a punctuationless monologue. She seemed to have been talking for some time.

"Yah and also me ordered a hearse car for taking her to de church a big one to drive slow tru de town me tinking she would have liked dat."

Marva's family took no more notice of her words than of the radio playing softly in the background. Cyril was making nonsense sounds, driving up the volume when he saw me come in. Derek glanced up from his grandfather's plate. I smiled and in return got a civil nod. Outside the screen door, Floria and Philip stood in the glare of an outdoor bulb having a quiet exchange. The air was redolent, the evening in motion.

"Sit down Addy dat coffin is nice," Marva said without turning around. "Me wanting one of you to check in at Roger's parlor before tomorrow night because me plenty busy. . . ."

Philip and Floria came in, he with a rusty milk crate and a folding chair in his hands, and began helping Marva pass out plates. They made a remarkable-looking couple, I thought, the kind that turns heads. There was about them both an aristocratic quality. Their bearing wanted a much grander room than that fatigued, decrepit kitchen. It seemed to me that Philip and Floria didn't really belong there any more than, for utterly different reasons, I did. The idea comforted me and inclined me again toward Philip. Still, I hardly felt at home, and took a seat in the corner, making myself as small as possible.

"Derek!" Marva suddenly barked, a serving spoon raised in the air. "Me talking to yah."

"What?"

"Me saying yah gotta clear up in yah room tomorrow for Denise de lady dat usually be a friend of yah mumma's from over in Priest's Bay Addy's in yah mumma's bed so me taking Cyril in wit me and yah cyan have de sofa."

Philip took several beers from the fridge and handed me one. I didn't want a beer. I'm a terrible and infrequent drinker. Besides, I thought I'd done enough damage for one day. But I didn't dare to speak, so I took the bottle and poured slowly into my glass. Philip winked at me, the flirt in him irrepressible. Floria took a seat at my side.

"Yah hear me, Derek?"

"I hear yah," Derek replied calmly, precisely working the knife and fork across his son's plate.

Marva came to the table, and the conversation ceased temporarily as Derek shushed his son. We linked hands for the saying of grace.

"For what we are about to receive, may the Lord make us truly grateful," Derek recited. His voice was tired, gray.

Before amen could follow, Philip broke in.

"And we pray for Louise up in heaven, who made this circle complete."

I glanced up and saw Derek's eyes lingering on the crown of his brother's bent head.

"Mmhmm. Amen," said Marva. "Me pass by Cora Pond's today, and she say enough flowers like to choke a horse arrived at Roger's parlor today. And dem come wit no card. Can yah imagine?"

This strange fact was met with complete silence, save for the sound of clashing silverware. Marva might just have announced a clement weather prediction. I couldn't tell whether everyone but me, and perhaps Cyril, *knew* who had sent the flowers, or they were all just too tired to care. When Marva didn't get a rise out of the others, she moved on to another subject.

"Me gonna fret about de headstone since yah haven't got it chosen today."

"Bobsled, down at the movie house, said him and his wife were sending flowers," Derek said, putting a slice of bread on his son's plate. "Did they come?"

"Don't know, but dese weren't old frupsy Bobsled flowers. Yah boys ought to know what dat head marker's gonna read. I'm not good wit dat kind of ting, yah know, but me told yah me wanting it to be pink." Marva hadn't touched her food. "But it's costing more, I know."

Derek looked at Philip, challenging him to respond.

"Whatever you'd like," Philip said quietly.

"When Mumma died, me wanted a pink stone, but dere weren't none in Pville. And for my Josephus me wanted one too. So. Now me getting my pink stone."

Marva's face took on a happy look, as though she were picturing not a grave but a double hot-fudge sundae, and the mood about the table seemed to brighten. Relaxing a little, I listened to Mr. Alfred's teeth clacking along and thought again of Coldbrook. I remembered how at dinnertime, Lou would sit with me while I ate and listen to my stories about school. Only after I was finished would she have her own meal, alone at the kitchen counter. Invariably, it seemed, she made herself a pork chop drowned by a pungent hot sauce. Smelling it, I would grab at my throat in exaggerated disgust, though dinner was Lou's quiet time and I usually left her alone then. If I entered the kitchen to ask her a question, she would put a hand to her mouth and nod or shake her head, unwilling to prolong the exchange. I was nine or ten before I figured out what made her so shy — when she ate, Lou removed her two front teeth, the ones banded together by a strip of gold, and clutched them in her palm. I stopped dead in my tracks the first time I saw her do this. I wasn't frightened or disgusted, but I felt I'd walked in on something utterly private, practically seen her naked, and I made sure never again to interrupt her at mealtime.

"Floria and me were speaking about the service," Philip said, glancing quickly over at his wife. "She'd like to sing something, a hymn. We could all pick it out or talk with Reverend Taylor."

Marva clapped her hands together.

"Yesss!" she said. *"Dat* would be nice."

"I thought Denise was singing already," said Derek, without looking up from his plate.

"She is, but just de one song. And Floria has a real trained voice. We should have two hymns, me tink."

No one said a thing.

Dat was Marcus "Taxi" Bickford wit "Paradise Riddem" in de numbah four spot dis week, boomed the DJ from the crackling radio. *Catch 'em next Saturday at Foxy's!*

"Foxeee!" shouted Cyril, until Floria put her hand over his to quiet him.

Derek drew a deep breath and seemed about to say something, but swallowed instead and nodded. After an interminable minute without conversation, Floria wiped nervously at the corners of her mouth and turned to me.

"Adelaide, have you ever been to the Caribbean before?"

"Yes," I answered, finding my voice strangled by my throat. "When I was small. But never to St. Clair."

"It's quite lovely. Down by Errol and Patrice's house is one of the nicest beaches around." She leaned across me to bring Philip into the conversation. "We should take her down there."

"Yah, why don't y'all do some sight-seeing?" Derek said, a faint smile on his lips. "Stop in on some of the local craftsmen. Or get yah hair braided nice."

Philip nodded earnestly.

"Yah, we could. We could. If that Clifton man can fix the Caddy. You say he's pretty good?"

"Well," said Derek, pausing to stretch and yawn, "he's all we got up here in *dah country.*" Derek pronounced the last words with an is-land accent thick as syrup. "He works better than he looks."

"Good, good. Because Papa doesn't know which end is up right now. He'll never find his way here by himself."

Marva cut her eyes at Philip.

"Here?" Derek asked.

Philip looked guiltily at his aunt.

"Here, yah. For the service."

Derek slowly put his fork down.

"Who said?"

"Me," answered Marva. "It's de proper ting."

The tension at the table had risen suddenly like mercury, and the room felt unbearably hot. When I reached for my glass of beer, I discovered I'd drained it to the bottom. Floria reached gracefully back to the fridge and handed me another.

"Proper," said Derek, shaking his head. "Please. Don't get me laughing."

Marva sucked her tooth just the way Lou used to do when I ir-ritated her. Down the table Cyril was tearing the center out of the slice of soft bread his father had given him. He spoke, mouth full of white sponge.

"Yah really assified, Papa."

A second or two elapsed as, except for the old man, everyone at the table turned to look at Cyril. Inspecting me through a perime-ter of bread crust, he didn't notice his father raise his hand and reach toward him with an open palm. The impact, to the back of the boy's head, wasn't strong, but it came by surprise and knocked the bread out of his hand. Cyril's mouth hung down, tears and drool rolling long before any sound came out. Philip slowly shook his head, but I'd seen the crinkled eyes before and knew his gesture belied a dumb amusement at other people's foolishness. I remembered what I hadn't liked about him in the first place.

Derek glared at his son, who was bleating now like a lamb, then shoved his fork into his food. He paused before eating and fixed Cyril with a cold eye of outrage and embarrassment.

"Dem limers Jossie usually be wit been learning him badways," Marva said, reaching over to wipe her father's chin.

"I know that, Marva." There was ice in Derek's voice. "It's why I'm trying to keep him up here wit me."

"I know you're *tryin'*, but dat girl is wicked."

"Mmhmm," interjected Philip, laughing now, "but sexy sexy."

Floria, busy wiping Cyril's face and encouraging him to eat, made no sign of hearing her husband.

"Listen, Derek," Marva said, speaking rapidly, deftly changing the subject, "yah cyaant miss work tomorrow? Someone's got to watch yah grandfather while me take a dress down to Roger's parlor to be put on yah mumma and den get to market for my callaloo."

Derek shook his head.

"I'm certain yah could, yah know, if yah just ask," Marva continued, prodding him.

"I can take care of him," I said, finally seeing my moment to be helpful. Derek blinked and looked at his aunt.

"Well, me don't know," replied Marva, watching her father. He was dozing, chin on his napkin.

"It's March, Auntie. Me not taking another day. I cyaant. Which dress?" said Derek.

"What do yah mean?" Marva responded, nonplussed.

"Which dress you giving Roger?"

"De yellow one wit de lickle stripe that she sometimes wore to church."

"What about the blue one with the white in front?"

"Dat one didn't fit her so good, Derek."

Philip spoke up, his mouth half full.

"The yellow one is nicer, I think."

Derek threw his napkin down on the table and stood up.

"Come on, brother," said Philip, conciliatory, "sit down and finish your food. Marva knows better. Let's talk about the rest of the service."

"Me telling yah," Marva said gently, "dat blue dress hasn't been so good since yah mumma was sick. It's too big. Hangs all over her."

"Gimme a break, Preacherman." Derek spoke from across the room. "Anyway, seems like yah both got it figured out already."

The screen door banged, and the roosters in the next yard began to crow again. Mr. Alfred looked up, startled. Philip sighed and went back to his dinner.

"Lawd," said Marva.

Philip apologized for bringing up the subject of Errol, but Marva shushed him.

"What sorry," she said, waving him off.

For the first time since dinner had begun, Mr. Alfred spoke.

"Where's Lulu?"

Marva pulled on the short hairs of her bun. An American pop song with an endless, whining chorus came on the radio.

"Yah want someting more to drink, Papa?" said Marva, slowly

getting up with the old man's plate. Philip began to describe to Floria the extent of the damage done to the Cadillac.

"Yah musta get driving down ya mumma line," Marva said, returning to her seat and refilling her father's glass. "Before yah boys were born, Mackie Goodson tried to learn Lulu to drive. Lawd, something crazy in her head, for she cyaant learn it. Poor Mr. Benoit next door like to shoot her. She runned over tree of his chickens trying to get out of de driveway!"

Marva began to laugh in earnest now, holding up her hand while she tried to compose herself. Her mirth spread about the table until everyone, including Cyril, was caught up in it. The old man looked from face to face, searching to discover what he was laughing about. In a circle of light outside the screen door, I could see Derek smoking a cigarette and listening.

"Mackie, him a give it up. Him say, 'Forget it, Lulu, you'll nevah drive a car!' But her a real rang-tang about it, yah know. Kept on trying till one day Mr. Benoit be crying, his fist full a feathers, 'Please, Lulu!' he say. 'I done run outa dishes to be cooking de chicken, so I'm begging yah to stop!' Ah, what a ruction she cause!"

Marva grabbed a dish towel from her shoulder to wipe the tears from her cheeks as she continued to laugh.

"Josephus, him a working den as a deputy down in town. Him a come home and tell me he don't want to lock his sista-in-law up, but if she don't quit driving, he gonna put her inna cell."

With laughter rippling around the table, Marva got up and went to the counter, leaning on it for support. The deep, chugging laugh that I'd heard from Marva earlier in the day seemed suddenly to take a detour. Her back quivered. She buried her face in the dish towel. Floria moved quickly to Marva's side. Only Mr. Alfred, lost in another dimension, continued his wheezy chuckle.

The table was cleared and routines continued without words. I snuck a glance at Philip and noticed that his eyes had become puffy and small, as though staying awake were suddenly a great challenge. Indeed, everyone at the table looked exhausted, spent by the weight of their grief. Pulling herself together, Marva began to help her father out of his chair. Taking a last swig from what appeared to be my third beer, I stood and moved to his other elbow. When I touched him, Mr. Alfred leaned away from me and shrieked.

"No, I say! Please! PLEASE!"

I stumbled back, hands in the air.

"Arright, it's arright, Papa," Marva said quietly, discharging me with a quick look. I turned, stunned, back toward the table and noticed that all the corners and edges in the warm room had softened and drooped. Gauguin meets Dalí, I thought, stifling a giggle. I was drunk. How charming.

Derek came back inside and lifted Cyril from his chair. He nestled the boy's head in the warmth of his neck and placed a long kiss on the top of his sleepy head. His eyes glittered in the dim light.

"Sorry, man," Philip said, trying to get his brother's eye. "Just tell me where to find Clifton. I'll go down and check on the car and we'll clear out of here as soon as we can."

"Yah won't find it," Derek said wearily. "Let me put him down and I'll go wit yah."

I went to Floria at the sink, took a towel, and began to dry, but she put out a hand to stop me.

"You go on with them," she said, glancing at the still-whimpering old man.

I walked outside, the door shutting affirmatively behind me, and leaned unsteadily against a rusted flagpole. There I waited, exiled from the realm of sensical thought, for Lou's sons to find me.

13

Who should I make one for now?"

"Have yah made a card for yah mumma?"

"Mom, Daddy, Dilly, Mrs. Cullerton, Edith . . . I know, I know!"

I do a little jig, try a headstand, somersault, and knock into Lou's dresser.

"Calm yahself," Lou says. She's picking the price tag off a flowered teacup. "Yah like to crack yah head open."

All around us on the floor, paper wrapping lies in shimmery reds and forest greens, gold and blue ribbon curling and streaming off the top of Lou's bed. The room smells of oranges and fresh-baked brownies she's brought in on a plate for my after-dinner snack. The radio is on, and a Christian station fills the room with choirs, harpsichords, "Silent Night."

"Philip and Derek," I shout, lying by the dresser, punching out the names.

I'm keyed up. I'm all in a pother, as Mom would say. Today is the beginning of winter vacation and now there is just one week left till Christmas. But that's not all, not the only reason I'm so fluttery.

This afternoon the fourth grade performed a holiday play, and I did not forget my lines.

At two o'clock we put on our costumes and made a line behind the music room curtains. I hadn't wanted to be a Christmas turkey, but the feathers that Mrs. Wishart pasted to my Dr. Dentons looked, I thought, sleek and pretty. I was glad after all not to be a big sweet potato, or wired shut inside of a papier-mâché ham.

Taking my place (Abraham at the front), I peeked out into the audience. Just beyond the stage, the first and second graders sat on the floor. Brian Sherry was pulling at Maggie Mabee's headband. Hayden Hurst, who licks his lips each winter until he chaps a broad doughnut of skin, worked his cracked mouth open over and over again. He looks like a scabby clown. The other kids were listening to Mrs. Labenski play our introductory music on the piano.

Most of the folding chairs were filled with grown-ups. Heidi Ostrander's parents had brought her baby sister, who was still in her snowsuit and giving in to a fit of crying. John Haberle's father held a big camera and talked with fat Mrs. Fusco, Colleen's mother. (Everyone calls Colleen's mother that.) Ellen Pierce's parents; Nat Marden's mother, who made our costumes; somebody's grandfather, I thought, to the side in a wheelchair. I stood on my tiptoes. Lili Arsenault pushed me *A-duhh now* and a clump of sticky feathers dropped to the floor. I grabbed the curtain and held on, peered over the first two rows. My heart began to gallop (I heard it in my ears, where it didn't belong). Finally I saw them, almost all the way in the back.

Lou was watching the stage, hands in her lap. She wore her best blue dress, sweater buttoned around her shoulders. Dilly, scratching his head, still had his coat on, though the windows were steamed with heat. (I think he's losing his hair and want to ask Lou if she thinks so too.) I let the curtain go and tried to breathe slow and easy, the way Lou taught me.

Pretend you're talking to an imaginary friend. That's what Mom said when she called last night. *Oh, Snooks, just have fun with it. You'll be great, I know. Are you mad at me? Hmm? Are you, baby?* She said she was sorry she couldn't be there. Sorry as the dickens. *New Mexico, honey, you can't imagine how beautiful it is here; the mountains are purple! A little Indian girl was on the set today; her father is consulting on the film. I invited her into my trailer for lunch. That's where I am now. Did your father give you the number? Oh, she reminded me so much of you!* I told her I had to go, had homework to do, but it wasn't the truth. Her voice was tinny and small like a voice on the radio, and I could hardly picture her out there. In a purple world, in a trailer, with Indians. Besides, Lou and I were midway through a game of spit, and I was winning.

Move it, mongoloid!

Lili pushed into me again and before I could think, I was out from behind the curtain, the rest of fourth grade trooping behind me.

Mrs. Fusco turned forward, arms resting across her bosoms as if she were leaning on a windowsill.

The baby cried.

Someone took a photograph.

I kept my eye on Lou and Dilly, sweat beading on my forehead. Lou jutted out her chin and nodded, mouthing my line.

"We are a traditional Christmas feast," I said, following her lips.

"I am a traditional Christmas beast. The turkey. Gobble, gobble, gobble."

When I flapped my wings, I hit Lili in the eye. But I'd made the audience laugh. *Look how well I growed her up, Dilly* Lou smiled at me as we drove home, the gold stripe between her teeth flashing in the rearview mirror. Maybe I'll be an actress too.

~

Night has come on purple over the Schroeders' snow-covered barn. Lou and I are making our Christmas preparations. She sits on the floor near me, filling a cardboard box with presents. Through the window above her, fat flakes of snow drift down in the dark like angel's tissues. I've been making one card after another, pleased with all the friends I have to draw for, pleased by success. There's a fizzy sweetness in my head; I'm a jitterbug of excitement.

"Philip and Derek, Philip and Derek!" I shout again, picturing the boys opening their presents. I leap up, pull at the corners of my eyes and kick a leg in the air as high as I can. "Everybody was kung fu fighting! Da-na, na, na, na, na, na." Dropping down, I land on the ribbed edge of the tape dispenser.

"Ow!"

Lou reaches out and grabs my pant leg, giving it a rough tug.

"I told you. Sit down now."

My foot doesn't really hurt, but I grab hold of it anyway and hop over to the bookshelf in the corner. It's here Lou keeps her special things. A bottle of perfume that smells like roses; a picture of a movie actor, his autograph written in neat script along the bottom;

postcards from England with lots of stamps and scraggly writing; a plastic Jesus on a cross just the size of my thumb; pictures of the boys in metal frames; a neat row of ticket stubs from every movie we've seen.

I kneel down before the pictures. Philip is older than I am. A year and three months older, which sounds like two years, since he is eleven and I am only nine. He plays with me anyway. But it is Derek who is my best friend. In the trip I've planned in my mind, the one I've drawn a hundred times, Derek and I are inseparable. Where we go is ever changing; what we do fills a drawing pad I keep on my desk.

I take him to the deep end of the pool and show him how to press all the air out of his body so we sink together to the bottom, enjoying an underwater conversation no one else can hear. We ride horses into the forest, and Derek saves me from a wood demon disguised in the base of an oak tree. He sits across the dinner table from me and shares a plate of spaghetti. We count raindrops on the car's back window, flash peace signs at passing cars. When night comes, Derek and I bundle under the covers and fear nothing.

"Gwan," Lou says, holding out the round-tipped scissors to me. "Make dem nice and den I'll be finished here. I've got to close dis box for Dilly to take me to de post office in de morning."

On Philip's card, I draw a fire engine and a picture of me in my turkey costume. Alongside the truck I make a giant Christmas tree, festooned with glitter and twinkly lights. Lou says there are no pine trees on St. Clair. I'll bring the boys a tree when I make my visit. For Derek, I draw only me in a dress, my skin a shade of brown darker than my own. I sit back and admire the turquoise ribbon on my smooth hair and the way my dress waves around my knees. But the nose is no good. It's too long and where it ought to be straight, I've drawn an ugly bump that makes me look like a witch. The more I try to fix it, the worse it looks. I scribble and scribble, feeling the heat rising around my chest and neck. I break the point on the crayon, then crumple the card and throw it across the room, narrowly missing Lou's face.

"Why are you trowin' dat away?"

My drawing is terrible. "Because I hate him!" I shout, stomping my foot and screaming until my throat hurts. "It" is what I meant, not "him." But that's what I've said. Lou gets up and grabs me by the shoulders.

"Yah stop it! Stop it right now!" Lou has never yelled at me before. When I look in her eyes, I see a terrible look. I fall instantly silent.

"Yah trying me completely now. I'm sick of it! Yah hear me? Yah cyaant hate Derek, and yah cyaant love him neither. Yah don't even know him! Arright?"

Without wasting any time, she recovers the card and smooths it out on the bed, her back to me.

"Now let's have a look, hmm? Let's look. Ooh, dat's nice, Addy. Sweet and dandy. Look, yah made de dress so pretty. Please let me send it to Derek?"

I can't answer her, can't speak. The snowflakes outside have gotten harder and smaller, and come down like spitballs.

I'm sorry, Addy, sorry I snapped at yah. He'll love dis. Please, Addy?

My eye falls again on the photo of Derek. A sunny day. He's standing in front of a fence, dressed in a starchy white shirt and olive shorts. With his hand, he's shielding his eyes from the sun. I get down low sometimes, to see what's hidden by the shadow, but I can never see beneath the swatch of darkness. I wonder if he's looking at me.

Lou puts the card in the box and turns back to her wrapping. Yesterday we went down to Danbury and Lou bought Philip a pair of track sneakers. She lays them in a square of paper, but instead of taping it closed, she runs her finger over and over along the stripes. She's been singing quietly along with the music on the radio.

Chri-ist divine.

Her voice breaks on the last word.

"Why is Derek only in the second grade?" I ask. "He should be in third."

Lou doesn't answer me. I've asked this question before and I know the reason.

"I said why is he only in the second grade?"

"I told you, Addy," she finally answers. "He was having some troubles wit his spelling and such. Dey left him back."

"Why was he having trouble? What's wrong with him? Is he retarded?"

Lou sighs, turns to me. Her face is streaked with tears.

"Quit it now. I'm pass tired. Just quit it."

I reach out for the rest of my brownie, though I'm not at all hungry. In fact I feel sick. When I'm done I squish the crumbs on my fingers. While Lou tidies up the room around us, I peel off two sections of the orange and place them in the back corners of my jaw, then get up and take a look in the mirror.

"And dey don't even call me de Godfadda," I say, thinking of the movie Dilly drove us to see last week. During the entire picture, Lou held her hands near the side of my face. When the scenes were scary or bloody, she flapped her fingers down over my eyes. We loved it. We'll go again another night. On St. Clair, Lou told me, she sees every movie twice. "So I can burn it in my mind."

"And dey don't even call me de Godfadda," I say again, turning to Lou, who isn't listening to me.

I walk over, sucking on the soggy orange sections, and sit on the bed where the grown-up scissors lie with the discarded paper. I stick the point into the palm of my hand, hard, until I see a tiny spot of red. Then I give the point a twist. The shock of pain runs up my arm. I twist the metal again, until it slices through my sickness, till it cuts away every single thought inside my head.

14

THE MOON WAS a white teacup by eight o'clock, the stars
emerging slowly and arranging themselves into constella-
tions. I followed Philip and Derek, the beer I'd drunk like a spring
tide on the banks of my brain. The two men walked along, their
heads bent identically, hands shoved into their pockets. For a long
time, no one said a word. The night air was still and close.

"Any word from Michael?" Philip asked his brother, who nodded his head almost imperceptibly in response.

"Did you talk to him?"

"Left a message."

"Where?"

"What do yah mean where?" Derek asked, annoyed. "At home.
Brixton somewhere."

"And?"

Without looking up, Derek veered off the road, leading us
through a cut in a hedge of coral vine. Here we met up with a loamy
path, different from the one I'd traveled earlier in the day, that
switched back and forth along a long hill.

"He called last night. Talked to Marva. He told her it was too far to travel. Couldn't get enough time off. Said he'd send a check."

I listened, vaguely, to the men and their conversation, paying enough attention to understand that Lou's brother was staying in England when he ought to have come home. But honestly, I can't say I cared much. I was too busy concentrating on the trail before me and pitying myself. Watching Lou's boys moving on ahead, talking of things I knew nothing about, chafed at me. I felt left out and determined to make myself known.

"What's too far to travel?" I said, trotting up to the two. Breaking off midsentence, Derek looked at me as though I were a troll emerging from beneath the woodbine.

"*I* came. No problem. I mean, New York isn't London. But still."

Neither man said a word.

"Your mom was so great," I said wedging myself between them and venturing a hand on Derek's back. It was obvious to me all of a sudden that I hadn't impressed upon him how I really felt. Knowing that Lou was truly loved would give Derek comfort, ease his anger and pain.

"Really," I continued, "she was the best. God, I miss her. Have missed her. All these years."

I looked at Philip, whose mouth was set in a frozen grin. Maybe I'd been wrong about Philip. He wasn't so bad after all.

"You know what she used to call me? Her white daughter. *You my white daughta! Fah true you are!* She used to say it just like that. And I'd call her my black mother."

Derek gave me a quizzical look. Did that sound strange?

"Not in front of other people," I clarified. "Just when we were alone."

Finally, walking between Derek and Philip, I felt I belonged. Lou had, after all, been a mother to me too. She loved me. But more than that, she *saw* me, like no one else had ever done. Lou looked beneath that tangled disaster of a little girl and found someone loveable. And I, because I was special in her eyes, saw *her.* I looked beyond Lou's skin color, her accent, everything that made her different. My parents pretended to, but they were just going through the motions. *I* was the one who really got it. For me, there were no distinctions. These men and I were siblings, truly, united at last. We were meant to grieve together. That's why I was there.

My mind was now tripping around all sorts of germane subjects, and it suddenly seemed I should explain something terrifically interesting: the world I came from.

"You know, most people in Coldbrook, I don't think they'd ever even seen a black person before Lou came to us."

Derek was studying me, listening intently, when Philip interrupted. God, he was rude! Skipping in front of his brother and me, he spoke loudly to Derek.

"You remember when Mumma wore that blue dress the first time?"

Philip bent forward to catch his brother's eye. I opened my mouth to continue speaking, but Philip jumped in again.

"Remember?"

"No. No, I don't," Derek finally responded as we reached the end of the path and turned onto a flat road. Philip started walking backward, his long limbs jangling about as he gesticulated.

"Independence Day. You, me, Papa, Mumma, Denise, Uncle Fry. Two other ladies. I don't know who. At Buck's Hill! You gotta remember!"

Derek shook his head.

"Before, in the morning, Mumma was clipping a tie on you and you started to cry. Remember that? She thought she hurt you but she couldn't get you to talk. Finally you say, all sniffly, 'You so beautiful, Mumma!' Damn, Papa and I laughed hard."

I giggled. Derek shot me a look that shut me up. Philip walked close to his brother now, nudging him with an elbow.

"You were small, like three or something. We got new shoes and my feet hurt so bad I thought I'd die, because we walked to Buck's Hill from the house. You remember that house, past Simon's pasture?" Philip was working hard to get Derek to join in the spirit of reminiscing, but his little brother wasn't biting. Giving up my own monologue, I fell behind a couple of steps. Philip continued. "The streets were full of people, nobody driving. Full! Everyone in their Sunday clothes, walking the hill. These big ribbons, in blue and red and green, wrapped around every tree in Eldertown. And fireworks. They scared you, so Papa carried you, and I got mad because it was me with the sore feet. When we finally got there, Papa put us up close, where all the ministers sat. He was in Parliament then, because we were inside a special box."

We passed beneath a house built into the cliffside, and music drifted out of its open door. A man stood in the darkness of his tilting porch. *All right,* he called out to Derek, who raised a hand in response. Though he hadn't said a word, I noticed that Derek walked now with his head slightly cocked. It seemed he was actually listening to his brother.

"I'm thinking how heavy that day was," Philip continued. "Intense. I didn't know what the hell was going on then, but I remember how everyone was really excited, but there was all this tension too. You could feel it in the air. There were soldiers everywhere, in front of the governor's house. And when Chesley came out, the crowd cheered. Papa and the rest of Parliament stood up. People threw flowers, and then on top of that I remember yelling. We couldn't see the Rastas protesting, we were too far forward, but they must have been making a shitstorm outside the courthouse. I saw them later, carrying some kind of effigy. Or maybe I just think I did since I've read about it so much. I do know that when the British governor started swearing Chesley in, Mumma told Uncle Fry she could see a fight breaking out behind us. Then you started to cry and Mumma had to take you out of the box. You didn't stop practically all afternoon. She kissed you and rocked you, bought you a sweet, but you wouldn't stop."

"His face was melting," Derek said, his voice rising over the crush of old seashells beneath our feet.

"Who's melting?" said Philip.

"Chesley. His face was coming off. I remember that. Me being afraid because he was white and then it got really hot out and he started turning black. His fucking face was coming off. Dripping. Horrible-like. Jesus, that scared me. Was that Independence Day?"

"Yah. Chesley wore some kind of makeup to look more white. And it came off during his swearing in. You remember that? Wow. Yah, it *was* noon in August. Stupid asshole. Ruined him. People were laughing, I guess, but I didn't notice it. I was too worried about my swelled-up feet."

"I was always expecting Papa's face to come off in the sun after that," Derek said, shaking his head. "Or sometimes I thought I'd turn white when I grew up. I never forgot that. Jesus."

"Yah, but Derek, don't you remember after that, the party? At Fort Charles? Went on all night. People were done up, doing the bamboula and bel-air, I don't know what all else."

Philip started swinging his arms around, laughing.

"And stick fights. It was a sweet night. Mumma and Papa danced, and Papa leapt around with you on his shoulders. He used to love to ride you on his shoulders. Remember? Called you his boonoonoo boy. Right?"

Derek spoke with quiet bitterness. "Unh-unh. No, I don't remember anything like that."

Charging ahead, Philip intercepted his brother's blackening mood.

"Anyway, night came. The whole of Eldertown lit up. Uncle Fry and the other ladies went off to drink and came back saying someone, a famous actor, was at the Sea Palace. Mumma screamed, and I'd never heard her do that before. We went over to look, but they wouldn't let you and me in the bar. Denise waited outside with us and we fell asleep in the grass."

Philip looked to his brother, hoping at last to have jogged his memory, then let the subject drop.

"Anyway, that was something, that day."

"Richard Widmark," I said.

Derek and Philip stopped beneath a streetlight and looked back at me.

"It was Richard Widmark. She had a picture of him, signed. It said 'Happy Independence Day. Best Wishes.' And his name."

I felt a flush of pride for solving the mystery. Despite himself, Derek laughed.

"Richard who?" he said.

"*Murder on the Orient Express,*" said Philip. "Yah, she's right. Mumma must have seen him at the cinema."

~

Minutes later we reached Clifton's. Behind a chain-link fence appliquéd with hubcaps, Philip's Cadillac sat up on blocks, open-hooded in the moonlight. Clifton was in the driver's seat, his head bobbing to a reggae-tinged rap thudding out of the car radio. A dozen other men lounged among the rusted appliances, car parts, and corrugated tin, the air rich with the funk of marijuana. We walked in from the back, unnoticed by Clifton. Derek was practically in the passenger door before the mechanic looked up through heavy lids.

"Colonel," said Clifton, his rubbery lips wandering into a tooth-less smile. His eyes were as yellow as egg yolks. Philip and I stood at the back of the car and Philip nervously pulled on his beard. This was obviously not his scene. Derek and Clifton began to talk in a rapid island patois, not one word of which I understood, and while Philip listened in, I walked around to the front of the car.

The place was illuminated by three clip lamps, hung off the fence and juiced by a string of jumper cables hooked to an overhead power line. The lights dimmed and flickered, nearly in time to the music. Nice disco, I thought. Not that I felt much like boogying when I saw the damage to the front of the Caddy. It was decidedly worse than I remembered. The passenger-side headlight winced at me, and the fender buckled up against both front tires. Through the windshield I could see Clifton peeling himself off the seat as slowly as physics would allow.

"Bakra Man," he said, ambling around the hood, "how come yah didn't say yah brothas wit de Colonel? Him and me partners from way back."

Philip smiled uncomfortably and looked at Derek, who said nothing.

"Well, you know," Philip answered, "he doesn't like me advantaging his good name."

Clifton snorted and scratched the little curls on his bare chest. His cutoffs slipped so low on his hips that I turned quickly away and looked toward the far end of the yard. In the shadows, someone was gesturing to me.

"So," Philip said, "what's the deal?"

Squinting, I could make out a dark figure with what looked like an enormous head, seated on a pile of tires.

"Clifton ain't nuh Detroit man," the mechanic was saying as I wandered away. "Ain't nuh assembly line here."

Getting closer, I began to see the contours of a tall man with a huge beehive of hair stuffed up inside a woven red cap. He was smiling, beckoning me with a long finger. When I got near and could see his T-shirt, I recognized him as the fisherman who'd been outside the bar that afternoon. He held out to me an enormous joint. I waved it off as casually as possible, feeling a familiar bullet of anxiety trying to pierce through my mild drunkenness.

"Yah don't lick corn?" he asked, with a floppy warble that, by comparison, made Clifton sound like Henry Higgins.

"Nah," I said, adding a lame just-not-in-the-mood shrug.

"Cool. Das cool. So what ya doin', den?"

"Hmm?" I replied, floundering. "Nothing. Not much. How about you?"

"Jes' chillin'. Jes' limin'."

I waited, figuring he wanted something. He lifted his chin. "Whas ya name?"

When I told him, he slowly shook his head.

"Addy? Nuh. You more a Pearl to me. Like yah skin," he said, pointing to my arm. "Yah. Pretty Pearl. I's watchin' yah before. Nice." He took a long hit off the joint, which glowed like a taillight in the darkness. Two other men, sitting on a washing machine not far away, laughed quietly as their friend hopped down and put out his hand.

"I Sebumbo."

I shook his hand.

"'Syah boyfriend?" he asked, gesturing vaguely in the direction of the Cadillac.

"What, him? No. Neither of them. No."

"Husband?" he asked leaning in close enough that I could smell his wicked breath.

"Nope."

"Yah dance wit me?"

The absurdity of my situation finally got to me, and I began to laugh. The truth is I was so uncomfortable at that moment I thought I might wet my pants. Encouraged by my laughter, Sebumbo put an arm around my waist. When I tried to pull away, he pressed me against himself. The music bumped and jived from the open car doors.

"Yah jes' chill, mama. Yah wit Sebumbo now."

Using his hips like a gyroscope, he swung me out onto his sandy dance floor. The more I resisted, the tighter he held me. His friends, whom I could see in the distance, were bobbing their heads in appreciation. "Relax," he whispered, following the music's heavy pulse and pulling my face to his shoulder. He put his hand on my ass, and I felt a spark of tension begin to blaze at the back of my head. I was having trouble breathing. The man smelled horrible. An unmistakable hard lump of an erection soon sprung up between us, and Sebumbo, making sure I didn't miss it, ground himself into my belly button. The song was eternal. I moved about gamely, tried to be cool, but beneath my silence I was hysterical. It was not a new tune but a firm voice that finally set me free.

"Bumba. Letta be."

My partner slowly unhanded me, and I turned to see Derek, arms folded across his chest. I was soaked with sweat. Sebumbo said something under his breath I didn't understand, but the purr of it was decidedly raunchy.

"Check yah latah, Pearl," he said as I moved quickly to Derek's side. Trying to recover, I offered a pathetic wave. Back in the light, Derek eyed my soggy frame and looked me in the eye.

"You arright?"

I nodded, rolled my eyes. My head was killing me. The good news was I no longer felt remotely drunk.

"He's harmless. Brain-dead."

Before I could thank Derek, he gave me his shoulder and walked away. Over by the car, Clifton had an arm around Philip, hanging on him and putting on a long face.

"Grievous sorry 'bout yah mumma, my man. I'll be fixin' yah car straightways. But it won't be fah tomorrow. Maybe de next day." Clifton lowered his voice, looked around his yard before adding, "And me not even charge you regulation price."

Philip nodded slowly, puckering his lips, then pulled out his wallet. As Derek and I began to walk away, Clifton shouted out to us.

"Colonel! Yah certain yah brothas wit Bakra Man?"

Derek nodded. Clifton waggled a pink tongue.

"Dere be a whitey inna woodpile, huh?"

The mechanic's laugh ricocheted off all the metal surfaces and followed us back down the long road.

～

Exasperated by me, my ex-boyfriend Daniel Moss once said I was like a Komodo dragon. Shortsighted, cold-blooded; you could be pretty certain I was dead until, unblinking, I stretched my maw and swallowed you whole. A born naturalist who wanted to be a travel writer, Daniel loved metaphors, especially when they rationalized my "primitive behavior." Hunger, lust, rage, I subverted every emotion into a strange, reptilian repose. I know he was trying to get a rise out of me with his armchair zoology. And I wish he had. The fact was, I didn't feel much of anything at all when I was with Daniel. And when we fell apart, over and over again, I felt even less. In a sense, his metaphor was entirely accurate. I flat-lined, then sucked him into the black hole of my trance.

He would have loved this moment: Addy unhinged, up a tree, in flight. He'd have laughed at my helplessness, and I would have let him. I think I would have put up with much worse to have Daniel there with me. My hands tingled, and my feet felt numb. I focused on my toes while we waited for Philip, who jogged up to meet us.

"Well, that ain't good," Philip said, hitching a thumb back toward Clifton's. Derek began climbing the hill, his older brother at his back. I fell in step behind them.

"Derek?"

"Mmhmm?"

"I'm meeting with the lawyer at noon."

"Yah."

"You sure you don't want to be there?"

"Yup."

"So. You think you might bring Papa up, then? When you come back?"

Derek stopped, halting the line behind him. He looked up at the sky and dug his hands into his pockets.

"Why would I do that?"

Finally angry, Philip marched up and stood nose to nose with Derek.

"Because he's your goddamn father. Because they loved each other, all right?"

Derek's eyes flickered. He poked his brother in the chest.

"Fuck off, Phil."

There was a smell in the air, of violence or of fear, that blew down toward me on the light tradewind. Derek's eyes flashed white, and there was tenseness to his body that made it tremble almost imperceptibly. For a long time no one spoke. Finally, without a word, the two men continued up the hill. I kept my distance, walking slowly. At the top, Derek turned to his brother.

"I don't want to talk about dis shit anymore, all right? None of it. As far as me being concerned, he killed her."

"Oh Christ, Derek. Come on!"

"Might as well, he lighting her up wit all dat talk. I mean, what do yah tink she was doing down dere, by de water, when she cyaant swim?"

"She was out of her mind, Derek!"

"He gave her ideas. Yah don't know nothing. I lived wit her. I saw her dat night! Yah don't know."

Philip put a hand on Derek's shoulder, but Derek pushed it off and walked on ahead. Before disappearing into the darkness, he turned back to his brother one more time, his voice dead calm again.

"And by the way, Phil, I know I didn't go to college, but I do know a few things. I remember Patrice that day, Independence Day. I remember Patrice being with us on Buck's Hill."

When we got to the house, Derek was nowhere to be found.

On the living-room couch, Floria slept curled within the folds of her dress. Seeing her, Philip forgot quickly about me. I snuck a last glance as he bent down to his wife's ear, delicately kissing it before whispering to wake her. I turned away and made for the bedroom door that had been left ajar for me. Marva shifted once but slept on. When my eyes had adjusted to the sheaf of moonlight coming in the window, I found my bag and quietly undressed. Then I lay down on Lou's bed beneath her collage of news clippings. Again the ghostly impression of ink emerged on the paper's edges.

"Growing smart as you!" it said beneath a story announcing Philip's place on the honor roll. Another, about the purchase by Errol and Patrice Hodge of the Eldertown Cinema: "Looking for a visit from my Cinema Girl!"

The last words I deciphered before my eyes began to ache were written on an aging photo of Philip, his back to the ocean. His hair was a mess, his expression surly and adolescent. A man's arm was draped around his shoulder, but the person to whom it belonged had been ripped away from the picture.

"We bought this boat for funning around. Please —"

it read, and then the jagged white line of torn paper interrupted. In my head, I tried to finish the sentence, but soon gave in to sleep.

15

~

SIXTEEN MUSSELS. THIRTY-two black-and-blue bruises. Or open coffins I've lined up in a sandy graveyard row beneath Edith's dock. Across the necklace of beach, kids are playing rag tag off the club pier. Leaping from pilons, they drop like bullets into green water, leaving on the air the rat-a-tat-tat of laughter and streaks of color piercing the haze. When I press my ear to the sand, I can hear a mermaid chorus and the volcanic rumblings of the sea.

How long? How long would it take them to notice if I left? Across the harbor, traffic rolls in a steady stream across the Bay Shoals Bridge, and I can see myself, tiny from here, walking the footpath across the span. Like a hobo, I could get a red bandanna and a length of stick. Or maybe just make a dive and swim. How long before they missed me? But then again, who cares? Face pushed into the sand, eyes closed, I fill my brain with a balloon of nothingness.

No noise; Cat has left for good, it seems. I'm all for nothingness now, nothing's biggest fan. Nothing is like our house in Coldbrook this winter past. Silent like death, and where there used to be people, only slippery ghosts. Laughing hollowly in the living room, whispering in the low-ceilinged hallways upstairs, breathing fog on the glass patio doors. I like this new silence, the nothingness that grows inside my head. I think I am beginning to disappear myself. I finished the year at the bottom of the fifth grade. I waited for my mother and father to react, but summer blew in beneath the doors and windows, and no one said a word.

Not even Lou. *Brugadung girl,* I thought she'd say. *You a brugadung girl, but me knowing you a smart ting. Yah just got one eye on trouble is all. One eye on trouble* Lou said nothing at all, only sighed and looked out through the window over the kitchen sink. A blue bunting pecked at the glass feeder, turquoise coat glistening. Lou fingered my report card with her wet dish hands, but her eyes were a blank. She is more and more that way, closed inside herself, lost to her Bible and pictures of the boys.

Below the dock, I scream nonsense into the sand, down farther and to the earth's core, where no one will hear me. I sit up, chew the pebbly grains.

Just above the seawall, my grandfather's studio is an old man, wrapped in a blanket of rose hips and briar. The windows forlorn, salty, tear-stained. The sign Edith has placed before the door looks like a pipe in the mouth. *PRIVATE PROPERTY. NO LOOKIE-LOOS.* I brush the sand from my stomach and elbows, leave behind the shell cemetery, and climb back up the rickety stairs. Lou is in town visiting the lady who owns the dry goods store *I'm wanting to drop in on old Mrs. Cohen, fi she gets very lonesome.* The afternoon is mine.

I'm an aerialist, a tightrope walker on this high stone wall. Look at me. Ssh. Don't say a word or I'll fall, tumble back down to the beach below. *Poor girl. Lost her footing. Dashed her head on those rocks right there. Yes, she was my granddaughter. Nothing but seafood soup now, though.* Poor Lou. There she is, standing by my coffin, raining tears. *My white daughter, she was my white daughter. Lawd, I should never have gone to town dat day.* And Mom, with her arm around Dad. When she faints, Dad holds her up, carries her to a chair. *Amazing grace, how sweet the sound, that saved a wretch like me*

Constable barks, once. Splayed beneath the studio stairs under which he spends his days, he cocks an eye in my direction, snorts, stretches, and falls asleep again. *Yes, ladies and gentlemen, another feat of derring-do by the one, the only Rat Girl!* I'm Harriet the Spy, hand inside the window's empty pane, fingers around the interior knob, pushing the rotting door toward me. Heavy mildew works its musty fuzz up inside my nose, coats my throat, and makes me cough. I've upset the dead. I can see only shapes, my pupils open slowly, slowly. Now more, and more still.

Two broad shafts of light thrust down from the highest windows, making dueling swords of dancing dust. Up above, in the rough-hewn beams, a nestful of barn swallows has been awakened. *Chee chee.* One bird makes a break for it, darts over my head and out the open door. A cannon goes off in the harbor, the beginning of a boat race. *I did, I got you, dickweed! You're it. Bwah-hah!* I poke my head back outside, check across the lawn, swing closed the door.

The place is tall and deep. Like a cathedral, filled somehow with echoes I feel but can't hear. When it was still a barn, the studio sat at the back of Edith's property, but my grandfather had it moved to the cliff's edge long ago. It's bigger than I ever imagined when I only peered in the window, obeying Edith's command not to go inside. But that was then, before there was nothingness, when I was still a little girl. Now I'm Bond. James Bond.

Holding my breath, I take it all in. It looks as if Edith has left the barn just as it was the day my grandfather died. The afternoon he went for his daily swim, came in for lunch, and dropped dead at the kitchen table. *Never one to make a fuss,* Mom said once, with an angry laugh. Someone came and took his paintings to a museum, except a couple of unfinished works up on easels. The room, half undone, reminds me of a person who stops his sentence mid-thought.

A long, low wooden table pushes up against the bank of windows turned out to sea. Messy piles of sketches, charcoal and ink, are scattered like leaves. An ashtray filled with old cigarettes is hard by a scallop shell, nearly overflowing as well. One two three four — four empty mugs. A shredded candy-bar wrapper, spotted with mouse poops. Pushy vines have made their way beneath the windowsills and climb up the walls, where my grandfather pasted and tacked pictures, postcards, maps, pinup girls in old-fashioned torpedo-bosomed bathing suits. A paint-smeared transistor radio sits on a high shelf next to a jar of Postum and a ceramic monkey. The flash of something human-shaped catches the corner of my eye. I wheel around —

A knight. In armor rusty and netted with cobwebs. Guarding the corner, holding an old straw hat instead of a sword. I've seen, in a picture, my grandfather in that very hat, on an empty beach. I hold my bony chest while my heart rackets around inside it like a squash ball. Beyond the soldier is an old bed, covered in ticking and a passel of small pillows thrown every which where. Up close, I can almost see the outline of Noah Kane's enormous body. How he lay there, one leg over the other, arm across his forehead, dreaming beautiful pictures. Thinking great thoughts. I lie down there myself, lie that very same way. My enormous nothingness grows bigger with every slow breath I take —

How do you do that? Hmm? Jesus, how

This. This voice cuts through the hollow in my brain. Sticks like a knife in my nothingness, my zero. I hear it all the time, can't make it go away. Like a trick candle I can't put out, it sparks and flares over and over. And to go with my father's voice, so soft and strange behind his study door, is my memory like a movie playing back in my head. Mom's on the phone, calling from California. I'm walking to his study to tell him. The hallway tilts crazily in the dim light of early morning. Is he sick? So soft, his voice a whisper, unlike him. Talking to himself.

You're like a flower, someamazingflower

My hand is on the knob, yes, I'm certain my hand is already on the knob, turning it to open, pulling the door from its latch, before the queer sound reaches my ears and makes me think of Cat. A cry but no, not. Something different but yes, animal. Have I called him? Have I spoken? I think I have but no, I must not have called his name. Dad. Can't now because my voice has gone away. I mustn't have said anything at all but only seen not Cat but something it takes me I don't know how long but feels like forever to understand. Shapes I can't untangle but then do. My father's naked back and bottom, on his knees, and before him a woman crouched like a four-legged thing. He's touching her hair like a petal, rubbing it like a leaf, and pushing up against her darkest place. Her eyes are closed, head turned back toward him, face strange and red, twisted mouth open, sweat dampening her long black hair. Her tiny breasts hang down like tulip bulbs. Is he hurting her? *Godyesjustlikefuckthat* no, I know it's something else. I don't know. The sound like Cat comes again from her mouth, and I close the door as she reaches back and holds my father's hairy hanging between his legs —

~

I'm looking at the studio ceiling. The baby swallows chirp for their mama, who reappears, darts back up to the rafters. I lie still on my grandfather's bed, a heavy feeling between my legs that makes me want to touch there, where I am still smooth. My hand is dusty, stained pink with raspberry juice. I tuck it beneath my shorts

~

— *someamazingflower* in the bathroom, the cereal I puke up swirls around the toilet bowl, little o's I haven't chewed spinning around whole. OOOOOOO. *Addy, where did yah get to, yah mumma's still on de phone. Dilly's waiting on yah, time for school! Addy!*

~

The ocean's an angry tangle in the painting on my grandfather's easel. One high window casts its beam, and I can see men lost at sea. A sinking boat broken in two. I can see what isn't yet on the canvas. I'm inside that graygreen sea, sinking down.

"Gotta light?"

I start, flip over onto my belly, tug my hand from my shorts. In the doorway of the studio is an older boy with a cigarette behind his ear. Constable stands behind him, tongue out, back end wagging. I've seen the boy before. *Townie,* I heard Sarah Conway shout at him. He's always alone, stands at the lip of the seawall, on the end of the dock, outside the movie theater. He hangs around, edgy as a Buck knife blade.

The boy wanders in, tossing things about on my grandfather's desk. Reaching into a drawer I hadn't noticed before, he pulls out a box of kitchen matches. He seems to know his way around. When he leans into the flare, a greasy sheet of hair hangs down over one eye. The other eye, the one I can see, is flat and dark as a coat button. A stain of mustache hair smudges his upper lip, threaded by a scar coming down from his nose. He tosses the match on the floor and looks out the window on the dazzling day. The tips of my fingers burn.

"Hate those fuckers," the townie says, tossing his head toward the army of kids on the beach club dock. He turns to me, looks me over where I lie.

"Know what I mean?"

My fingers glow like coals, hot like the trigger of a gun. I nod in ready assent.

16

My first morning on St. Clair, a heavy rain spilled down on the Alfreds' roof like marbles on a can. From Lou's bed, I watched the old man I'd seen on my arrival riding his mule across the ridge road. He tilted his straw hat over his eyes and tapped the animal's haunches with a piece of cane. The mule flicked a long ear and continued, bent under the rain, as slow as time. It was still early, barely light, but Marva was already up and gone. Through the wall, I could hear her in her father's room, her patient tone rising and falling with the strain of moving him about.

I felt entirely hollow lying there. Cored like an apple. My head hurt; I remembered the beer I'd drunk the night before. The rest of my body was heavy with sleep. I lay still beneath the thin blanket, pulse throbbing slowly against my temples, and took some time to try and parcel out what had gone on around me for the last twenty-four hours.

That's not to say that I understood much. The scene between Derek and Philip on the walk back from Clifton's seemed like a squall spun off from a much larger storm. I doubted that when Derek had implicated his father in Lou's death, he was being literal.

It seemed that her accidental drowning was an established fact, a terrible mistake precipitated by her unsound mind (or body, if Marva's intuition was right). But something had Derek convinced differently, that the malignancy lay elsewhere. Maybe his was just the bitterness of an angry son. Or maybe he was right. What did I know? Nothing.

I lay on that white sheet, bedded down in my nothingness like a pair of old pajamas, for I don't know how long. I looked above me at the news about Lou's life and the lives of those she loved, smelled her musky scent still on the bedclothes, and felt as perfectly alone as I'd ever felt in my life. There was virtually no one to whom I felt bound. No place, physical or spiritual, where I connected with anyone in the world. I was, it came to me like a vaporous genie rising from a bottle, inessential. And if I'd hoped to make my mark with Lou's sons, I'd surely blown it by acting the night before like a drunken boob. The bottom line was never simpler to me than at that moment. God, I was sick of myself.

The sound of an engine turning over finally rousted me, and as I sat up, I saw the little blue car heading down the road. Derek, in shirtsleeves and a tie, reached behind himself to adjust a jacket that was swinging from a hanger, and then took off. Not surprisingly, he looked as if he was in an awful hurry to get away from home. What *did* seem strange: I felt a little sorry to see him go. As I dressed, Mr. Alfred and Marva moved around outside the bedroom. Their conversation reached me in little threads.

"Dey might have right to de tree of life, and may enter tru de gates of de city."

"Yes, Papa, yah right. Hush now."

"It was Vain-Hope, de ferryman, dat helped him ovah."

"Come in de kitchen," Marva whispered. "Me fix yah up some-ting."

"De ferryman. I'm de ferryman. Toot-toot. Memba how we used to call it? Toot-toot, Marva."

Mr. Alfred laughed and shuffled slowly along the hallway.

"Yes, Papa. Toot-toot. Commere. Philip and Floria are in de liv-ing room. Let's not wake 'em up, now."

I sneaked out of the house through the front door. The sun coming up over the mountains had broken through the rain clouds and warmed them to a Vermeerian pink and amber, promising an-other hot day. I followed the sound of children's voices around to the dirt yard where Marva and I had sat the day before and found Cyril with a barefoot bean stalk of a girl.

The two children stood face to face. The little girl, her skinny arms stretching out of a soiled yellow dress, held the boy's hands and stomped her foot against the packed, wet earth.

"Little Sally Water, sittin' in a saucer," sang the girl in a quick, brassy voice. "Cryin' and weepin' for someone to come."

Attentive and quiet, Cyril looked up at the girl and let her swing his arms.

"Rise, Sally, rise, Sally, wipe your weepin' eyes, Sally. Turn to the east, turn to the west, turn to the very one that Sally loves the best."

The girl kept singing, and as she did so, I heard Lou again, smelled the lilac bushes of a Connecticut spring.

Me sing you de song. But we cyaant really play de game witout tree people to make a circle.

Sing it anyway, Lou, please sing it.

Dere's a brown girl in de ring, tra-la-la-la-la, dere's a brown girl in de ring, tra-la-la-la-la; dere's a brown girl in de ring, tra-la-la-la-la, for she look like a sugar and a plum, plum, plum. Show me —

Hey, what's so funny out here?

Good, here's yah mumma now fi join in. Den we'll have a circle and one fi be in de middle. Come on, Addy, come be in de middle! Show me yah motion, tra-la-la — Addy, commere! Put yah hands on yah hips like I showed yah — ADDY!

It's all right, Louise. You all go ahead.

But we cyaant, witout dere bein' tree to play de game. She's just showin' off for you. Addy? Arright, den, nevah mind. Yah gwan and play by yahself, den.

❧

I walked up to the children and slipped inside the circle.

"Let your backbone shake," I sang, tipping forward and back in the tiny space between their arms.

Cyril broke free and jumped back, giggling and holding his head.

"Come on, Cyril," I shouted, planting my feet and letting my hips go. "Shake it to the east, shake it to the west, shake it to the very one you love the best!"

Cyril busted up laughing and looked at the Crazy White Lady with astonishment. The little girl took my hands in hers and swung me out wide.

"Went to Jamaica, to buy brown paper!" I called, my memory working itself out of some deep groove.

"Magazine and me and you!" responded the girl, using her foot to change the tempo of the dance. We began to move around in a circle, half skipping, half dancing, and I followed her moves with surprising ease. The song was fast and tricky, but the harder it got, the more confident — and louder — I became.

The boy's eyes sparkled. He rushed at me and reached up to clamp his hand over my mouth in protest of my lousy singing, but his face was flushed with mirth. I had bobbed out of his reach and started the next verse when the screen door whined and Floria appeared, taking in the spectacle. She hung in the doorway, a shawl around her shoulders. With the exception of her bare feet, the pink soles like ballerina slippers against the brown of her skin, she was as perfectly arranged as the evening before. If I hadn't seen her asleep on the couch, I'd have thought she'd passed the entire night upright, surveying the house in some swamilike posture of calm and wisdom.

"Cyril," she called, politely averting her gaze as if I were a naked bather, "it's too early for such noise. You all go play somewhere else."

Cyril flashed his eyes and screeched one last time before running out of the yard with his friend. I remained frozen, mortified, my hands still high on my hips.

"There's coffee and fruit, if you're hungry," Floria said, unblinking, then disappeared back inside.

I walked out to the edge of the hillside, wanting to catch my breath. Halfway out in the harbor, two trawlers, one cherry red and the other gunmetal gray, chugged away from shore. Far up in the rusty rigging of the gray boat I could see a man tying knots in a shredded net, oblivious to the altitude. A bloated white ocean liner cruised east along the horizon, and for a moment my perspective made it look as though the big ship and the gray boat might collide. I shut my eyes. When I opened them again, the fishermen were leagues from danger.

Farther ahead, northward still, lay my tiny life in New York. It came to me suddenly, cramped and defeated, its white flag hoisted and fluttering. The thought made me a little woozy, but I held my ground. I hadn't traveled anywhere in years, I realized. By closing my circle of movements, I felt I'd somehow mastered the chaos that had once ruled my life and built a little citadel against its possible return. No one came in, nothing went out.

So what did I have inside that marvelous fortress? A cruddy apartment for which I paid half my salary, a few friends, none of whom knew me well, and my job. My job. Which was? A corner, on the top floor of the museum, under a dome of filtered skylights. And in that corner I succumbed each day, in the exacting ritual of my craft, to a kind of self-hypnosis. I swabbed and dusted and scraped, looking for secrets, trying most of all not to leave my mark. When I'd done my finest work, I was invisible. I could stand back and say, *This is good because I am not here.*

Once upon a time I'd wanted to be a painter. I'd studied and dreamed and strived toward some imaginary goal of artistic perfection, my shoulder bent to the task with grim determination. But my work was always too careful, too exacting. Ultimately, it fell flat. I had no access to the currency that connects a good artist to her audience, didn't, I guess, speak the language of the heart. My last year in college, I began to recognize my deficiency and retreated from the whole endeavor. I couldn't, however, give up art altogether, and when I discovered restoration work, I rejoiced. It seemed that I'd found an arena perfectly suited for turning my shortcomings to advantage. There was reward for my obsessiveness, my precision, and on very good days I felt I had a real calling. But since my recent debacle, even that faith had flown without tether into a void as white and deep as the hole I'd made in the painting's sky. I was a glorified janitor, really, spent my days cleaning pictures made by a bunch of dead white men. And I wasn't even very good at that.

What would Lou make of me now? Would she be proud of what I'd become? Might she draw me to her bosom and, with a suck of the tooth, dismiss my flaws and praise my virtues?

Addy, yah a fine girl; don't yah listen to dem old pissy chilren, because yah gonna grow and be de best, yah hearing me? Numbah one at whatever yah choose, and dem be jes' scratching around —

Not likely. I thought again of Errol, of the boys. Of Lou's broken family and the disturbing truth of my complete ignorance.

For the longest time, Lou had been the standard by which I measured and defined love. I'd maintained a childish but convenient philosophy of absolutes: Some people got love right; others did not and never would. The Abrahams were most decidedly of the latter sort, love handicapped. Lou, however, without seeming too corny, *was* love. The very embodiment of that emotion. My conviction about my own otherness allowed me a sort of safety, a certainty about what I was not and could not have. Now, after a day on St. Clair, nothing held its center. That I hadn't ever considered the possible reality of Lou's life, *why* she was apart from her children and so far from home, stunned and shamed me.

The dogs in the neighbor's yard began to bark, and I heard the Alfreds' front door open and close. I slipped quietly through the kitchen door and searched out a tin pot of coffee warming on the stove. Hearing voices, I peered into the living room.

Mr. Alfred, in a pistachio-colored short-sleeved shirt, was seated in his chair. Beside him, Marva held a Bible and turned her squat, sturdy frame in the direction of the front door. She was watching, patiently, a small man who shifted from one foot to the other, fiddling nervously with the brim of his hat. His brown suit, which overwhelmed his narrow shoulders, had about its lapel the shine of years, and he wore his fraying collared shirt without a tie.

"Well, well, well," the man said, his voice quivering as he tried to smile. He reached up and touched his hair, which grew in two thick wedges from his head like wings. His neck was bent, eyes cast down.

"Minerva. Mr. Alfred, sir. Me here wit a heavy heart today. De Lord has surely recalled an angel. Took her right from us. From you specially."

He cleared his throat, squeezing and torturing his hat, but didn't look up from the worn floorboards. He seemed to be choosing his words with exquisite care, and I could see Marva, a bemused expression on her face, waiting.

"Nevah thought me see dis day." His speech faltered. "Me jes' suspected . . ."

Marva put her father's Bible in his lap and began to walk toward the visitor, but he waved her off. I took a seat at the kitchen table as soundlessly as I could, sliding my chair back where I couldn't be seen but still had a partial view. Backlit by the window, the man's features were in shadow.

"No, no," he said, without looking up. "Don't expense yahself. Me come to set by, to comfort *you*."

The man drew a deep breath and moved into the room, resting his hat on the arm of the couch and walking toward Mr. Alfred with renewed purpose. As he got closer I was able to see his face more clearly. He was dark and delicate, with a full graying mustache that grew like a carpet down and out over his sunken cheeks. The sorrow woven on his face gave him the most pitiful aspect I'd ever seen. His big eyes were red and wet.

"Mr. Alfred, it's yah old friend here, Mackie Goodson, from nearby. Remembah me?"

Mr. Alfred moved his jaw about, either searching his memory or rooting out the breakfast he'd just finished. If he recognized Mackie Goodson, he wasn't letting on.

"Me jes' as sorry as me cyan be about yah daughta. She was a great lady. Her and me were friends for so many years, me cyaant even figure. How you doin' today?"

"Pretty good for an old man, tank you."

Mr. Alfred smiled slyly, oblivious to the weight of Mackie's question.

"Well, tank de Lawd for dat," said Mackie, his voice whittled down to a whisper. "And you, Marva . . ."

Unable to finish his question, Mackie backed up onto the couch and buried his head in his hands, his courage spent. His grief wound toward the kitchen and pulled at my heart. I held onto my chair, feeling like a lonely moviegoer in the back row.

"Dere, dere, Mackie," said Marva while she propped her father with a pillow. "S'arright. Have yahself a cry."

She sucked a tooth and shook her head. Mr. Alfred appeared blissfully unconcerned.

"De Lord does his work in mysterious ways, don't he now?" Mackie said, sobbing, feeling for a handkerchief. Marva sat down next to Mackie and put a big arm around his shoulder.

"Yes. Yes, he does."

"Me miss her so already," Mackie said. Though he could not have been under sixty, Mackie looked like a lost little boy crumpled against Marva's breast.

"Well, she loved yah, Mackie." Marva gave him a squeeze, her face still and calm. "Surely as day follows night she did."

"Do you tink?"

"Mmhmm. Mmhmm."

His face brightening ever so slightly, Mackie sat up and looked Marva in the eye.

"Yah know, Marva, me wanting to tell you someting. Dere was a time when I asked yah sister to marry me. Yes, I did."

Marva nodded with an unconvincing display of surprise. Mackie sniffled, then fiddled with the edges of his handkerchief as he spoke.

"When she came home to Pville, and her having dose boys to care for, after dat man treated her . . . Oh, I don't even like tinking on it. Cyaant speak his name. Me cyaant, Marva. It jes' about dead me."

"It was hard times den."

"And dis before she sick, Marva. Well, me knowing she didn't love me dat way, de way for marrying, but I did love her. Truly, since we was lickle tings. And me wanting to care for her. By de time I reach fifteen — *fifteen*, Marv — me making my own way."

"I know, Mackie. I know."

"And my business was doing very fine. So one day, after her and me were working out some numbers for me buying de store dat usually be next to mine? Remember she was always helping me wit my books? On dis one day, me jes' in a mood, brave, and I ask her flat out. 'Would you do me de honor to marry me, Louise?' Dat's how me ask. And you know, Marva, what she done? She put her hand to my face and her say, 'Yah de finest man, Mackie Goodson,' and den she begun to cry. Me knowed den she was saying no. But I needed a proper answer, and so me gwan go ask again. She say, 'No, Mackie, no, I cyaant put dat on you.' I figured she meant about Derek, and how he was back den, de devil's own instrument. Jes' as hard and mean on his mumma as de devil hisself. But I say please, me wanting to be a father to de boy, learn him well. But she wouldn't have it. Oh, I know all dat ruction is what made her sick, Marva. After dat time, we never spoke of it again. But she was ever only de one for me. For tru she was."

Mackie was weeping again, and Marva drew him close. In the kitchen, I felt stuck, bayoneted by the man's despair. At last, Mackie managed to pull himself together and, after one tremendous honk into his kerchief, he gave a trembling laugh and looked about the room.

"Where is everyone?"

"Derek's gone to work. Philip come up yesterday and he's down doing some business." Marva leaned back and sighed. "Him and Derek been scrapping about Errol."

At the mention of Errol's name, Mackie set his mouth and looked down at his hands, threading and unthreading his fingers.

"Is he coming?"

"Is who coming?" Mr. Alfred shouted suddenly. Startled, I tipped my cup, splattering hot coffee on my sundress. I pulled the dress off my lap, flapping it in the still air.

"Nevah mind, Papa," said Marva with a wave of the hand. "He was. 'Cept yesterday Philip, him a crack up his car drugging his papa's old boat down to de harbor. Me not knowing what to do 'bout it now."

"I do," Mackie said.

Marva batted him with the dishcloth she had slung over her shoulder.

"Come now, don't be an old frupse."

"Sorry. Sorry," he said, frowning, his voice now laced with anger. "Me jes cyaant abide him. He a face-man."

Marva stood up and moved to her father's side, fussing needlessly with his collar. The sun had shifted its angle and cast a harsh glare across Mackie's tearstained face.

"Don't yah talk like dat about Errol now, Mackie," Marva said. "I'm not having it." Just as she'd done with Derek the night before, she brought the discussion to an end with stunning speed. She looked at her watch. "Hear me, Mackie," she said abruptly, all traces of displeasure immediately gone. "Me needing to go down to Eldertown, to market fi making my callaloo. Dat lickle girl from de States, de one Lulu usually cared for, is here, but Papa fears her. Cyan yah watch him fah me?"

"De girl's here? For tru?"

Marva laughed and began clearing the cups next to Mr. Alfred's chair. I sat frozen, knowing I was too far from either door to slip out unheard.

"Yah," Marva continued, stepping into the kitchen with her hands full. I was too surprised to move or make any sound of warning. "She a real fenky-fenky. Always's tremblin' about."

Just as Marva finished her sentence, getting a big chuckle out of Mackie, she caught sight of me in the darkness and stopped in her tracks. Issuing a holler, she drew her hands to her heart, which upset her load and sent an empty cup bouncing to the floor. I leaped to my feet, following the cup as it rolled along the sloping boards and across the room. Mackie appeared behind Marva, halting by her side.

"All hands on deck. All hands on deck," shouted Mr. Alfred from the living room.

On my knees, I reached for the errant cup, which had lodged itself in a greasy spot between the ancient refrigerator and the edge of a cabinet, all the while apologizing prodigiously and claiming that I had just at that moment walked in. By the time I'd recovered the cup, Marva had calmed slightly and Mackie was softly patting her back. As he did so, he stared at me in disbelief.

"Jesus jumpin' Judas," Marva said, a faint smile coming to her lips. "Like to dead a person fi fear."

"Are you de girl? Adelaide, right?" Mackie said, looking at me as if I were an apparition.

"Course she is," said Marva. "Like me telling yah. Fenky-fenky."

Mackie came toward me tentatively, watching me and straightening himself to his full height, which was no higher than my shoulder.

I put out my hand and he looked at it for a moment or two, then at last took it in his and made a deep bow.

"A pleasure to be making yah acquaintance."

Marva sucked a tooth.

"Mackie de king of England now."

Mackie stood back a pace and looked me up and down.

"She's not what me visioning, Minerva. I cyaant believe a girl so frail woulda done de tings yah say."

"Hush, Mackie," said Marva.

Mackie leaned in close, as though trying to peer directly inside me.

"Yah really bit a lady once?" he whispered. "So she bleed?"

"Yup," I answered plainly. Mackie whistled and laughed. He didn't seem to be judging me as much as taking me in with wonder. He made me feel interesting. I let him look me over until Marva began to move toward the back of the house.

"Marva!" I called after her, surprised by my own boldness. "Can I come to town with you, come to market?"

Marva kept moving, and for a minute I thought she was ignoring me.

"If yah don't stand dere like a poor-me-one, yah can. Eldertown bus is twice a day."

Mackie was still laughing when Marva and I walked out the front door into the blaze of morning.

17

G UESS SHE TAKES after me. I was always dreadful in math
and science," says Mom, including me in her conversation
with a swivel of her long neck.

She smiles at me, then back at Mrs. Akins, her teeth shiny and her
mouth hard, like it's strung with wire. I do not know just who she is,
this woman who looks like my mother. Since she's come home *not
going anyplace, lambie, just going to spend time with you and Daddy* I've been
pretending she's someone or something else entirely. Lou and I have
seen a movie like this. Robots, mechanical creatures disguised as
wives and moms. I think she is one of them. She wanders about the
house now, surprised by what she sees, as though the stuff around
the place is unfamiliar, not hers. She redecorates, moves bits and
pieces about, rolls out new rugs, and rehangs pictures. But soon
enough they don't suit her, and she sends them back to the store,
only to begin again. The more she fusses, the messier things become.
The house is upside down, everything out of place. And she is one
long, coarse edge, doesn't fit with anything. I'm convinced it's because she's never been here before. She's a spaceman, metal and machinery stretched over with human flesh.

"But of course, that's no excuse," continues the thing impersonating Mom, her smile melting under Mrs. Akins's gaze. "She'll have to work harder, I know."

Mrs. Akins nods once, definitively, and twitches her mouth like a rabbit. (Mrs. Bunny Akins. That explains her name.)

I have been caught. Weeks ago Mrs. Akins, the headmistress of the private school to which I've been transferred, sent a note home with me. I placed it on my mother's desk, where it stayed until she came back from shooting. I didn't tell Mrs. Akins that Mom was away, didn't tell her I wouldn't give the note to my father. That if I did, he might notice me. And if he noticed me, the nothingness I carefully tended would explode in a blistering fire of *what kind of idiot* and *just like your mother* and *outrageoutrageoutrage*. So I dropped the letter on Mom's desk, where it disappeared under weeks of other mail. Then it was homecoming and clatter and boxes wrapped in bright paper and *Oh, you're getting so big, I missed you so much* and days more till Mom found the envelope with Mrs. Akins's crisp cursive on the front. *Gosh, Snooks, what's this? This isn't like you at all.*

~

I've never seen these dishes before, or the silver service that Lou took from the high cabinet and polished yesterday. Please come for Sunday tea, Mom wrote to Mrs. Akins on one of her thick blue notecards. As if we do such things all the time. Sit around in our best clothes sipping from china every day at five. The crinoline lining in the dress Mom brought me from someplace *You will too wear the dress, Addy, I-am-your-mother!* is rubbing a rash on the back of my legs. Mom fidgets with her locket, primps her hair, and keeps talking, though I can't hear her anymore. I'm watching Mrs. Akins, who studies the furniture, the walls, my grandfather's paintings, while Mom babbles on. This was the wrong idea, inviting her here, the silver, the paintings. This will only make things worse. Mom is a dumbhead, just like Dad says. *Your mother is a dumbhead. Look what she's done this time. My God, Addy, what was I thinking?*

"We're not into excuses, Mrs. Abraham. We like to look for solutions," says Mrs. Akins with a sigh.

"Of course. I just meant, well, I read to Addy all the time and she's such a terrific reader. We're readers, Mr. Abraham and I, and of course visual people. I just meant I'm not very good at the other subjects myself, so —"

"If you'll forgive me Mrs. Abraham . . ."

"Barbara, call me Barbara, oh yes, please!" says the Thing. She looks suddenly like the baby squirrel I found in the driveway, her eyes still darting about though her body has gone still, lifeless. "What do *you* think?"

"I don't take any pleasure in this kind of thing, but, well, I'm wondering if there isn't something bothering her, something at home, which might account for her grades."

"No. At home?" The Mom Thing looks to the air, searching, shakes her head. "Nothing at all, nothing I can think of. Is that what you think?"

My ears have begun to ring. They are speaking about me as though I am not here.

"I don't know. But I have found that to be the case when children, when they work below capacity. When they are in distress."

"Mmhmm. Yes, I see," says Mom, nodding. "You know, I have been away a bit. Perhaps —"

I am a cockeyed painting, a surprising sofa Mom has never seen.

"— she's just missed me."

Mrs. Akins looks at me and twitches her pink nose.

"Perhaps."

Mom's taut face lights up. She likes this idea.

"Come here, Snooks," she says, gesturing broadly with her arm. Robotic. "Come on over here. Have you been missing me? I'm not working at all this summer. My husband wants me home *someamazingflower* and then we'll be going to my mother's by the shore. I'm certain seventh grade will be better for Addy. Sit here, sweetie. No? You don't want to sit down? OK. Let me — here — let me fix your barrette. Oh. All right, that's fine *hatethosefuckers*. Yes, Bunny, you know I think you're right. That's probably the whole thing. I know I hated it when my mother traveled. Have you missed me, lambchop? It's been rotten of me to be away. Have you missed me?"

"Get off me."

"Sweetie —"

"Fucking let go!"

Mom, finally, is silent. I can hear my own blood in my ears. Mrs. Akins looks down at her teacup, runs a finger along the brim. A little gust of air pushes through Mom's nose. She touches at her throat, looks at Mrs. Akins, and smiles weakly.

"Can I go now?" I ask, wanting to run and somehow leave myself behind. Get away from me.

"Um. Sure," Mom says, her hand again on her locket. The

veins in her neck pulse beneath her opalescent skin. Real looking, human.

"Sure, Addy," she says. "You run along."

~

In the kitchen, Lou stands over the sink, a crisp tang of early spring coming in the open window. She is singing to herself as I come up quietly beside her, taking a carrot and peeler from the cutting board *I do not ask, O Lord.* Lou moves over to make room but doesn't look at me. Under her dark hands moves the greasy yellow goosebump skin of a chicken.

Joy is like restless day but peace divine like quiet night

The peels drop and stick against the wet metal basin as I turn the carrot round and round. Lou's body is warm next to mine. She gives a tug and out pop the giblets, which she scoops into a bowl. Beneath the spume of running water beats the chicken's heart still. Thump thump thump.

Lead me, O Lord

When I've whittled the carrot down to a fine point, Lou places her long fingers over my hand.

"Dat's enough, Addy. Yah too lawless wit it. Make dem halves and den yah do de others."

Till perfect day shines

The insides of the chicken quiver as Lou lifts the bowl to the side. I'm stripping another carrot when Lou stops me, flecks of chicken skin stuck to her nut brown hand.

"Yah jes' expressing yahself now?"

She gives me a gold-tooth smile, jabs her hip where it meets my waist.

"Dat teacher is only trying to learn yah. Yah a lucky girl and aren't even knowing it, yah know. Wit all dat you got and yah fussing and scrapping. Some people don't even have a mumma who loves dem. You a smart girl. Too smart."

Lou doesn't know what I've done, what I've said to Mom. I want to keep this from her, my badness, most of all. I move the carrots to the butcher block island so I can halve them as Lou has said. When my mother's heels ticker-tock on the polished wood, I tilt my head back to my task. *Sorry.* There it is, jammed up against the back of my throat. Not moving.

Mom carries a checkbook, which she lays on the counter before tearing the paper from its binding. Her face is hard again as plaster. She is startled suddenly by the pots hanging above the island. Where-did-those-come-from? But she doesn't look at me.

"Louise, don't let me do this again," she says.

"What's that, Mrs. Abraham?" Lou replies, holding in her hands the shining, now lifeless heart.

"I'm late paying you, aren't I?"

"Oh, it's arright."

"No, it isn't, not at all. You ought to be paid promptly. For your work." She places the pale green rectangle beneath my nose. Lou's name dances across the page in Mom's curvy hand. In the lower left corner, my name. FOR: ADDY. A fresh thought, unforeseen, stings me like a spray of gravel to my face.

"Louise."

"Yes, Mrs. Abraham," says Lou, turning now. The shiny black curls on her head have wilted from steam off the hot running water.

"We're going to spend some time together, just us, in the evenings. As a family. So I want you to think of the nighttime as yours. To do what you want. OK?

"And Mr. Abraham is very cross with the amount of television Addy watches. I'm putting a stop to that."

"Yes," Lou says, chewing the inside of her lip.

"I'll finish up here, all right? Why don't you take a break."

When Lou leaves the kitchen, I move back to the sink. Dropping the carrots — like body parts, like fingers — in the disposal, I watch them whirr away.

18

MARVA, I DISCOVERED that day, knew everyone. All along our route to the Eldertown bus, townspeople stopped whatever they were doing and offered their condolences. *So sorry, Mrs. Cassell,* they said, or *We prayed for yah last night, Marva, we and de chilren both.* Her bag held firmly in the crook of her elbow, Marva kept up a breakneck pace across the ridge road, responding to each neighbor without a hitch in her stride. *Bless you, Opal. See yah tonight,* she called over her shoulder. *Have faith in Jesus, Mr. Lewis. She nyah suffer no more. Come on by tonight.* And *Arright, Daphne, arright. We'll see yah tonight.* Marva was not lacrimose or sentimental; her mind was too firmly fixed on the next order of her seemingly endless business. Her breakdown at dinner the previous night was, I would have bet, the only crying she'd done over her sister's death.

At the final turn in the road before we reached the bus stop, a barefoot woman in an amazingly dirty housedress appeared, walking in the opposite direction. Keeping hard up against the dense overgrowth of green along the side of the road, she shuffled along with her head bent low and dragged behind her a pallet of burgundy-colored nuts. When she sensed us near her, she stopped and turned her head fully away, like a child sent to the corner.

"Good morning, Olive," Marva called, slowing up at last.

The woman cut her eyes toward us, and I could see a deep scar running along one cheek all the way back to a puffy brown cauli-flower ear. When she at last recognized Marva, she lifted her chin and her brow gently softened.

"Yah taking care of yahself, dear?"

Olive was still for a long moment, then covered her eyes with her hand.

"Yah bring in dat washing me left on de line, and me be seeing yah Monday."

Marva and I continued on, leaving Olive just where she stood with her face buried in her hand. Marva waited till we were around the bend before she spoke again.

"She retarded, dat girl. She got herself married to Vere Edwards, mean and foolish man from de big Edwards family on de hill. He used to beat her till he nearly dead her. One night she took his gun and when he came at her, she shot him. After dat nobody was speaking to her because she kill him and he an Edwards. She cyaant barely care for herself. Wanders around in dat pitchy-patchy dress. Sells nutmeg to de ships, and gives herself to de boys back of de school. Me help her wit chores, make sure her eat right sometimes."

Marva sucked a tooth, shook her head. I wondered how many other luckless people Marva did for, how many hours in the day there could possibly be to prop and mend and apply balms of every nature. Maybe Lou's death was some tiny secret relief. I suspected that it would be for me anyway, a thought I tried quickly to banish. It wasn't much longer before we rounded another curve and the oily smell of an old diesel motor drifted in on a breeze.

Looking at it from the outside, I found it hard to believe we were getting on that exhausted gray whale of a vehicle. The hubcaps pressed into the tar, the front end listed, even the stairs looked already filled to capacity. The Eldertown bus resembled not so much a bus as a tin of pressed ham. I got in line behind Marva, breathed once, twice, and tried to ward off my inevitable attack of claustrophobia. This was not going to be easy, I thought. But by the time I grabbed the railing, the clot of people had magically disbanded and the stairs had become an open pathway. Inside the bus, dozens of women somehow pushed toward the back and made an empty row of seats for us. Marva, head held high, moved into a window seat and motioned for me to take the one beside her. I noticed that with the exception of the bus driver, there was only one man on his way to town. The women looked at me, then bent their heads in private conversation. An enormous woman about Marva's age, with a box of mangoes in her arms, made her way forward and leaned down to us. Her breasts, at my line of vision, were titanic.

"Where you get dis milkweed, Marva?" the woman said, looking me over as if I were a goose going to market.

"Lulu's lickle girl she cared for. Came fi de funeral."

The woman leaned back to get a better look at me. I was getting used to this weird St. Clair ritual of inspection. Losing interest quickly, she leaned back in to talk to Marva as the bus made a perilously sharp, speedy turn.

"Annie came home yesterday." The woman began to whisper,

checking this way and that to see if anyone was listening. "Say she hear Errol acting funny, yah know, strange, down at Foxy's."

Marva put up a flat palm.

"Don't bad-talk him, Termuda."

"Me just saying, yah know."

Thermuda straightened herself up and started talking with the woman at her elbow. I got a bad feeling and began to think maybe Derek hadn't been talking in metaphors the night before after all. For all I knew, Errol could be a homicidal maniac, a Raskolnikov in a prison of his own making. I didn't know what to think.

"Philip and Derek had another fight last night. On the way back from Clifton's," I said quietly to Marva, who had turned her attention to the countryside passing by the window. She sucked her cheeks. Taking the plunge, I continued.

"Do you think Lou, Lulu, would want Errol to be there?"

"Of course," Marva said. "What stupid question is dat? Of course."

"Well, Derek said Errol killed her. Or practically did."

Angry now, Marva turned and looked at me, eyes bulging. "Kill her? Lawd. Dat's pass ridiculous. Dey were going to be together again. Me cyan sure you of dat. From jes' four days pass me knew it was true." She spaced her next words out, to make herself perfectly clear. "Dey were going to be together. Believe me. Believe me. Kill her? Errol did no such ting."

"But God, Marva, they'd been apart for so long."

"Only because her so stubborn. If her weren't so headstrong, she could have back dat man. Believe you me. He was *always* wanting her."

"What makes you think she would have had him back? Now and not before?"

"Because I know! She my lickle sista and I know! She having a change of heart. She dress up when she fell in de water like dat? Well I know where she thought she were going. She had a change of heart! For years seemed like she wouldn't see him. For years! He wrote her, sent her flowers, lickle stories about Philip. Ting and ting. He tried to see her, but she would nevah let it. Philip, he begged her finally, say to her, 'Please, Mumma. Life is too short and he suffered and he's sorry. Do it for me, leastways.' And Philip is right, you know? Life *is* too short. If I could have one day, one *day*, wit my Josephus again!" Marva pressed a hard finger into her breastbone. "Me give up everyting for it. Me swearing it. And dere Lulu, refusing dat man."

I don't know what made me so contrary, but before I could stop myself, I'd waded deep into the conversation.

"Yeah, but Errol married someone else," I said.

Marva shook her head in exasperation and then began to root around in her purse.

"Patrice? Of course he married Patrice!" Marva was looking for something, pulling her Bible, a fat comb, a small bottle of hand lotion, from her ample bag, pushing wadded up Kleenexes around, unzipping compartments, and all the while talking so that soon the entire bus had their eyes trained on her. "He have a child wit her from de first!"

"Before Lou?"

Marva sucked a tooth.

"What dem boys been telling yah?" At last she found what she was looking for. From a leaf of Kleenex that had been tucked into the smallest pocket of her handbag, Marva drew a thin gold braided band, one that looked vaguely familiar to me.

"Yah see dis? A promise ring. Errol, him a give it to Lulu long time pass. She weared it till him gwan married Patrice, den she put it away. Since her sickness she too drawn to wear it anyway. It woulda fall off. But not even one week ago, she ask me, she say, 'Marva, can yah get a lickle bitty chain? Me wanting to wear dis round my neck.' She was going to be wit him again. I know. Now I don't know how Derek and Philip tell it, but it's complicated. Not some simple ting. It's not."

~

During the hour or so we spent on that overcrowded bus, traversing the St. Clair hills, Marva set me straight. Hearing her talk was a little like traveling somewhere you've only known from a picture postcard. The happy people aren't as carefree as they look, the sun rarely sets so brilliantly, the shining palace turns out to be a shambling relic held together with cheap mortar and tin. And, standing perception on its ear, neither is the distant vista what it appeared in two dimensions. The undistinguished, fuzzy background turns out to be the gateway to an entire, unimaginable ecosystem. Ultimately, Marva's version illuminated for me, unrefracted, a vast landscape that had been wholly, stubbornly obscured.

~

"I'm not saying she have a choice," Marva stressed after she'd explained what Lou's boys had managed to omit over the course of the previous day. "She loved him before she knew, and den it was too late fi turning back."

Apparently, at the time that Errol first set eyes on Louise, in Bobsled's back office, he already had a wife. Not a wife in the technical sense, but with Patrice he shared an apartment owned by her father, Foxy, and a two-year-old little girl named Christine. For a man who had grown up without much but his looks, it was an arrangement too good to pass up. He was glad for the security, for the job, and not least of all for the companionship. "He liked de performing, but even more he liked being wit a body," said Marva. "Errol always hated to be alone. Dat was what he couldn't abide." As time passed, however, he became restless, and chafed at the ordinariness of it all.

"Yah have to know," Marva continued to explain as we bumped along the high road, "dis was a crazy time down here. Before independence. A spirit went and catch us all back den. We all of us were seeing a chance for tings bigger and better. We didn't want anymore to be owned by a person. And you know Foxy, he really *owned* Errol. Even if Errol felt comfortable on de one hand about it? Him still struggling to be free like de rest of us. So when he met Louise, and Michael, him want him for Parliament, it was just a kind of — Boom — like it all come together.

"Lulu, she was young den, only seventeen when she went down to live wit Michael, but she weren't foolish. She was always a very serious girl. She didn't go a lot of places or have too many friends. See, dat was always me wit all the friends and people around, because I have a spirit dat's outgoing. But she was smart and surely going to be a teacher. Our mumma had it all planned like for her.

She worked at Bobsled's while she was doing preparation classes for college. Lawd, she was doing great till Errol came along. When Mumma found out, she was so raging mad, she like to dead Lulu. Mumma was always very strict, even I say stricter than you need to be wit chilren. Very hard on us. Anyway, she never forgive Michael for promoting Errol in his sister's affections. And she swore Lulu up and down about it, but she was shutting de barn door after de asses done got out."

Marva laughed at her own joke, and sighed. But when she spoke of Lou and Errol's love for each other, she was contemplative and serious in a way that revealed years of consideration. Marva believed fervently in her sister's romance but was ever mindful of its consequences.

"Sometimes I wonder on Lulu's life if she hadn't met dat man. But it doesn't advantage to dwell on what didn't. It's did dat matters. Lulu was a good Christian. She was, though maybe some people don't tink so. And yah know her love fi Errol really wreck her in de end. She nevah let go de guilt she feeling for Patrice and dat lickle girl. It mash her up, yah know, made her sick. But deir love was too powerful to be denied. She tried. She turn away from dat man plenty of times. It's even why she went away to de States. But she couldn't run away from dat love more dan from a speeding car."

Lou and Errol began seeing each other in the winter of '64, though quietly at first. Errol's nascent interest in politics proved a good cover. The Caribbean Federation had by then collapsed, the British interest in their island colonies was rapidly waning, and St. Clair's future looked increasingly up for grabs. The country was vulnerable in every way; Michael and his cohorts saw their moment.

They set hard to work grooming Errol as the first candidate of the National Labor Party of St. Clair. Hungry for revolution, they were nevertheless smart enough to know that the European influence would not die easily. Errol and his creamy skin were a godsend. By the end of that year, the NLP had taken off. Errol's face was on a poster in every bar and grocery across the island.

That's when Lou got pregnant. Errol was still living with Patrice and Christine, still singing at Foxy's, and the situation sent Lou into a tailspin. "She came to see me and Josephus, and her go cry like a damn hurricane. I feared for her life den, she so distressed." For his part, Errol was paralyzed. He was deeply in love with Lou, had been from the first, but couldn't deny his obligation to Patrice. And, as Michael was quick to point out, his political future relied on clean resolutions. St. Clairians, like most Caribbean people, were tolerant of unconventional families, but few people would set much confidence in a leader with such a distracting personal life.

"Me tell Lulu to hold on. Me tinking it would work out," explained Marva, shaking her head at her own advice. "Errol, I expect he was wanting Patrice to pitch him out. Dat's how men is. Dey never leave, but if dey wanting out of someting den dey fatigue you till you want to dead dem. Patrice, she was stubborn about him, she wouldn't give him de satisfaction. So for a time he kept wit both women, and dey played a waiting game upset all tree of dem. Dat changed when Philip was born. Ooh! He looked jes' like his papa. And yah know, it did the turn. Errol finally done it. He left Patrice, left Foxy's. For a time him and Lulu were happy. Dey were. Real, real happy."

Not surprisingly, Lou became Errol's greatest asset. "Dat quiet girl, she did all de work," Marva crowed as our bus made another in a series of rattling stops along the lush mountain road. The rest of the passengers had gone back to their business, and Marva and I were able to disappear into a world of our own. I was stitching the pieces of story together and every now and again felt besieged by a recollection or flash of insight I didn't have time to explore. It was as though I were racing through time on a bullet train, monumental events melting down to smears of color.

A far better scholar than Errol, and with more conviction as well, Lou did much to create the Errol Hodge who won a seat in Parliament in 1968. The year before, Derek had been born, and the family left Michael's apartment for a tiny place of their own. Between the limitless tasks of caring for her two boys, Lou dressed her man, gave counsel on party issues, and late most nights sat at the kitchen table writing position papers and speeches. Michael set the agenda; Lou gave it words, though she herself stayed in the shadows. Still pained by the conflict she felt she had caused, she avoided being seen by Errol's side whenever possible. She also encouraged Errol to spend time with Patrice and their daughter. Theirs was a fragile, but working, arrangement, until well into Errol's first and only term. Marva admired her sister's generosity of spirit, but she would never be convinced of its wisdom. "Lulu should have smelled trouble coming when Patrice started being around."

At the reminder of what St. Clair's independence had brought to bear, Marva's features tightened as though they were being twisted from within. "It was nineteen seventy-one. My husband, Josephus, jes' became a deputy. Tings were dangerous around here. Chesley stayed in as governor, but from de very first day he bad as week-old fish. Tieving and such. Michael and him rude boys were getting angry, began making a head of trouble. Pretty soon dey were tinking about righteous fighting, like Panthers, like Rastas. Violence was boiling up all over de West Indies, yah know, just like de States. Errol was set fi making peaceful change, but not Michael. Him go leaning on Errol for dis law and dat policy, wanting him to push Chesley around, but Errol wouldn't do it. He's a gentle man, Errol. It was maybe de only time when his weakness kind of served his favor.

"Dem two really fell out den. Oh, it was a murderation. Michael get real ignorant wit Errol, calling him whitey and a pig and such. Awful. Michael and his boys stirred a ton of trouble. Me always knowed my brother would gwan mash up someting wit his angriness. Anyway, dere was a bombing in Eldertown, April nineteen seventy-two. A man in a bank was killed. Dey nevah knew for sure who did it, but one of dem boys telled Errol it was Michael, and pretty soon Michael left fi good. Went to England and nevah came back. And dat's, you know, what probably killed our mumma in de end. She didn't really live too much longer than that."

It appeared that the commotion of her mother's memory would silence Marva, and I wished for her sake that she'd change the subject. But instead, she barreled ahead, gaining some sort of strength around her already vibrating self by carrying on with the tale.

"Well, me won't lie to you. Tings weren't gwan too terrific after dat. Errol for sure lost his seat, connected as he was wit Michael. And he took a good deal of dat burden, of de killing, on himself. Errol did. Put dat wit de other tribulations, wit Lulu and Patrice both wanting him, and he turn to drinking pretty quick. For my sista it just seem to her like a proper punishment from de Lawd. She climb up in herself even more dan before, and all de light around her faded.

"Errol tried his hand at a few jobs after dat, but nobody was really wanting him for anyting good. Hotels were coming up here and dere, and he tried singing again, but he showed up late, or drunk, a couple times, and dat was dat. For a lickle bit he was driving a taxi, but he got in a accident one night coming back from somewhere and him go lose his hack license. Lulu took back up working at de cinema, but it was too anguishing bringing de boys along, having dem fall asleep in a chair or on de office floor. Me like to say it was Errol's fault, but yah know it takes two. Trouble is, Lulu tried to make dat man into someting he weren't. He weren't a sticking man, and she should have seen dat. We all should have seen it. Cyaant make a four-penny nail six.

"Before long, Errol was liming down at Foxy's again. He go down to call on Patrice and de lickle girl but end up staying. Lulu didn't see how she could complain too much about it. Before long seems like she was losing dat man to his old life. It pained her horribly, but she had de boys to feed. Finally she decided to leave. Her have a friend June, was caring for some chilren in de States — well, you knowed dem — and she tell her to come up fast for maybe she can get Lulu a job. De night she went and telled Errol, she had to search all over before she found him. He was in a back booth at Foxy's. Wit Patrice and his old movie friends. I learned dat much later, from our old friend Fry.

"Errol, he didn't fight her on it, which maybe hurt her most of all. He nevah was a bad man, just weak. Me tinking he felt like he was hurting people every step he made, so he jes' gived up. And Lulu maybe hoped if she left, Errol would miss her so much he'd call her home. But dat isn't how it went.

"De boys went to stay wit Mumma, though she hadn't barely spoken to Lulu since she took up wit Errol. Me and Josephus were saving up for a car, but we gave de money to Lulu for plane fare. And her and me went shopping for some new dresses, a winter coat. I remember dat coat, brown wit a lickle fur round de collar. Lulu wouldn't pick it out. Jes' kept shrugging her shoulders till I had to grab her and tell her to look at it as a opportunity, yah know. Seeing de world. Poor Lulu. Seems like she was just dying on de inside.

"De night before she left, we all up at Mumma's getting de boys settled in, and me find her out back, looking out at de ocean. She holding dis lickle bitty shirt of Derek's in her hand and she smelling it, and crying. When me went to her, she wouldn't speak, but she didn't need to. All her sorrows was out dere plain to see. Her looking at me like ghosts dancing in her eyes. Like she saying nothing was evah gwan be de same. I knowed her well enough to understand she was saying dat. And she was right. Noting *was* very good for her pass dat.

"At de airport, Papa saluted her like a sailor, but he wouldn't hug her. Mumma neither. Dey disapprove of her very much. Derek, den jus' a bitty ting, he held on to her knees, just crying and crying. Pitiful. So sad. Fi he was really still a baby. Philip tried to act de big boy, but you could see how it was ripping him up too. As fi Errol, it looked for a time like he wouldn't even show up. Finally he walk in de terminal, pissing drunk like me nevah seen him. Him couldn't look at her he so ashamed. It was Lulu had to tell him it was gwan be arright. She have to tell *him*. Lawd. What a day dat was."

Marva, who had been so deep in her story I wasn't even sure she knew who she was talking to, turned to me suddenly and patted my knee. "Dat's when she came to *you*," Marva said with forced brightness, half hoping with her weak smile to soften the truth she was revealing. She pulled a handkerchief out of her purse and offered me a fruit candy. In the look we exchanged at that moment, however, there was, I thought, a decision that we were too far in for niceties. Our bus was making the last of its switchbacks down onto the island's outer road as Marva related the events after Lou's departure.

"De boys cause a stir wit Mumma, getting on de ropes wit her till finally Philip went down fi live wit Errol. He had taken back up wit Patrice den full-time, Foxy gave him his job back, and Patrice say she could care for Philip but not de two. I knowed Derek took dat hard. Seems he thought Patrice chose Philip because he had de good skin like Errol and she. I suspect he was right about dat, though me knowing Errol nevah felt dat way. Errol did miss Lulu terribly. He wrote and he called her up dere, saying he still loved her and he was sorry. But me tink he couldn't figure how to fix tings, so he let dem slide. My mumma was getting sicker, wit diabetes, and she having a hard time wit Derek. He was into a lot of mischief, just like Michael once was. Finally all de pain of it was too much for Lulu. In seventy-seven, she came home. Couldn't stay away from her babies any longer.

"De boys went deir separate ways den. Philip was doing real

good down at de Eldertown school and he didn't want to come home. Lulu could see he had all de advantages, so she let him stay, even though it hurt her. And Derek, he punished my sista hard for leaving him. Dat made Lulu sick in de end. I know she felt a lot of guilt for so much, and it all came and put dat infection in near her heart. Left her open for cancer, and den went and made her crazy. Poor Derek's been angry wit his papa and mumma so long, now he's just angry wit himself.

"Errol been trying to win Lulu back all dese years. It's funny about love, because I really believe dat man loved her to his core, but he couldn't do de hard ting. He chose de easy one wit Patrice. Living was just easier for him down dere. But he wrote and call my sista all de time, sent her lickle tings, flowers. Lulu didn't study him, though, she couldn't. She cut him dead, for it was de best way to get along. Patrice died a few years back, and we all thought maybe she would take him back, but it didn't happen.

"But den, out of nowhere, last week, she ask me about de ring I showed yah. About getting a chain. Next night, we sitting out after dinner and Lulu looks at Derek. She say, 'Let's take a ride, Errol.' Just like dat! She was in a lot of confusion in her head dese past years, tinking one person for another, but I nevah heard her speak dat man's name. She say, 'Let's take a ride, Errol. I love de sea.' Me went and phone Errol and said it was time. His time had come. Him and her talked. She sounded just like a schoolgirl again. It's why poor Philip bring dat boat up here, yah know. Errol asked him to put it inna water fi him and Lulu to take a ride together. Since his mumma pass, Philip been tryin' to ease Errol's pain. Figured jes' to go along for the time being, pretend a lickle like it didn't happen.

"Oh, it rips me up, Addy! Even when Lulu was crazy, I *gots* to believe Lulu knew dat love is hardship. People are nevah perfect. Love is a mortal pain, but yah *gots* to love. Yah gots to love or yah aren't wort yah flesh on de open market. She was going to love him again because she *always* loved him. If she only hadn't gone off in her craziness dat night. I still cyaant believe it."

Marva turned her face away from me, toward the window. Along the windy coastal road on which we traveled, the pastiche of prickly grass and moraine began slowly to give way to shantytowns and homemade road signs. We were hurtling suddenly, much too quickly, toward the hustle and life of our destination. Now, as the bus made another of its wheezing halts and the ladies shifted places, calling good-byes, Marva quit her narrative and began smoothing her balled-up handkerchief across her lap. Thermuda hovered again, zeppelinlike.

"Is dere anyting we cyan do for yah, Marva, before tomorrow?"

"No, but tanks. And God bless."

"You going to see him, den?"

"Who?"

"Errol."

Marva cocked her head at Thermuda thoughtfully and smiled. "No. Doesn't look like I am, Termuda. It's de boys' business and me not interfering no more."

"OK. Well. Annie and me be seeing you tonight."

Thermuda pushed her way out the back door and, pulling out a ring of keys from the voluminous folds of her waist, made her way across the road to a whitewashed concrete rotunda. *MRS. HOT DOG*, read the sign, and below in a red script, *Only Jesus Saves. Have a Godly Day.*

"Damn busybody," said Marva, recovering her old fire. "Her daughta been following Errol around since de day Lulu first bringed him home. Worked his campaign just to be near him all de time. She ain't nevah married, and all her teeth are gone; she so ugly now. Tss."

I leaned back and watched out the window as Thermuda's hut vanished. The bus tipped dangerously around a rotary, and moments later we were in Eldertown proper. The hollow feeling I'd had that morning returned, billowed like a curtain on a windy day. The bus came to another halt. Marva stood up and, numb, I followed her out into the high sun, realizing at once that I'd left my hat on the rusty rack under which we'd sat. But when I turned around, the doors had closed and the bus was shuffling away.

19

~~

DEAr MUMMA. I AM FInE. THAnK YOU FOr THE
gUITAr I WAnTEd ALOTT. THIngS IS HArd HErE.

I lie on Lou's bed and peek beneath her arm with one open eye.
The nubbly spread is damp against my cheek, the air still thick and
wet with the bulky heat of the day. Lou's room is the warmest in
the house, and though the sky is end-of-the-day pink, the fan turning its lazy head offers no relief. It only moves hot air and flutters
the paper in Lou's hand. Under the sloping eave sits June, knitting
tiny cream-colored booties. She listens and nods as Lou reads from
the letter.

I AM PLAnnIng To BE VEry gOOd So yOU COULD
PLEASE COME HOME nOW. I WILL dO no QUArILIng
Or CryIng AnD SUCH.

Lou halts and a couple of tears make their way down her nose,
dropping on the letter before she can wipe them away.
Cat.
There he is. Cat, away for so long. He enters the room, makes a

dead run for the corner. I close my eyes tight, but when I open them he is still there. Taking his yellow-eyed fill of me.

Today. Todaytodaytoday. Today is the Fourth of July. *Oh say can you see*, sang the lady on the podium, after the parade. I sang along, tried to teach Lou, but she wouldn't pay attention. At the fair, the Coldbrook Volunteer Fire Department had a booth, DUNK THE KID, WIN A PRIZE, and Lou let me climb up onto the chair. I screamed for her to watch, but she kept looking down at the envelope clutched in her hand. When Teddy Rubinstein pitched the softball on target, I let my breath out under the frigid water and felt my head turn to bubbles, filling with whiteness, with air. A fireman pulled on my T-shirt and up I came. Faces smiling, hands clapping.

Teddy has gone to a baseball game in Germantown. Mom has gone away too. Again, yesterday, somewhere, out the door and down the drive before I could change my mind and ask where. I've been giving her the silent treatment *Please, Snooks, stop. Stop giving me the silent treatment.* Beyond my toes, beyond the foot of Lou's bed and out the window, my father kneels in his summer garden. I can see him turning brown earth with gentle hands *someamazingflower* and stopping to caress a new pink petal. Cat hisses, plucks at the screen.

IT SEEMS LIkE I AM nOT nOWIng HOW yOU LOOk FOr IT HAS bEEn SO LOng. DO YOU rEMMEMbEr ME? I rEMMEMbEr yOU grAnny AgnES IS FEELIng POOrLy nEErLy EVEry nIgHT nOW. SHE IS nOT nICE AND bEETS ME SOMETIMES. I gOT gOOd MArkS THIS QUrTEr.

Lou thinks I'm asleep. Thinks I can't see the fine blue paper and the blocky words that wander a sloping trail to the edge of the page. The paper is not like the paper I use to write to Owen. I use lined white notebook paper, and he writes me back on the other side. Owen Prowse 354 Woodlawn Street Bay Shoals, Mass. Today is the Fourth of July. So seven, fourteen, three weeks before we go to Further Moor. Owen says he'll teach me how to drive this summer. Owen is waiting for me, he says in his letters. You're the only summer dink I like, he says. *Hatethosefuckers.*

I AM ALWAyS LOVIng YOU MOST.

Lou and I will go to Further Moor. It will be all right then. It will be OK. Cat meows like he is sick. Lou wipes her eyes and keeps reading to June.

ALSO PLEASE SEnd SOME MOnEy FOr I AM nEEDIng THIngS. PHILIP SAY HE HAVE A nEW MUMMA nOW BUT I AM yOUr dEVOTEd SOn

dEREk HODgE

Folding the crepey paper between her cocoa fingers, she tucks the letter gently again into the ribbon-edged envelope and presses it like a dying bird to her chest. Outside the window, Dad gets off his knees and wipes the dirt from his jeans. He's wearing the shirt I bought him for Father's Day. A shirt to cover his white chest and back, to cover himself. I rattled the money out of my jelly jar for it *Well, peanut, how about that. Isn't that something?* Yes. Something.

197

"When I sleep, June" — Lou's voice is nearly a whisper so she doesn't wake me; her hand, wide and warm as coals, strokes my hair — "When I sleep, June, I'm dreaming dem small still, like when I left. Babies. June, I feel I'm like to split inside."

Andtherocketsredglare thebombsbursting inair

"I knowed it," says June.

"And true she isn't wanting me here anymore, interfering wit her and de girl."

"Yah."

"I cyaant stay here no more. I cyaant."

"Mmhmm." June nods.

❧

Up prickles Cat's back. *Land of the free and the home of the brave* Yellow eyes. Claws spread.

Red belly

above me

Slick wet smell of fur.

20

THE ELDERTOWN MARKET lay before us, a local bazaar the size of a city block. The place was crammed with people, busily buying and selling on rusted card tables, in wooden stalls, and under umbrellaed kiosks sprinkled with road dust. Marva clutched her bag and waded into the crowd, but I hung back, feeling strange and distracted. The story Marva had told me on the bus shook my brain so that everything inside it was suddenly awry, out of kilter. I worried what I might stumble into if I moved too quickly. Instead I let my eyes wander beyond the market to the U-shaped promenade skirting Eldertown harbor. At the top of the curve, wedged into the cleavage of two green mountains, sat the behemoth of a cruise ship I'd seen off the northern coast that morning. It muscled up against the town dock, pressing its gleaming white hull into the pier. Insanely out of scale with the town, the boat transfixed me.

A long stream of people moved down the gangplank like a rainbow-colored army of ants, turning this way and that into narrow streets. I could see someone still on deck, diving from a platform into a serene blue Olympic-sized pool. The *pim-pam* of steel-drum music blared from speakers that resembled giant white-wall tires. The portholes were planetary in a white sky.

This sight, with all its state-of-the-art grotesquery, pulled at me and filled me with crazy longing. Why was I not a girl on a cruise? With a ticket to ride? I wanted to swim in that pool, lounge on one of the countless white deck chairs that lined up in perfect sepulchral rows (as though in paradise you did not die but napped and tanned for eternity). I wanted a straw bag and a clean polo shirt; I longed to eat lobster thermidor, whatever that was, beneath the frozen spume of a whale carved from ice; to be at sea, going nowhere, deciding between activities, asking the purser for an extra pillow, archery lessons, directions to the disco or the shuffleboard area. With just the slightest turn of the dial, I could be that: a white tourist on vacation who didn't give a rat's ass about the faceless blur of black people whose water I was befouling with my tons of bilge and gasoline. Just a pink American grooving on the incredible scenery and enjoying the hell out of myself. *Out* of myself. That was the operative phrase. Temporarily blinded by my daydream, I caught sight of Marva's bright pink dress disappearing down the market midway just in the nick of time.

When I met up with her, she was standing above a table so pungent I thought it might asphyxiate me. A woman in a rubber apron was fingering a row of sardine-sized fish, smoked and brown, with one hand while with the other she shooed away flies the size of grapes. Her knuckles were gouged and swollen, striped white with scars. Marva stuck out her lower lip and scrutinized the wares.

"What yah want for dese?"

"Dollar apiece," answered the woman, lovingly straightening

a scaly tail. Trying not to inhale, I inclined my head over the table, where the woman's small umbrella offered a tiny bit of shade. Black flies whizzed around my face, landed on my sweaty brow and neck.

"Dey coming from which boat?"

"*Carrie-Ann*, just dis week past."

Marva held up one of the little fish, sniffed it, and then slipped it under my nose. Both women busted up cackling when I gagged and drew away. Out from the umbrella, I fell back under the sun's merciless interrogation and looked again toward the ocean liner and the town it dwarfed. Squinting, I tried to make out what lay in the boat's shadow.

"I've lost my hat, Marva," I told her. "I'm going to look for a new one. OK?"

Busy selecting her catch one by one, Marva didn't turn around.

"Bus leaves at tree. Sharp."

Reassuring her I'd be back in plenty of time, I moved off, shielding my face from the sun and the sickening smells of the market. I scuttled along, darting through the hucksters and the fishermen, vendors calling to me, *Yams here! Kokobeef, jump-up-and-kiss-me!* my sights set on the white strip of walkway ahead. When I reached the promenade, I leaned against a pylon, my heart speeding along. The air felt like a wet sock in my lungs. I stood there for five minutes, maybe, and waited to pass out. The concrete would definitely bang me up, but I couldn't move any farther. I prepared for the veil of fog, the spike in my head, the oncoming whiteout. But I was, it seems, out of luck. My heart slowed its manic pace, my throat cleared, my head didn't hurt a bit. And then, nothing. I wasn't being hit by a wave of anxiety but something perhaps the inverse of it. I was having a calm attack.

My senses, all of them, were painfully acute, crystalline. I found myself longing for just the thing I had so often dreaded: the eclipse of consciousness. It seemed I'd had a useful escape hatch. Now, unceremoniously, that route had been closed. There I was, left out in a white-hot blaze. If I'd had a gun, I would have taken a marksman's aim and shot out the sun.

I walked along the promenade, listening and looking. Each object floated with intense singularity, set off against the blue of the sky and the green of the water as if pasted in place. The world to me was a Magritte-ish one of unreal hyperclarity, strange and obvious at the same time. Traffic, vehicular and human, rang orchestral in my ears.

Near the center of town, I came to a pay phone hitched to a lamppost and lingered there. My head filled with peculiar ideas. I wanted to make a call, wished there were someone expecting to hear from me. *Addy? Oh, yes, operator, I'll accept the charges.* But who? I would call Daniel. Yes. Why not? Did I still know his number? Of course. I picked up the receiver, dialed 0, and only thought better of it after I'd been connected to New York. I hung up at the familiar hum of his answering machine but before I had to suffer the sound of his sweet, gravelly voice.

What, after all, could I have said? *Hi, it's me. I'm down in the Caribbean. Listen, what was it exactly that I told you that evening? You remember. Downtown, near the mission, where you used to hand out dollar bills like business cards to the old drunks on the sidewalk. Even when you were stone-cold broke. Can't remember the name of the restaurant now. We used to go there all the* time. *Anyway, what was it I said to you? "My heart just isn't in it." That was it, right? Came at you out of left field. "I'm sorry, but it's that simple. I just can't imagine my life with you. It's not your fault." Good God. You looked at me, stunned, like you'd been struck with a two-by-four. "Well, let's not worry about it for now," you said, unbelievably enough. "I love you." I focused on a small crease along your brow, like a nail wound, so I wouldn't have to look you in the eye. You tried to hold my hand and laugh a bit. "I'm willing to take what little I can get."*

I was pissed with you then, for making it so hard for me. "I have nothing to give you," I remember saying, hoping it would be enough. You know you made me ill at that moment. I might as well confess. I couldn't wait for dinner to be over, and that goddamn French place was so slow with our food I thought I'd die. "Please, Danny," I said, "don't make me say something that will insult you." Ha. As if it weren't too late for that.

"Oh," you offered, fingertips on the table, scrutinizing your untouched soup as though you'd seen a fly dive in. "Oh." That was it, before you placed a couple of twenties on the table and got up. I think I tried to give you a hug, not because I wanted to but because I thought I should, but you pushed me away. You were crying, for fuck's sake. Jesus, that made me feel awful. It really did. I wanted to torch you then for making me feel so bad. What could I have done, Danny? I was doing the best I could. Saying good-bye is never easy, right? By the next day, I was just so relieved it was over that I barely thought twice about you. I figured you'd be fine, better in the long run. I have thought of you so rarely since then it's a wonder you ever existed. It's true. You always appreciated my honesty. There it is.

So, like I said, here I am on St. Clair. And I'm calling you because I miss you. Isn't that strange? I don't suppose you'll ever forgive me. Do you and my mother still talk? Barbara was always crazy about you. Has she told you how terrifically I'm doing, about my promotion? How hotsy-totsy things are? Well, the funny thing is, they're not. Not at all. And I was just thinking that, well, that if you still loved

me I might feel, well, real. Like a living human being right now. I might believe that
I'm a person standing here in this infernal heat and not just the fast-moving smoke
from the real thing. Not just a disappearing vapor. If you loved me, that would be
proof, wouldn't it? I know you don't owe me any favors, and nothing's changed,
really, so don't get the wrong idea. I'm just looking for something, just a small place,
maybe, cool and dark, where I could lie and be very, very still. Where I could feel
my heart thump against my chest. Because then I would be certain of it, certain I
was here on earth.

I looked at my feet, at the hair on my pale arms, the moons rising in my fingernails, the blue lacework of veins along my hands. It
seemed I'd never seen them before, that they were the features of
a stranger. Spreading my fingers, I raised them to see if sunlight
would pass directly through.

Across the harbor, spelled out in giant bulbs like an old Broadway marquee, was the sign: FOXY's. I squinted through the shimmer-
ing haze of the day, thinking it could be a mirage. The building was
taller than any other in town and sat up on a bluff over a wedge of
white sand beach. Foxy's might easily have been something else, a
fort or a plantation house, once upon a time. The two stories of
stucco gleamed bright white beneath a red, cupolaed roof, and a
prim line of international flags waved against the facade. It was
smart looking, robust, an irresistible invitation. I fooled for a moment in my head with the letters — F O X Y — rolled their
sounds about in English, in French. What did they mean? Was this
a sign, or was it a Sign, a dadaist perversion made up in my head?
The old familiar heat rose from my chest, and I moved off with a
sudden purpose down the walkway. My hat would have to wait.

21

Lou is sitting on the dock, a dish towel in her hand, and I am waving good-bye. Edith drives the boat out of the harbor. Behind Lou, the staircase back up the cliff to Further Moor tilts at crazy angles. Cold water rushes up through the slats of the running boards, where I'm sitting in my bathing suit, a long-sleeved shirt and canvas cap between me and the August sun. Down my nose, white with zinc oxide, I admire my knees, which have become bony and sleek, like a teenager's, since I turned eleven. When we take the bluff, the ocean becomes choppy and white, and I lick the salt spray from my chin.

My mother and grandmother are up front, Edith at the wheel. Mom absorbs the ocean movement expertly, bending her knees, hand across her eyes as she scans the horizon. Today she is forty. Like every year, Edith is throwing a party, though I've heard Mom say a dozen times she doesn't want one. The tent and tables came this morning, and Edith painted all the guests' names on seashells we had gathered. The sky is cloudless, but the air feels jagged as a bread knife.

Mom doesn't make movies anymore. She sleeps till lunch each day with a black mask across her eyes.

Edith takes us into the sound and cuts wide around middle ground where the sandbar is marked by orange buoys. She opens up the motor.

Fucking baby

I hear Owen's voice and what he said to me when I wouldn't let him *I can't* and feel him up against me, his breath hot like steam from a faucet *I have to go; Lou will be mad* his hand inside my suit wet and sandy, the smell of warm beer in a can, and a cobweb dangling from his dirty bedroom loft *Who cares, she's just a* fingers like razors up inside.

someamazingflower

I cyaant stay no more, I cyaant

It's been eight days since I saw Owen. I stood on his doorstep on Wednesday and peered inside the screen, but he wouldn't let me in.

As we come up parallel to the rocky little island of Unkatena, Edith pulls back on the throttle and we cruise slowly into Blueberry Cove. Mom undoes the scarf around her head and lets her hair roll out loose around her shoulders. I can see her birthmark sneaking purple across her throat. When she looks in my direction, I turn quickly away and drop my feet into the foamy wake.

Edith cuts the motor and drops anchor while my mother unpacks the lunch basket. Beyond the bow of the boat, near the shore of Blueberry Cove, the ocean bottom is sandy and smooth and you can stand without fear. It's no good for snorkeling but nice for headstands and underwater tea parties. Here, though, where we're anchored, the water is congested with fingers of spongy seaweed and green tangles like mermaids' hair. The warm weather and last night's rain have brought schools of jellyfish up from the deep, coating the surface of the cove. The harmless jellies, orange and fuzzy like peach pits, circle like planets around the radiating suns of giant pink stingers. I kick my legs slowly and watch their dance.

"Ready for a sandwich, Snooks?" asks Mom. I hear the crinkle of unwrapping foil. I've got my eye on two glassy orbs the size of saucers.

"Addy doesn't talk to me anymore, have you noticed that?" Mom's voice is breezy, as though she doesn't care.

"Addy, your mother is speaking to you." Edith sounds like a bulldog.

Without turning around, I tell them I'm not hungry. One of the jellyfish billows his tentacles, puckers.

"She doesn't do it with Hank, you'll see."

"That's because she's afraid of him. You let her run roughshod over you."

"Well, I don't know what to do."

My mother's voice cracks a little on the last word. I've twisted the corner of my shirt into a tight little ball. "Honestly, Mother, I don't. She hates me."

"Nonsense," says my grandmother, dropping ice from the cooler into her vodka and lemonade.

"It's not nonsense, Mother. Watch her. Louise is the only one who can get her to do anything. The only one she seems to like. Now, if she goes home . . ." Mom sighs. "What have I done?"

"Home? Where?"

"Where she's from, Mother." My mother's voice gets softer and she turns her back to the wind. I can hear her just the same.

The sun is too bright, and my eyes begin to throb and ache. The wake from a passing boat sets us slowly rocking. One jelly flutters like eyelashes along my ankle and in its brown center, I can see Derek's face.

"Anyway," continues my mother, drifting off.

"Well, no sense worrying about that now," says Edith.

"I just don't know what to do, Mother."

"How long is Hank staying? Briefly, I hope?" Edith always changes the subject when my mother gets upset. She lights a cigarette and hands my mother the pack.

"Just till Monday, I think. He's got a conference or something in the city Wednesday."

"Hmm," says Edith. "Can't stay for the Chiltons' clambake?"

"Don't think so."

"Then you can go with Will Conway."

I've counted thirty-four jellyfish, big and small, off the stern of the boat when my mother accidentally drops her glass.

"Shit," she says, and I turn around to see her, hands in the air, tomato juice bleeding into the skirt of her two-piece. She begins to cry.

"Mother, I don't want to go with Will Conway," she says, rubbing vigorously at her suit. "Anywhere. At all." The red liquid sluices down the fiberglass deck and pools around the fishing-rod holders.

"Well, darling," Edith says evenly, "why not? I suspect he and his,

what is she, Oriental, friend would want you to have some fun.
Hmm?"

I've pulled off my shirt and feel the sun taking aim at my white
shoulders. Mom is bent down, trying to clean up the tomato juice.
Edith hands her a towel. I drop quietly into the ocean.

Floating on my back with my eyes closed, I can hear the underwater hum of boats out in the sound. I concentrate on my weightless body, anticipating, listening to my own breath. At first I sense
only the tickle of tall seaweed on the backs of my legs. *yOU-
COULDPLEASECOMEHOMEnOW.* Then, along my left fore-
arm, comes the first sting. It is quick but dull, like an extinguished
match pressed to flesh and held there. A second flash bursts at my
heel, radiating up my calf to a third flame burning near my knee.
YOUrdEVOTEdSOn At the top of my other thigh. Near to my bottom. *Fuckingbaby* Again at my neck, and then my cheek. I roll over,
slowly, and lie like a dead body, bloated, white. A sensation like a
hot raw egg settles on one eyelid, and there it sizzles. My whole
body glows, I imagine. Even my belly burns, though it's covered by
the film of my suit. I turn back over and breathe through my nose,
even and deep.

Only my face is above the water's surface, and the sun dries the
salt till my cheek feels hot and tight. A voice is carried to my ear
along the surface of the water, and when I sense the too-close rum-
ble of a boat's motor, I open my eyes. A teenage boy and girl are
looking over the port side of their Boston Whaler at me.

"You OK, kid?" asks the boy, leaning over so I can see the letter
B on his Red Sox cap.

I nod and smile, touching with my hand a tender spot on my

shoulder. I've drifted across the cove and through the glittering sun can just make out Edith and my mother on the deck of our boat. Edith has one hand on her hip and the other on my mother's shoulder.

"Shit, Dale," says the girl, peering over the top of her sunglasses, "look at her shoulders!"

"Jellyfish," says Dale, looking at me with his mouth open.

I slowly swim the breaststroke back to Edith's boat and climb up on the running board. Out of the cold water, the stings heat up and catch fire, accelerated by the heat of the sun. My teeth begin to chatter, and when Mom bends down and puts her hands on me, her lips apart but wordless, I cannot stop myself from falling into her arms.

22

~~~~

I HAD A THING or two to tell Errol and though I wasn't exactly sure what those things were, I was in a big rush all of a sudden to say them. By the time I reached Foxy's Palace, I'd worked myself into a pretty good lather. Stoked with anger and propelled by my new mania, I determined a hazy course of action that got me as far as the tall, cambered front door. The now familiar voice I believed to be Lou's urged me on. The rest I left to fate, praying that my plan would reveal itself when I met my destination.

I spent a disorienting ten minutes wandering through a broad antechamber that served as the entranceway to Foxy's restaurant and beachfront. The hall had a schizophrenic personality I found both spooky and depressing. Lit by chandeliers hung from mahogany rafters, the Moorish room was a monument to colonial domination, and thick with shadows. I could almost see the liveried servants standing in their alcoves, hear the rustle of long skirts across the heavy terra-cotta. The plastered walls had turned dun, cleaved and blistered with years of neglect. But like an old drunk in a party hat, Foxy's entryway had been halfheartedly improved with already outmoded nightclub decor. A neon Ladies sign swung, broken,

from over an imposing door; one-armed bandits stood about looking like handicapped and abandoned children. If not for the smell
of new paint, which drew me around a curve, I might have thought
Foxy's was out of business.

The man I found up on a ladder was working his way back from
the farthest end of the hallway. A fresh white coat of primer glis-
tened over old water spots. As I approached, he was laboriously
scraping the trim off a sign — Gentlemen Will Kindly Wear Neck-
ties and Jackets — that hailed from a lost era.

"Is the proprietor around?" I asked the painter, who seemed to
enjoy the interruption and slowly got down from his perch to answer me.

"Yah mean de boss?"

"Yes," I replied, impatient.

He considered my question as he wiped his hands with great de-
liberation on a rag hanging from his waistband.

"De boss is on de beach."

Finally, after a bit of coaxing, he directed me out a side door,
where a staircase led me away from that museum of history and all
its decrepitude. Charging onward, I caught sight of my shadow on
the building wall. It looked like a launched cruise missile.

The beach was blazing. A handful of umbrellas tilted about,
making tiny pools of shade for a dozen people sane enough to seek
them. But largely what I found below was a long, uneven line of
sun-blasted beach chairs filled almost to capacity with tourists
slicked up and roasting. Near the chaises lay identical white bags
emblazoned with the cruise ship's logo: a cartoon dolphin wearing
an exaggerated grin, leaping through a bejeweled crown. No one

looked to be in charge, and so, setting my eye on the beach's other end, I began to make my sun-drunk way along the strand.

Had he flattered her that she still looked the way she had when they were young? Told her all the mistakes he'd made along the way, how age and sorrow had changed him? What had made her say yes now? Was it the lure of a promise unfulfilled that had taken her down to the beach that night? Or had he urged her to return to him for old times' sake and nothing more? No clever entreaties, no snap and patter. Either way, I'd decided I was going to take hold of the dinner jacket lapels I imagined Errol in and hurl him headlong into the surf. Quite suddenly, I had a mission.

"Hey lady! Watch it!" barked a man into whose chair I rammed. Catching my foot on the stubby metal leg, I pitched forward nearly on top of his enormous belly.

"How could I miss it," I spat back. Righting myself in a huff, I continued down the corridor of flesh. A girl in a bikini riding a Jet Ski made a sharp turn just before hitting the shore and splattered me with a cooling spume of seawater. I stopped to wipe my face and catch my breath. A few chairs away, a young couple was placing an order with a man who had his back to me. He wore a white coat, short pants, and kneesocks, and carried a spotless silver tray.

A rum and tonic — no, just give me a Coke. You got Coke? How about you make it a rum and Coke? Good rum — don't gyp me arright? Whoa, hold on, boy. Babe, what are you having? You got piña coladas? Are they good here? She likes 'em sweet. OK, good, we'll take that and

The man on the chaise was bird chested but alarmingly tan, the color of liver. A turquoise bathing suit stretched taut over his lumpen assets. All the time he spoke with the waiter, he slowly caressed his own broad rug of chest hair, lovingly tracing each glistening whorl. His girlfriend, nearly matching him in skin tone, kept her face to the sun, eyes invisible behind her large gold-rimmed glasses. She yawned and spritzed herself from a bottle of oil while deciding what to have. The man continued talking and touching himself.

Lemme get some kind of sandwich. Real simple. You got something doesn't have any of that fruity shit you people put on your food? Can you make me a sub? You know what a submarine is?

I waited till he finished his order, then reached for the white-jacketed shoulder of the man whose boss I sought. For a moment or two time unhanded us. The tiger eyes that met mine flickered, unblinking, and in their seamless reflection I could see my mouth in an ovoid of shock. Derek's face glittered with sweat, his jaw hard as granite. He gave me his back again, after which I stumbled along while he charged through the maze of beach chairs.

Derek was up the stone staircase and well across Foxy's balustraded terrace before he yielded to my entreaties, turned, and practically slammed into me.

"What is your problem?" he said in measured, combustible tones.

"My problem?" I shrieked, my voice curdled by embarrassment and rage. "*I* don't have a problem."

Derek began to walk away, but I pulled him back and forced him to face me. I couldn't believe what I was doing. I hadn't fought with anyone since I was a kid, had always gone to enormous lengths to avoid a confrontation. My hand clutched Derek's arm, and I could feel my whole body shaking. But now that I had his attention, I wasn't sure I could say any more. Derek, for better or worse, didn't give me much of a chance.

"What do yah think you're doing here, anyway?" he said, pushing my hand off his sleeve as if he'd been splattered with crap. "Just why in de blazing hell are yah here?"

"I came down with Marva," I said, thrusting a finger in the direction of the market.

"No. Here on St. Clair. At my mumma's funeral. Why did yah come?"

Beads of perspiration dripped into Derek's eyes. He squinted them away.

"Because I thought it might help," I sputtered. I felt as if I were being dangled by my ankles out a window, searching for a line with which to save myself.

Derek pursed his lips and turned away again. In my head, my voice was a roar. But what came out when I spoke was closer to a plaintive sort of murmur.

"Why do you hate me so much?"

At this, Derek wheeled around, unable to contain himself anymore.

"I don't hate yah," he said, his voice calm but pregnant with rage. "I do not hate you. Me don't *give* a shit about yah." He turned away, then turned back again. "Me gwana tell yah someting, OK? Yah tink yah were special. Me know. Like she loved yah and oh, ain't it sweet how yah loved her so much. Yah black mother. Yah. Yah proud of yahself, right? Treated her just like one of yah own, after she gwan and wipe yah uptight white ass for a couple of years."

"No, Derek," I protested, hopelessly.

"Wait. Now yah come down here and doing us all a big favor in our time of grief. Well, listen. Thanks, but we not interested."

"Derek —"

"No. Let me *instruct* you." He narrowed his eyes at me and tapped his temple. "So yah stop misunderstanding yahself, all right? I understand yah and *here's* de real shit. Get dis. Yah *nevah* stopped tinking of her as beneath yah. Nevah stopped looking down on her. Right? Maybe yah feel a lickle sorry for her, like she's a puppy or some such, because she's black. Maybe it made yah love her *more*, even. But de shit of it is yah *nevah* once looked at her witout tinking, 'She's black and me whiter dan white.' Did yah?"

A memory washed in like bilge, crowding my vision.

"Yah tink she woulda wanted yah here? She wouldna given a shit. Don't yah get it?" Derek poked the air with an emphatic, trembling finger. "She was paid to be caring for yah!"

"So what?!" I shouted, feeling myself unraveling. "I still loved her. Regardless of what you think of my love, Derek. Of the *quality* of my love! Or the, whatever, *color* of it!"

"Den where yah been?" he shouted back, bringing his face up close to mine. "All dese years. Hmm? When she was sick, crying from pain like a baby. When she gwan fucking crazy, not knowing who she was. Hmm? Dis ain't about she, yah coming down here. It's about *you*. If yah loved her so much, where were yah? Tell me, do yah *evah* tink about anyone but yahself?!" Derek laughed. "Yah must tink yah de only person in de goddamn world. Yah sure as hell ain't doing her much good now she's dead." He took a breath and began at last to back away. "And tell Philip to do his own work. Not to send yah down here like some goodwill goddamn ambassador."

"Philip didn't tell me to come here," I said, my voice now no more than a strangulated whisper.

He held up a hand.

"Yah know what? Me don't care."

With that, Derek turned on his heels and, dropping the metal tray with a bang, walked back down the beach. A couple of birds alit on the railing, their heads cocking this way and that. They chirped and flitted away, their song punctuating the relentlessly cheerful island music that wafted from somewhere inside.

~

I saw my mother in a movie once, playing the girlfriend of a desperado. It was a forgettable picture for the most part, a racy western with a lot of violence intercut with endless scenes of ribald saloon merriment, conquest, and seduction, followed by more gunplay and galloping into the sunset. My mother's character doesn't show up till well into the second act. She's the prostitute who eventually wins the heart of the handsome gang leader, only to watch him be killed in a border skirmish with a bunch of banditos. As always, Mom looked beautiful but lost. No amount of acting could hide what she was: a Smith girl on a Hollywood back lot, trying more gamely to keep her dignity with every layer of satin and lace she shed. It was pitiful, really, but there was one scene I've never forgotten.

Kit, the outlaw, and Lily, the harlot, have made love for what will turn out to be the last time. Lily lies on the bed while Kit pulls on his boots and holsters his gun with elaborate gravity. She can see her own reflection in the mirror on the wall. Kit knows he's not going to make it out of this fight alive and as he dresses he tells Lily/Mom how much he cares for her. All the while, my mother is looking not at Kit but at her own face, running her finger gently along her throat. Mom was wearing a lot of stage makeup, but I knew that beneath the place she touched was a birthmark the size of a small eggplant. It was claret colored and spilled from the side of her neck to a spot just above her clavicle. She always hated that spot, said it reminded her of a rodent, or a hairless baby possum. Her birthmark was, as far as I could tell, the only physical flaw she had, and I never saw her leave home without concealing it.

In the scene I remember, Kit tells her there are other cowboys on the range, that she'll meet someone new and forget about him, throws her a few manly clichés. Lily/Mom's eyes are a hundred miles away. For her, he's already gone. She seems to be seeing herself years into the future, alone. Or perhaps that's just what I imagined. Anyway, in the end Kit leans in to kiss her good-bye. Lily, a prostitute again, won't give him her mouth. Instead, in an acting choice only Mom could have made, she presses the actor's mouth to her neck so that he'll kiss her birthmark. As he does, she keeps her gaze on the mirror and tears roll down her face. It was an incredibly honest moment and it moved me so that I wept. I'd never told her I saw the picture and that I knew what was going on in that scene.

~

As I followed Derek down the sandy strand, the gap between us rapidly widening, I thought of that movie. Just past Foxy's, where the beach was empty, I gave up my pursuit and stopped near the high-tide line. Maybe I was crazy, I mused, but didn't Derek look a little like the actor who played Kit? I could never remember his name. R something, Ray, Ron.

A biplane made a slow arc around the harbor, pulling a banner advertising new waterfront condominiums. The old motor racketed above as I began to clear a patch of hot sand around me. With my fingers I plowed even furrows, concentrating, to the exclusion of all other thought, on the trueness of each row until, finally, I had a precise rectangle the length of my body. I sat down carefully in the center and turned my sights on the sparkling water. Lou appeared there, in a vision that had, I suspect, been forming for days in my head. Walking into the sea, back to me, her dress fanning out about her like a lily pad. I would have followed, but the earth's pull rooted me to the spot.

23

⁓

THIS DAY HAS a hole in it. It began. The sky was sunny and clear. No wind blew. But still, it's as though a rip ran the length of hours and now everyone has gone out with a sucking gust. Everyone but me. I'm thinking about the hole when I wake up. I'm trying to picture faces, but I can't. It's like Alice in Wonderland, only they're all down the rabbit hole and I'm alone beneath the spread of a tree. Or maybe it was all a dream.

Eight-twenty says the clock. The butterfly ticker tocks. Bambi grazes with his head bent down near the minute hand. I can hear music *Oh how my heart sings, these foolish things* and see rougey light from the Chinese lanterns coming through the tent ceiling. I slipped away off Edith's boat. Yes, that happened, that happened today. I swam through a sea of jellies. There is a birthday party for Mom out on the lawn.

⁓

My father was here, before. Yes. I'd been dreaming, in a drifty place, soft and blue. Flat. Clean. Swooping then up to a sky of honey clouds. A picture formed, I made it with my hands, painted it with a brush. It was a ball of snow and I held it when another hand came near, waking me. My father's and the mmm-sweet smell of his breath. Scotch on ice. My bedsheets were pulled back and I was bare.

Christ, Barbara, where did you say this was?

Shh. Blueberry Cove. Mother and I were talking and

Hi, peanut, hi, Daddy's here. Why are her eyes like that?

The doctor gave her something

Christ

How long are you staying? Mother is counting heads for

I don't know. Just leave me alone

I don't care, Hank, it's Mother. You can do what you like for all I care. Honestly

Mom went. *Bye, Mom* and ahh, *pinkle* was the sound in the tin bowl the washcloth

There, baby, there. You'll be all right. That feel better? Hmm? Oh, God, what a mess. You think so too, don't you? You're right, peanut. Too late now toolate toobrokeforfixing

Open the shade, Daddy

The studio. A hunched old man. No invitation to the party. No Owen, still.

I closed my eyes and a red-eyed gull scratched the sand, flapped and cried against a hot sky. The face of a man in a picture ripped in two. Could not stay. Exploded. The sky tore the picture and the wind began to howl.

⁓

Eight-twenty-three. I remember my father was here, felt his hand in mine. *What a mess. Toobrokeforfixing.* Since then I've been dreaming.

Dreaming of the hole and its tattered slit. Lou is in the door, here beside me.

"Addy, you awake? Cyan yah take a lickle food now, darlin'?"

When I turn to her voice, a thousand tiny prickles dance along my shoulders, back, and legs. It isn't pain anymore but more like a sprinkling of rain. Lou puffs the pillows and helps me to sit up. I drink in her warm Lou smell. The sleeve of her white sweater brushes my cheek.

"Dere yah are, Miss Shirley."

She is just before me, close enough to touch. I'm out of my dream and Lou is back through the hole. Little black freckles dot the brown skin of her nose. Her pencil eraser–sized mole moves when she smiles. I can almost see myself in the gold strip between her teeth. I only need to stay right here in the reflection of gold, not move an inch. Ever. But suddenly she steps back, taking her smell, and the lamplight cuts across her glasses, hiding her eyes. *Back home. Where she's from, Mother* Lou's disappearing again, fading from view. My heart tugs toward her, out of my chest, until it hurts. I have to turn away and look back out the window.

"So what yah tinking? A lickle soup?"

The music plays on. I am not thinking. I'm breaking up into tiny shards. The moon is a rusty blade.

"Addy. Look at me. What's dat buggly face for? Watch it doesn't stay that way, now. OK. I'm going to make yah some lovely dinner. Jest a lickle someting light. Yah rest now."

Cat is in the corner, playing with a mouse, batting it from paw to paw. I've had enough of Cat. Tonight I'd strangle him if I had the strength.

When Lou is gone, I peel back the covers and lift my nightgown, inspecting my body. I am not in pieces like a broken mirror. I am just me, covered in calamine. Pale and pinkish like an oyster out of her shell. My chest, where Owen wanted to touch but I wouldn't let him, is only two little rosy caps. I should have. Let him. They are nothing and neither am I. Now it's too late. *Fuck off,* he said when I stood on the steps outside his house. *Fuck off.*

Ladies and gentlemen, Rat Girl like you've never seen her before! Let's give her a big round of applause as she prepares to do the impossible! To kill mighty Cat!

Over by the window, I look down on the green expanse of Edith's lawn and watch the guests under the party tent. Mr. Grose is showing a woman the backside of his tie, where there is a hidden pocket and a zipper. Aunt Susan is in her stocking feet on the dance floor, holding her square-toed shoes by their thin straps. *It takes two to tango,* the bandleader sings now, clutching the microphone, his skinny arms too long for his stripey jacket. *Two to really get the feeling of romance.*

Funsy, Mom would say. The party was funsy. Except I can see her next to the buffet table, in her swirly green dress, listening to Mr. and Mrs. Harding. She doesn't look like things are funsy at all. She's smiling her robot smile, and her hand is at her neck, where her birthmark is painted over. I lean against the glass and close my eyes, remembering how she held me on the boat. She was there and I felt her arms against me. I was something to hold, to be pressed against. I was not nothing after all.

I've greased the window with my forehead, made a smudgy triangle with my nose. Ha-ha-ha, I say to the glass, and leave behind a misty curtain. When I swipe it away with the sleeve of my nightgown, my eye is caught by a flicker of light on the seawall. A blaze, darkness, and a blaze again. From a cigarette lighter. My stomach turns a circle, a revolution. *You say you want a revolution, we-ell you know* Owen is holding the flame beneath his chin and waving his arm in a slow arc. At me. When I wave back, he slips his hands into his pockets and walks off toward the studio. My stomach is like a washing machine.

I'm halfway out the bedroom door before I think again and turn around. On a hook inside the door is my party dress. My arms are crusty with calamine that stains the sleeve holes as I pull the dress down over me. I don't bother with shoes but rip a hairbrush across my head. Quick, quick, quick. When I fumble and drop the brush on the hard floor I hold my breath and pray Lou hasn't heard me. *No time to lose.* I can pull Owen back through the hole in the day. Take back time and begin again. Press something against me. No time to lose.

Outside my bedroom, the second floor is silent. *Hush folks, this takes the utmost concentration, now.* On the left, Lou's room, which I peek into, making doubly sure she's not there. My skin tingles again so that I shiver. My brain feels big but light, like a Thanksgiving Day float. The back stairs lead to the kitchen. I tiptoe by them and scoot down the long hall, past the upstairs window seat, where Mom smokes and naps and traces little whirligigs in the chenille quilt while the sunny August world goes on outside. Swinging my hand around the smooth newel post, I'm down the main staircase and out to the gravel drive. Back behind the garage is where I can sneak and then follow the tall privet as it runs in a crisp line at the edge of the lawn, far from the lights of the tent.

In school this year we learned all about Kaspar Hauser. The story swam around in my head like an electric eel, slippery and giving off thunderbolts. I wanted to hold on to the details, bite down on their tails with my teeth so that I could taste each one. I listened to the story with hungry ears. Kaspar lived in a box until he was sixteen, Mr. Spooner said. When he appeared one day from the woods outside a German town, he could barely walk. And he didn't know how to use his fingers. Just as if he were still a baby. "I want to be a rider like my father," was all he could say. But he said it in German.

Picking my way in the dark through the grassy alley next to Edith's garage, I start thinking of Kaspar and how he couldn't see in the light. Daylight blinded him. It made him faint. But in the darkness, he could see almost everything. Once, after nightfall, he pointed far away and showed his teacher a tiny bug caught in a spider's web. I think about Kaspar and the electric eel comes alive again in my head, lighting up the ground in front of me. I start to run toward the studio, dewy grass clippings stuck to my toes *Thank you. The band and I are taking a little break and I'm going to turn things over to your hostess, Mrs. Edith Kane. Mrs. Kane?* Across the lawn, the party continues.

Owen has lit a candle. I can see the jitterbugging light as I close in on the studio. At the door, I nearly stumble on Constable, lying in his familiar spot. He's stolen a lobster, and his long tail swings crazily across the grass when he sees me. His jaw is clenched hard around the big red creature. The shell will make him sick. It always does. But I've got no time for tug-of-war.

Inside, the light is dim and ambery. Owen's shadow is a gray giant on the farthest wall, and my heart rocks hard in my chest to see it. He's looking at my grandfather's unfinished self-portrait, head cocked to one side, a paintbrush in his mouth. With a little dab into a broken tube of holly green paint, he's coloring in the collar of my grandfather's shirt. I've never seen Owen do anything gently. He is hard and flat as a counterfeit nickel, and doesn't care about "girly shit" like art. But in the winter, when the summer people are gone, Owen is in the studio all the time. He's told me that, and other secrets too. Now I see he's been painting when no one is around, and it makes me like him more, though I know what he is doing is wrong. I like and I hate Owen both, and just now I like him like crazy. When I push open the door, Owen jumps back from the easel. He sees it's me, turns, and gives the easel a little push so that the painting falls to the floor.

"Fuckin' scared me," he says.

"Sorry," I say, wanting more than anything for him not to be angry with me. Back under the tent, Edith is talking into the microphone. *And so I want to raise a glass to my daughter. What? Oh. Yes, I guess. All right. Sorry, friends, before we toast, someone else wants to say a word or two. My daughter's shall I say erstwhile husband, Henry Abraham. Come on up, Hank.*

Without looking at me again, Owen throws himself down on the cot, back against the blue-and-white ticking. The bedsprings hee-haw. I can hardly make him out now, in the dark. But I want suddenly, desperately, to be up close to him again, to breathe his loamy, sour smell like the one that comes from my father's garden when he turns the soil, black and rich. *Thanks, Edith, thanks a lot. I don't really have anything prepared. I just wanted to say . . . what? To tell Baby that I love her* I thread my way through the shadows and sit down on the edge of the cot. Owen's pulling at a bottle of liquor, the expensive kind that Edith drinks. I know where he got it. After he gulps, he squeezes his eyes shut and shakes his head like a wet dog. He shoves the bottle toward me and I tilt it back, the clear liquid blazing like a brushfire down into my belly. *Most of you have known Barbara even longer than I, but it's been, wow, I can't believe more than twelve years ago when we met. God, she was so fantastically beautiful, IS fantastically beautiful, and, well, I'm sure you all can imagine. Here I was this impoverished Ph.D. candidate in some kind of fetid getup from which I hadn't likely changed in weeks — didn't even have the money to do my laundry back then — just quite a mess, and here comes this creature to talk to me at this Morningside Heights ratfuck, excuse me,* anyway I'm crawling across the bed. I give the bottle back to Owen and reach up, wanting to touch his scar, which runs like dental floss from the edge of his nose down to the bow of his lip.

"Get off me," he says, leaning away and flicking his cigarette off into the darkness.

Quiet. If I sit still and be very quiet, I can stay here, close to Owen and his dirt smell. Owen drinks from the bottle again. I keep my head down and taste the bitter fire at the back of my throat. It reminds me of the pink jelly Lou puts in her hair and how I tasted it when I was smaller. I don't want to drink from the bottle again. *And she says, "Mr. Abraham, I'm Barbara Kane, I heard you lecture at the New School, and I just wanted to tell you how interesting I thought your talk was." So I'm thinking, Ah well, I'm interesting. THAT won't get me laid. What? I'm sorry, Baby, but that's the truth. In any case, I was wrong. One story I can tell* I'm very quiet, my back against the wall, and now Owen has his hand on my knee. He's rubbing my leg and I don't look at him, because if I am very quiet he will stay. Cat nestles on the beam overhead, looking down with a Cheshire smile *just after we got hitched. Oh, how utterly perfect the moment was, because here we were in the goddamn White House of all places and sweet Baby asks the president which of my works the guy likes the best. Well, it was the longest ten seconds of my life, because of course he hasn't actually read anything of mine, and my wife barrels ahead with her gorgeous enthusiasm* I've tilted my head back, crown against the wall to stop my trembling, and Owen's face is on my neck, wetting my skin with his open mouth. *Finally she takes a breath, and the president says, "I'm told you're Noah Kane's daughter. I'm such a fan of his!" And then he turns his shoulder to me to speak to Baby in private, and the First Lady says, "If you'll excuse me, Mr. . . . Kane, is it? Lovely to have met you." Now I'm standing there alone* He's whimpering like an enormous, angry baby and his hot, sticky hand is on my wrist, pulling me in to touch at the hardness in his pants. I can feel sickness rising up in my stomach and throat, and I have to swallow hard so it doesn't come up. But there, there with all his smell and hard touch, Owen is up against me, and I am not nothing. We are together, up from the hole. His fingers are under my party dress and pulling at the waistband of my underpants *Yah wash everywhere. Keep yah punani clean or de gibnut will come and get yah!* I know what they look like, his fingers, the nails all bitten and the corners shredded and raw. They're poking and straining at the V between my legs *someamazingflower.* With my head pressed against the wall I'm not trembling, but the light from the candle is. It jiggers and sways, makes a lion-size shadow of Cat on the ceiling, his white needle teeth like great long spears. *Click click.* He's using his claws to sharpen his teeth. *Jesus, I have loved her. She's a goddess. A goddess, for christsake. And I a mere mortal. Right, Edith? Ask my mother-in-law. Baby, I bow down before you. I'm your humble goddamn servant* I close my eyes against the sight of Cat's shadow as Owen's fingers begin to pull apart where I do not know what's on the other side. I'm hollow like the hull of a boat, and his fingers scrape at me like oars. I'm afraid there's nothing inside me where Owen is trying to reach. Constable barks once outside, and Cat wails a wail of death. I'm sliding down across the mattress, and my legs are at the strangest angle so I feel just like Raggedy Ann on the bench in my Coldbrook room, her arms and legs all splayed where she hasn't been held or moved for the longest time. Owen is moaning, his fingers like Cat's long claws. *How could I ever compete? How could I ever —— I'm sorry I'm going I'm gone. Happy birthday, Baby* Cat, on the beam, flashes his yellow eyes, rolls them back, is about to pounce till Owen springs back and an oval of flashlight exposes his sweaty face.

"What's that? What yah do ——? Oh, Lawd. Get out! Get outta here, yah nasty boy!"

The seam in the day splits wide open. For a time, I don't know how long, everything is perfectly quiet. Like a silent movie. In one quick movement, Owen is gone. Not pressed against me, not inside me. Gone again, like he was never there. The band starts playing.

I sit up. Lou is in the doorway, her hand over her heart. Her eyes have a drowning look. Just like Mom's. Cat is flying through space, his claws like spokes of a wheel. Everyone is going again and there's nothing I can do. Like they were never there.

"YOU get out," I scream.

My tongue is a spit of flame. I'm lighting the tattered hole on fire.

"Addy ——"

"YOU get out. NIGGER!!!"

～

Nothingnothingnothing. Cat lands at last. His fur covers me. Once I breathe. Twice. We're burning everything beyond us. Cauterizing the fluttering hole in the day, slipping inside a box that closes, smooth and firm. *Bang bang.* Nothingness is ours.

24

I WAS BURNED, sensationally sunburned. When I at last got up from the sand, a nearly radioactive wave of heat rose from my body. My arms were crimson and inflamed. Walking on uneasy legs back to Foxy's, I tried to judge the hour from the angle of the sun. I had no idea how long I'd been down on the beach, wandering in the dark thicket of my mind. I only knew that I felt as lost as any castaway.

Climbing the terrace stairs, I found my way into the restaurant, cool and empty in the stillness of afternoon. A plump banquette under the ceiling fan beckoned me. Completely overheated, I leaned back against the vinyl and felt my last reserve of energy rushing away from me. Lying there, I drifted off for a bit, grateful to the darkness, and woke to the sound of clacking shoes on the heavy tiled floor.

"Bubbupbup. Don't yah move," came a voice behind me. Weak and uncomfortable, I complied and lay back down.

"Yah just rest now."

A damp cloth was placed across my forehead. I closed my eyes and drank in the scent of bay rum that wafted from the body close by me, and tried to focus on the motion of my lungs, their lift and descent. I was such a shambling wreck at that moment that I wasn't even entirely sure what was going on. Eventually, though, propriety spoke and I forced open my eyes, wanting to set myself straight. The man who was applying the compress took a seat beside me. When I saw his face, the hair instantly rose on my arms.

Of course. Of course I'd seen Errol before, knew him intimately beyond even the tissue of my deflated brain. His square jaw and smooth brow were just the same, though his hairline had beat a retreat and lay in a thin and graying crown about his head. Just as Philip had said, Errol wasn't white. But neither was he black in any categorical way. His sloping eyes and angular cheekbones, his smooth, light skin and broad nose made him the ultimate exotic, polymorphic, pandemic. He was still stunningly handsome. His image had riveted me as a little girl; the sensation of him lingered long after I could recall the context.

Lou didn't keep his picture on display. It was stashed in her bureau, beneath her slips. I discovered it as I was snooping one morning while she took her bath. I had thought, at first, that he was my father, not because the figure looked like him but because I was a child and he was a man. At some point I realized my mistake but was more excited by the feeling the picture itself gave than the truth of the subject's identity. It interested me that the photo had been ripped in two then carefully taped back together. I liked the paper, its thick stock and scalloped edges. But mostly I was preoccupied by something I couldn't name, the very Him-ness of the person looking out at me. He didn't belong in that drawer, I remember thinking. He couldn't possibly be contained by it. One day he would certainly levitate, explode through the wood, and go away forever. The man in the picture couldn't be trusted to remain in that static and lovely state for good.

Through my fritzing mind came an old hunger, unbidden. Errol handed me a glass of water.

"Yah an angry red, aren't yah? Feelin' badly too, I cyan see."

His voice was a near whisper, and he smiled warmly as he spoke. I tried to remember an imprecation or two I'd intended for him, but when I opened my mouth, the words had fled away.

"That's arright," he said, "'sarright. Is it paining you? Just rest. Errol's here now."

Reaching into a pocket of his trousers, Errol drew out a handkerchief. I noticed that his hand trembled. Carefully, he wrapped the fabric around his finger and began to blot my tears, which were apparently trickling in streams down my face. I tried to stop them, but it was as though I were paralyzed. Each time he touched me, I cried more. I had no control whatsoever.

"Yah got in a piece of trouble, didn't yah? A piece of trouble. Don't fret. Don't yah fret now."

I remembered some of Derek's words to me and an invisible fist socked me in the stomach. My crying continued unabated, though it felt as if only my eyes were engaged. I didn't make any noise. Powerless, I lay still and watched Errol through my tears. He leaned into me, dabbing the handkerchief along my temple and hairline, but his eyes were flat, unfocused, and seemed to look beyond me. After a while, he leaned back in against the upholstery. His shirt hung loose over his broad shoulders, as if he were a hanger, and his trousers bunched up under his tightly cinched belt. He was disappearing inside the folds of his clothes.

"I'm Addy," I said finally.

They were the only words that came to mind. Errol nodded, un-surprised, and continued to sit peacefully on the banquette. Besides the idling of his hands, he was motionless. His skin glowed, and I thought he looked beatific, otherworldly. I don't remember being aware of anything else in the room except Errol. Stirring briefly from my torpor, I tried once to sit up, but he placed a shaky hand on my ankle and I quickly relented. His touch dissolved all my var-ious aches and pains, and time moved in an indeterminate wave. When Errol spoke to me again, it was in a private way, as if he were letting me in on a great secret.

"I cyaant stay long. I'm sorry, but I cyaant. For I got to see my sweetheart."

I thought of what Thermuda had said on the bus, about Errol acting crazy. He didn't seem crazy so much as sad and dreamy, like a man talking in his sleep.

"When?" I asked quietly.

"A piece later," he replied, nodding. He sat back and looked off into the middle distance.

"That's nice," I said, at a loss.

A smile spread across his face.

"We're going for a sail. Cinema Girl and me. My boy say he gonna put out the boat, and then me and she are going for a sail. Yes, we are."

Oh Lord, I thought. Turning again, he stared me right in the eye, his brow furrowed.

"How you think I look?

My throat felt like I'd swallowed a rock.

"Swell," I answered. "You look swell."

Errol looked down at his sunken chest and smoothed the front of his shirt. Then he nodded again and looked back out into nowhere.

"Gonna have to look my best. My girl, she wants to see me again. Said she'd go for a sail."

My head seemed to lift away from me. All the questions I'd had for Errol were suddenly meaningless. They drifted out and away on the moist air.

"Set me as a seal upon thy heart," he said, a dreamy smile playing across his face. "Yes, indeed. As a seal upon thy arm. Mmhmm."

After that, Errol was silent, and in time, I dozed. When I woke I found myself alone, uncertain Errol had ever been there. The clock above the bar read half past three, and with a groan I realized I'd missed Marva and the bus. My arms and legs were murderously painful to the touch. After a couple false starts, I gathered myself and made my way through the empty restaurant and back down the Eldertown promenade.

25

A DDY?"
The sea today is glass, smudged with gray. After rain. In
the box where we sit, Cat and I, the surfaces are also flat, but made
of harder stuff. No door. No in, no out. In this box we move ourselves about, and it seems, if you look at us, normal. But that's a
trick. We know better. We know better, in the box.

"Snooks? Her taxi's waiting. I want you to come out and say
good-bye. This instant. Do you hear me?"

Cat pulls up and down, up and down on the skin of my thighs.
Elongates his body, makes the slow crawl up my chest toward my
face. Soon he'll cover my eyes and the wet, sticky fur will clog my
throat. This is how it goes in our box. There will be darkness where
only I can see. In the light, I am blind.

"Oh, Addy."

OhAddy. Up rises Mom's voice, then down. Down, sad, disap-
pointed, mad. Too, too bad. Nothing I can do. Clitter clatter of her
shoes on the stairs.

We'll miss you so, Louise, and again, I'm sorry —

Front door closes; the taxi driver, *whoosh,* opens his van. Cat's fur on my tongue tastes of all the badness I know. I turn away from the ocean view, before nothing closes over me entirely, and watch Lou climb into her taxi.

I knock, once, but my box is hard and closed.

Prrrr is Cat. Against me.

That is all.

26

In the twilight, I made my way back to Eldertown's center where the cruise ship docks met the main avenue. Before I had left Foxy's, a tour around the restaurant turned up neither Errol nor Derek. Lunch was long over, the dinner hour not yet begun, and except for two women chopping vegetables in the back of the kitchen, the place was empty. At the sink behind the bar, I drank a glass of water and splashed some on my face. Then I moved along as swiftly as I could, mindful of the approaching evening and Lou's wake.

Outside, the air was warm and heavy, but the sun had thankfully disappeared behind the hillside. Figuring that Marva hadn't waited for me, I hailed the first cab I saw. The driver, with a look of alarm on his face, moved more quickly to open my door than I'd seen anyone move in two days. I understood his urgency once I'd finally settled in the cab.

"Whereyouwannago?" he said, eyeing me in the rearview mirror while simultaneously careering around the town's central rotary.

"Petionville," I said, hoping I'd recognize the Alfreds' house when we were near.

My answer wasn't what the driver expected. He made a quick,

hairy right turn at the last minute, away from the harbor road and the big hotels.

"Petionville?" he repeated, slamming on the brakes.

I nodded and, in the rearview mirror, got a good look at myself. Pretty Pearl, as Sebumbo had called me, I definitely was not.

All of my exposed skin was an angry red. The neckline of my dress, under which I was still paper white, exposed the extremity of the contrast. My face was swollen, so much so that my cheeks had puffed up over my lower eyelashes, partly obscuring my vision. Even the tops of my feet and my toes were fried to a crisp.

The next stages I could predict. My skin would turn oily at first, coming to a greasy sheen like that of a roasting pig. Then the burn would begin to subside, the dead skin turning from a dry and crusted brown to gray before it began to fall away. The peeling process would take weeks, and under the flakes of brown would be the pink, defenseless, easily scarred new layer. I would shower dead skin like a snowfall. I sat up in my seat and made myself stare into the mirror one more time.

Brugadung girl. Damn foolish brugadung girl.

"Petionville. Yes," I said, leaning over from the backseat and trying to smile. "Whatever way is quickest."

~

Derek of course was right, and now that I was fully conscious, the truth struck me as if I'd been beaned in the head with a brick. Words and images — the long tale Marva had told me, Derek's tirade, Mackie Goodson's grim face, the lost musings of Lou's true love — all lay over and against one another. Bright, dark, some bleeding together, others hard and painful to touch, broken at the edges. There were all these people, I thought, strangers to me, who were joined together in every crack and fiber by one woman, whose face I was still struggling to recall.

What in the hell *was* I doing there? The sharp blade of Derek's pronouncement — that I didn't much matter in the grand scheme of Lou's life — cut me with deep force. I had loved Louise Alfred. But was that why I had come? Who was I really mourning?

My taxi driver was patient while I made an effort to direct him along the back roads of Petionville. A big, burly post of a man in a gaily colored Hawaiian shirt, he seemed mostly relieved I hadn't expired in his cab. At last, after several wrong turns, I spotted the Alfreds' house. All the lights were on inside, and the faint sound of many voices grew ever louder as we made our approach. On both sides of the narrow road, cars were parked bumper to bumper.

"Yah going to a party, den?" said the driver, grinning back at me. I could tell he was surprised that a white girl, a tourist, was making the scene on this side of the island.

"Sort of," I said, feeling a wrench of nervousness in my stomach.

"So you gwan have a fine time! We knows how to party on St. Clair. Believe you me!"

"Listen," I said, interrupting him and pulling some cash from my wallet. "Would you wait a few minutes and then drive me back to Eldertown? I won't be long."

The driver craned his head out the window, cocking an ear in the direction of the back lawn. Someone was playing a pretty melody on a steel drum. A joyful cry rose above the beat.

"Why you wanna go, man? Dat's nice music."

Plainly, he was waiting for me to invite him in.

"Just give me five minutes!" I shouted, leaving him idling on the road as I scooted inside.

The front of the house was empty, and I was able to sneak down the hallway to Marva and Lou's bedroom without detection. I slipped inside and went immediately for my bag but was stopped by what I saw out the window over Marva's bed. I shielded my eyes from the light in the room and leaned up against the screen.

In the greenish glow of the bug-stuck backyard floodlight, I could see Philip up on a chair. He was holding the end of a string of little Christmas lights. Laughing, he shouted back to Mackie Goodson, who stood by the side of the house, holding the plug and waiting. When Philip gave him the thumbs up, Mackie connected the wire. The backyard lit up, twinkling like the Milky Way. A roar came from what I could now see was a crowd of people gathered about the Alfreds' small square of yard.

In all, there were maybe seventy-five people. Nearly the whole village, I guessed, and some from elsewhere too. Holding beer bottles and plastic cups, they stood about in thick bunches, talking and laughing, enjoying themselves. A three-piece band, set up on the edge of the cliff, began to play again, and soon everyone seemed to catch a festive spirit. Over by the drum set, I could make out Clifton and Sebumbo, looking hopelessly awkward in crisp collared shirts, nodding their heads and tapping feet in near perfect unison.

Near the back door, I caught sight of Mr. Alfred seated in a slightly elevated spot, a blanket around his legs. Two women on either side kept him company. Cyril ran by the window in a flash, dressed in a suit with short pants that he'd already managed to rip at one pocket. Shaking up a bottle of soda, he was chasing a smaller boy in and out of people's legs until someone grabbed him by the shoulder and pulled him in close. Marva stood by a buffet table with Floria, filling plate after plate and robustly dismissing a couple of women who were trying to relieve her of her job.

I don't know what I'd expected. A wake. A hushed household into which I would have to apologetically crash. But as with nearly every other assumption I'd made on this trip, I was mistaken. The Alfreds were throwing Lou a good-bye party. They were celebrating her life. As I leaned against the window, it began to come to me. Lou had *had* a life. Where was mine? Not here, I thought, aware suddenly of Lou's rich smell still hanging in the room. Not here. I turned around and just for a moment, I could actually see her, remember her face, feel her right there before me. With hot tears again on my cheeks, I began to gather my belongings.

When I'd finished packing, I found a scrap of paper and scribbled a note to the family. It was a cowardly thing, full of dumb apology and thankful for their kindness. The paltriness of my sentiment left a bitter taste in my mouth, but at that point I was beyond a solution for myself.

I took one last look out the window. Among the hubbub of the party, I could see a half dozen young girls in pressed cotton dresses, standing together as space was cleared around them. Marva was hugging a new guest, drawing him into her big arms and the circle of her family. Sick with sadness, I grabbed my bag and headed back out into the hallway.

I didn't get very far. My hand was not yet on the front doorknob when the same door swung open and I stood nearly toe to toe with Derek.

"Watch yah head, Papa," he said, standing aside as Errol, so tall he had to stoop, made his way inside the Alfreds' house.

Wearing a checkered sport coat now, his thinning hair groomed perfectly back, he looked far more like the elderly man he was than he had appeared to me at Foxy's. His movements were halting, unsure, and he stared nervously down at his shoes while he waited for his son to direct him. Closing the door, Derek saw me in the shadows and, without betraying any reaction, led Errol my way.

"Papa, this is Adelaide Abraham. From the States."

Errol looked up, distracted, and gave me his hand in a thoroughly automatic way. His face was lined heavily with sorrow, his eyes deep in their sockets. He clearly didn't remember me. Something had changed; he'd come back from his state of shock, I suspect, and the hard facts of death had wrung the day right out of him. Derek and I said nothing to each other.

"Nice to meet you," said Errol, his voice weak and reedy.

"And you," I said, taking his outstretched hand. "I'm so very sorry."

Errol nodded. And then, all at once as he was still shaking my hand, he began to cry. The tears coursed down his cheeks, and his lower lip curled, trembling.

"Oh God," he said, barely getting the words out of his quivering mouth. He looked up to the ceiling. "Oh God. I just loved her."

I stood holding the man's hand as he kept trying to control his outburst. For a second, Derek and I locked eyes. Then I watched as his gaze traveled to my bag, slung over my shoulder. He looked back at his father, and it seemed to me as if he might break apart at any instant. Clearing his throat, eyes layered with tears, Derek put a gentle hand on his father's back.

"Papa, I got to check on something, OK?" Derek's voice broke. "Yah want to sit here for a minute?"

"Let's get you a little tea," I said, fishing a Kleenex from my jacket pocket.

Without looking at me again, Derek took his father's elbow and transferred the man's weight from his own hand to mine. Errol didn't hesitate but, like a little boy, seemed ready to do what he was told. Breaking into a jog, Derek went down the hallway and closed the door to his room behind him.

"Come now," I said, leading Errol into the living room. "It's going to be OK. Let's just have a seat."

Errol bent his long frame into one of the low chairs, knees nearly level with his shoulders. He continued to weep, and I dabbed his eyes once before handing him the packet of tissues.

"I am a fool," he said, his mouth full of teary saliva.

"It's all right," I said, smoothing his brow and then slipping out for the tea.

The kitchen was empty. I rinsed a pot, putting water on to boil. Hearing the sound of rhythmic clapping, I moved over to the back door and leaned out. Marva turned and smiled, touching a cheek out of sympathy for my sunburn before turning her attention back to the entertainment. The mourners stood off to the sides of the yard while the little girls fanned out to form a broad circle.

Clapping in unison, the children began to move, to the left a turn and then the right. All the grown-ups, following the girls' lead, clapped along. After a couple of turns, the girls began to sing. Their voices, precise and high, were easy to follow, though I couldn't grasp the meaning of their words. One by one, the girls jumped into the center, singing a solo verse. They sang:

Nou ka mouté anro-che lapé
Eliza Congo!
Mouin ka mouté anro-a ché lapé
Eliza Congo!
Ay jou-joup, jou-joup, jou-joup
Nou ka mandé
Eliza Congo!

On and on went the song, to the left and to the right went the circle of girls, their bright faces fixed in concentration. Many of the older women nodded and sang along. Cyril, who had plopped himself down on the ground, followed the girls' movements, mesmerized. When the song was done, the mourners burst into applause, and then one girl moved to the center of the stage. It was the girl in the saffron dress I'd seen with Cyril that morning. In a tremulous soprano, she delivered a mournful solo.

Green gravel, green gravel, a bow
Shall be,
And a bow shall be and a kiss to you.

Will you get up and look at your hands and face,
And a bow to me, and a kiss to you?

The song subdued the mourners and though they applauded, most seemed given over to their loss. I brought the tea to Errol, who had managed to compose himself a bit and offered me a shy but handsome grin.

"Where's that party at?" he asked, looking up at me.

～

We walked outside under the twinkling lights. Every head had turned when the back door opened, but among all the faces, I saw not one that betrayed any displeasure. A couple people lifted their hands to Errol in silent greeting, others looked politely away from his evident sorrow. Marva, her body loose with relief, marched forward from the crowd and embraced him.

"I knew it," she said, grinning as she rocked him from side to side, "I always knew it."

Errol allowed himself to be held, by Marva, then by Philip, and finally by Floria, each one drawing him further into the net of people waiting to greet him. As he was taken into the crowd, I retreated to an empty spot near the buffet table and soon found a job for myself dishing out food. The simple activity made me weirdly weepy with happiness, if such a thing as happiness could be had that night. My sunburn became a bearable pain. Soon enough, the band started up again and the yard began to buzz. I hadn't forgotten about the taxi driver; I spied him with a group of other men, sharing a joke and swaying to the music.

I was still near the kitchen door, filling plates, when Derek came out, holding a small piece of paper in his hand. He kept his head down and moved straight for the ice bucket, not looking up when Philip came over and wrapped an arm around him. I heard Derek say, gruffly, as he cracked open a beer, "I just didn't think he should be by himself is all."

"Well, thanks," replied Philip, and without commotion, he backed away. Derek got under the fluorescent light and cleared his throat.

"Excuse me, people! I just wanted to say —" he called out loudly.

A whistle from the back of the crowd stilled the group.

"Excuse me, people! Thank you. I just wanted to say. I just wanted to say that we're glad to have you all here with us." Derek's voice quivered slightly, but he was dry-eyed now, graceful in his manner, and spoke carefully. Once or twice he consulted the piece of paper in his hands, but I don't think he needed prompting. His thoughts seemed to flow from his heart in an even wave.

"My aunt, my grandfather, my son, Cyril, Philip and me — we're grateful to all of yah for being wit us through this. We don't really know how Mumma died. And I guess we'll never know. But I was tinking this afternoon and I figured out how it doesn't really matter. Dat's not what matters. I took a long, long walk and me feeling angry at a bunch of tings." Derek looked down and scuffed his shoe in the dirt. Then he looked back out at the crowd again. "And me tinking why. Why dis? Why dat? And den I remembered dat saying about how ours is not to wonder why. When I was a boy I had a chance to tink about did my mumma love me enough. I troubled myself a lot about dat. But it's now I realize it doesn't matter if yah are loved. It's enough to love. Whether yah loved back or not. Yah don't ask why, yah just *do*. I tink dat's de way my mumma always lived. She loved all of yah here tonight. So. Anyway. I just wanted to say that, and thank you all for being here with us. Stay and we'll celebrate her."

Derek raised his beer to the crowd of mourners, and they lifted their glasses back, tears flowing freely down each and every face. Then they came forward and opened up, drawing him into their collective embrace.

～

I stayed. We all stayed, late into the night till the moon was high and children fell asleep on the grass. The music played on, and Lou's friends danced until they couldn't anymore, trickling home to bed in the early hours. Inside, Floria made a poultice of something that did wonders for my burn, and after sleeping for an hour or so in a chair, I woke feeling a good deal better. Then just past dawn, as the bells rang for Lou, I followed her family as they made a procession down the steep slope to the church. Small boats charted their solo courses on the flat sea, cutting thin wakes that rippled and finally disappeared. We walked oceanward to say good-bye.

P ICASSO ONCE SAID, "It takes a very long time to become young." I don't know if my suggestible state was what he had in mind, but I thought of that aphorism when I visited my mother the summer after Lou's death. Suddenly the simple words made sense to me. I rode the Bay Shoals ferry feeling as if I really ought to have had an ID tag around my neck and a chaperone to hold my hand. I couldn't remember ever before feeling like such a child. I walked down the gangway with my eyes trained on my mother's windmilling arms.

"Addy lady, you made it!" she shouted with glee, compounding my sensation that I wasn't old enough for such a feat. "Bravo!"

She was wearing a tennis dress under a strange little sky blue windbreaker and a big-brimmed hat tilted at an extreme angle against the August sun. *She looks a little crazy,* I thought. My analysis brought me up short, broadsiding me with disappointment. I'd imagined it all different. Better. Fixed. I'd imagined *myself* better. There was still so far to travel.

My hopes cinched in a notch, I held on as my mother rushed forward, pressing herself against me in a big, awkward hug. There was a strangeness, I thought, a particular difference to our physical arrangement, and when I figured out what it was — Mom was shorter than I was, she was shrinking — I pulled back in distress. She did a convincing job of pretending not to notice.

"Oh gosh, you look terrif, Snooks!" she exclaimed, breathless with excitement. "Your hair! Wow! *Very* Jean Seberg. I love it!" And with a mad sort of abandon, she clutched me in another embrace, held just a moment too long. I breathed in lavender and the polite, perspirey top note of ladies' tennis. *Whoopsy daisy*, was all I could think as I staggered under her soft weight.

"How *are* you?" she asked, ear to my chest.

"Fine," I replied, my voice weak. "How are you?"

My mother stepped back and threw out her arms, smiling heroically.

"Hotsy-totsy, now that you're here. Hotsy-totsy!"

Whoopsy daisy.

~

Back at Further Moor, I took my bags straight up to my old bedroom, closing in on the familiar scent of mothballs and rose water.

"You have to decide what you want in here," Mom said, following me up the back stairs. "I'm going to redo the whole place this fall."

For four years, Further Moor had belonged to my mother. Her siblings, older than she and still married, had their own summer houses in and around Bay Shoals. When Edith died, everyone agreed that the Baby (at sixty-one, Mom was still called the Baby by her two sisters and brother) ought to get the house. It was nice of them. Mom had not only lost her mother, but her second husband, Bruce, that year. Grateful for the offer, my mother took over the old house and quickly made it her year-round residence. The place had continued its leisurely decline but hadn't been fundamentally altered one whit.

My room, with its pine furniture and water-stained alphabet wallpaper, was frozen in time. Ribbons I'd won in the Agricultural Fair junior art competition still hung in faded strips over the lampshades, and jars of sea glass on the windowsills made dappled light across the white painted floors. I sat on my old bed and looked around. A flock of downy pillows sighed behind me. There was no museum, no garden, no place in the world lovelier to me than that room. I didn't even want to imagine it rehabilitated.

"You don't have to do anything to it," I said, ashamed by my sentimentality. I scrutinized the hands on my old Bambi clock for signs of life.

"Oh, but it's so *fusty*. It can be any way you like!" Mom replied with a magical twirl of the hand.

We'd had this conversation before, and nothing had ever come of it. But still, I thought, who's to say this time won't be different?

"I like it this way," I said, trying for firmness. Simplicity.

"Come on. Your taste is so much better than mine." Mom was energized. Hands bracing her lower back, she surveyed the moldings. "How about color scheme?"

"Whatever," I answered. Her sunny will, as always, had depleted me. *I don't live here.*

"I don't live here."

Mom let out a wounded hiccup of a laugh.

"Hmm. What an odd thing to say." She sounded genuinely puzzled. "Well. Get settled. I'll be downstairs."

I heard the back door and through the bedroom window watched her, still in her blue jacket, crossing the lawn to the seawall. When she wrapped her arms around her waist and stared out at the ocean, I turned quickly and, disgusted with myself, went to the business of unpacking.

~

I would be staying a week. It's what I do each August. I much prefer Bay Shoals off season, but August means my mother's birthday. It's also, I've discovered, a likely time for peace between the two of us. We've always had a better chance of surviving each other's company when there are distractions, other ways to occupy ourselves. That particular August, though, after St. Clair, I wasn't very sanguine about my visit. Or anything at all.

My life had more or less returned to normal. I'd gotten past my hysteria over the damaged predella and, working sometimes eighteen hours a day, finished the restoration only slightly behind schedule. Emmeline thought I'd done a great job. And, truth be told, even I could no longer see the discrepancy that had upset me so. I moved on to other projects, and did some experimenting with Grenz ray analysis, a little-used technique that had baffled everyone else in my department. By April any lingering effects of my sickness had vanished.

The only sign that my life had turned turtle, besides the impetuous decision to shear my hair, was that I'd lost some sort of resistance to myself. Louise's death, and my three days on St. Clair, had, ultimately, undone me. I was in mourning, and I was unspeakably lonely, and the feelings hung on me with the permanence of a second skin. There were days when I was literally sick to my stomach with loneliness, nauseated by an emptiness that felt just like hunger eating away at my stomach wall. And for the first time in years, I actually wanted to go home. Whatever I thought that was.

I loitered in my room at Edith's for a while, looking at pictures, picking through the flotsam of drawers, making sure my memories were in their places. I needed to go slowly, to take things in doses. Finally, when the sky turned sapphire, I gathered myself together and went downstairs. The dining room table, where we seldom ate, had been set for two, and the meager place settings made the echoing room seem even more vast. By my plate, Mom had put little gifts wrapped in tissue, as she'd always done when I was small and *she* came home from far-off places. Seeing them made my heart flutter. The packages were rarely more than trifles. Soap, or tea, perhaps some chocolates. But there they'd always been at the first meal upon her return, a persistent challenge to my conviction that I'd been tossed off, forgotten. Their consistency maddened me, even as I lusted after the beautiful ribbons and paper. Often, I feigned indifference, then waited until I was alone in my room to greedily unwrap the boxes, with a care all out of proportion to the gifts' value. I wanted the little things so, but prayed no one would know that I'd wanted them at all.

Mom was in the kitchen, still in her tennis dress. The light was lousy, mostly coming from the gaping refrigerator door, but it wasn't hard to see she'd already deranged the room completely. Half a dozen grocery bags from the gourmet shop spilled their loads onto the linoleum, pots burbled on every burner, and I noticed something buttery making a slow, dripping journey from the counter to the floor.

"Won't be too long," Mom said, consulting with a bag of rice as I walked in. "I don't think."

She appeared to be making risotto. A gob of something, maybe a mushroom, flecked her hair. I shut the fridge and flipped a light switch.

"Thanks," she said, looking up at the ceiling with surprise.

Now I could see why we weren't eating in the kitchen. The top of the round oak table was invisible beneath a mountain of stuff. Newspapers, dirty coffee cups, fruit, and their accompanying flies. Where Edith had once presided with a drill sergeant's precision every morning, an undisciplined basket of laundry now lollygagged, waiting with the mail to be attended to. I eyeballed the sink, already overfull of dishes. As I moved toward them, Mom stopped me.

"Leave it, honey. Carla comes tomorrow morning."

My mother's dinner production was not half over yet. Carla, I thought, might have trouble getting in the door by tomorrow morning.

"Your uncle Larry said he might come by later and say —" a short scream from the blender swallowed Mom's voice — "think Siri isn't feeling well, so I wouldn't count on it."

I pulled up on the handles of a shopping bag and watched as it split in two, the brown paper soaked by three sweating pints of melting ice cream that rolled across the floor. Mom bent to pick up a container at her foot, exposing a flank laced with red spidery lines and thick veins like bluish rope. Their trails were mesmerizing, like a road map. Been places, going elsewhere. My knees did that, too, curved in funny at the sides. Didn't they?

"Addy!" Mom said, jolting me back. "There's cheese, yummy Brie, in one of those."

Methodically, I began to put away the groceries. I made space in the fridge, shifted and stacked and threw away, created order out of the cans and boxes in the pantry. I could usually count on organization to soothe me. Mom talked *they waited for the committee boat for more than an hour and what with the rain* and I straightened up. When the groceries were put away *coming in third is not worth the flu* I pulled out a platter and balanced it gingerly on a stack of printed paper.

Mom had been doing her travel research. Glossy brochures for walking tours in Ireland, African safaris, birding expeditions through the Azores, were strewn in blazing color about the table. She and Bruce used to travel every winter after they retired. Each time a new country and a different kind of adventure. Since Bruce's death, Mom had asked me over and over to accompany her, but I'd always begged off with some excuse or other. The truth, that I hated the *disruption* of leaving home, was too stupid to admit.

My eye was caught by something else on the table: checkered squares of newspaper, scratched and inked. She'd been doing crossword puzzles. A lot of them. When I was younger, there would never have been time. Now it seemed there was just a little too much.

OLEO LIANA ATWATER
"Addy?"

I turned around. She was holding up a bottle of red wine, pointing the neck in my direction. I demurred. She pushed out her lower lip. "You sure?"

"Yup. I don't drink," I answered, and began trying to disunite plastic wrap and runny cheese.

She refilled her own glass and, up on her tiptoes, lifted a pot top. Dubiously inspecting the contents, she hesitated, then replaced the lid with a gentle drop. She looked to me like a little girl in front of her Easy Bake oven.

Bruce had taught Mom to cook. Or encouraged her, anyway. He was a soap opera director who had wooed my mother into joining his cast after Dad had gone. Not feeling like there was much left to lose (I had already won the fight for boarding school), she came out of retirement and agreed to a one-year contract. At the end of the first season, she and Bruce were married on the soundstage, and her year turned into seven. What I remember of their wedding day — I was thirteen and the ungainly, unlikely maid of honor — was limited to two items: I got my period for the first time, and I flipped Bruce the finger when he asked me to dance.

Bruce was actually a decent, probably a lovely, man. When he died, my mother's grief had seemed bottomless. I finally realized she'd had a life with him as long as the one she had shared with my father. With Bruce, Mom was flat. Contained. And being the snob that I was, I had scorned them both, christened them stupid and dull. Now I looked at my mother's hand against the copper pot, Bruce's pretty solitaire on her finger, and I thought how much she'd lived. How lucky she was.

Maybe if you want a game of Scrabble later

Mom was still talking, turning the crank on the salad spinner. I was lost. I licked the Brie off the heel of my hand and picked up a cracker. Beneath a brochure for the Okavango Delta, a piece of yellow stationery peeked out. My father's name, in Mom's loopy handwriting, caught my eye. With a sticky finger, I slid the paper out.

Dear Hank, it began,

Chalk it up as just another mash note from an old fan, but I think the new book is absolutely perfect. Just splendid. Really, each chapter knocked me out.

Mom went on, citing passages and ideas, warning my father not to listen to any of the critics.

They're only jealous. Always have been.

She had her back to me. I pulled the letter out farther till I could see the whole page. The last paragraph read this way:

I'll never forget what you wrote when Bruce died. And I quote "There are revelations great and good, Sweet Pea, to be found in the darkness. Take it (if you can) from the Old Pissmire himself." Well weren't you right, O.P. So. Back at you.

With l and d,
Your Gal

I looked up toward the stove. My mother's eyes were on me, anxious and expectant.

They were hazel. Her eyes.

"What?"

"I *said* what do you think?"

Mom was holding a spoon out to me, her head cocked to one side and her brow furrowed. I got up and tasted the risotto. What I *thought* was that I didn't know where in the world I had been. All this time when my mother and father had been busy being kind to each other. Where had I been?

"Good. It's good," I answered.

My mother sighed. She put her hand to my cheek. Her palm was soft and cool. I could not remember ever feeling the inside of her hand. My teeth chattered.

"I know you're sad," she said.

Scooting away, I assured her I was fine, and pulled a singed baguette from the smoking oven.

"I think it's so good you went, Ad. I don't think I could have done it. But you're so much better than me that way. So generous."

We hadn't talked about St. Clair. And now I wasn't certain I could handle it. The blackouts had, I knew, deserted me for good. I cut the bread in diagonal slices, keeping my shoulder to her.

"I'm sure they were so glad to have you," Mom continued. "You were probably such a help."

Out the kitchen window, the moon was rising over the harbor, orange and fat as a prize pumpkin. I began watching it and, in relation, felt breathtakingly tiny. It seemed my entire world would fit on the head of a pin.

"Not really," I said.

Mom was ladling the risotto onto plates. The moon cleared the treetops across the harbor, creating a spectacular nightscape.

"Well, you may not think you were, but I'm certain of it. You don't know, Addy; when someone dies you just want people there. It makes such a dif —"

"They didn't. Want me there."

"Oh, but Louise loved you so —"

I couldn't help but laugh. Not at her. At myself.

"You know what, Mom? They didn't know a thing about me."

In the harbor, a coast guard cutter was steaming out to sea with her searchlight on. The long beam caught the windows of my grandfather's dilapidated studio and, for an instant, illuminated the old barn as though by lightning. I could not turn around but knew my mother had stopped what she was doing.

"Oh, come. You were a daughter to her," she stated emphatically.

"No. I wasn't a daughter to her."

"But —"

I took the plates from my mother. Her hands were empty now, turned out toward me.

"Let me do this, Mom," I said, ready to move on. "It's OK. I wasn't."

Her eyes were soft, almost sleepy, as though something unwieldy had just been lifted from her back. She smiled.

"Well, you loved her, Ad. That's what matters."

As we walked into the dining room, Mom threw one last question my way.

"Were the flowers nice? At the service?"

We spoke very little at dinner, neither of us knowing how to bridge the new landscape that had begun to reveal itself about us. I'd like to say it was an enjoyable reunion, but it was instead a funny kind of agony. We were giving painful birth to something. When we had finished eating, I didn't clean up. Leaving it instead for poor Carla, I stepped outside into the warm August night. My mother, lost in her own thoughts, repaired to the living room and soon a sweet, jazzy tune shimmied out the screen doors.

Edith's two giant elms still kept their posts before the sweep of the porch. I passed between them and let the green perfume of new-mown grass fill my head. Each step I took felt like the circuit of a year, running backward. And by the time I reached the cliff's edge I was small again, when Further Moor was not a place of subtle shades but of primary colors. Of blinding light and monumental shadows. I turned around and stood looking back for the longest time, allowing myself to remember.

Acknowledgments

I would like to acknowledge the enormous debt I owe to friends, family, and others who have helped me to tell this story.

My terrific editor, Michael Pietsch; agent and friend Esther Newberg; Judith Taylor; Helen Schulman; Charlotte Hale; David Michaelis; Susan Minot; Bridget Tobin; Michael Barclay and Sydney Bachman; Marjorie Bowen, Mavis George, and, of course, Daphne Lewis; my siblings, Susanna, Polly, and Tom Styron; my extraordinary parents, Rose and Bill Styron; the late, great Selma "Nana" Burgunder; Ethel and James Terry, wherever you rest; faithful Wally; and my husband-to-be, Ed Beason.

At last, words seem insufficient. Thanks to you all.